The
WHITE LIE
Assignment

Books by Peter Driscoll
  The Wilby Conspiracy
  In Connection with Kilshaw
  The White Lie Assignment

The WHITE LIE Assignment

Peter Driscoll

J. B. LIPPINCOTT COMPANY

Philadelphia & New York

c.3

S

Copyright © by Peter Driscoll, 1971
Printed in the United States of America

First American Edition 1975

U.S. Library of Congress Cataloging in Publication Data

Driscoll, Peter, birth date
    The white lie assignment.

    A novel.
    I.   Title.
PZ4. D7816Wh 3   [PR6054.R53]   823'.9'14   72-688
ISBN-0-397-00904-6

For Angela, with love

The height of cleverness is
to be able to conceal it.

ROCHEFOUCAULD *Maximes*

The
WHITE LIE
Assignment

1

Tom Blakeney made a bow before the unopened bottle of Scotch.

'This is with the compliments of the Red Army,' he said. 'Let's drink their health.'

Ceremoniously he stripped off the seal and uncorked the bottle, then poured about eight shillings' worth of whisky into each of four glasses on the desk in front of him. He pushed them round to us with nervous, jerking movements. Silent with fatigue we picked them up, settled in our chairs and took our first sips.

Yvonne, twenty and blonde, an artless sort of flirt, made a face. Then she took a healthy swallow, set the glass back on the desk and crossed her legs, sending the short lime-green skirt a few inches higher up her thighs.

Nathan the darkroom boy, seventeen, took a manly pull at his and swallowed without tasting, but couldn't prevent the tears starting to his eyes.

Tom and I, for whom neat whisky couldn't be called a novelty, drank it absent-mindedly. No-one could be bothered to fetch water from the darkroom tap.

After Tom's toast we were all silent for a minute. The sounds of late-night traffic came from Holborn through the open window of our office. The light of a single bare bulb shone unsympathetically on the chaos around us.

Paper, of one kind and another, lay everywhere. Spread across the lino-covered floor, draped over our three desks and two filing cabinets, tumbling from an overturned waste-paper basket. There were sheaves of soggy prints discarded for better ones, mounds of copy paper both blank and typed-upon, curled sheets of carbon, big brown envelopes, duplicated caption slips spewed from the Roneo and pages pulled and scattered from that day's evening papers and early editions of the next morning's dailies. These pages held, at least in token, the rewards of nearly twelve hours' work, the rewards we were celebrating among the debris.

Spread over one page on the floor beneath the desk, with a large black footprint superimposed on it, was a photograph of a Russian T-54 tank. A full-face photograph, so to speak, with the cannon reared in silhouette against the dawn sky and, framing it on either side, the dark shapes of two buildings in the centre of Prague. I had taken the picture, among many others, early that morning.

'Three thousand quid,' said Tom into his glass, draining it. 'Three thousand before the second-use payments start dribbling in. That's my estimate. Do you blame me for toasting Comrade Brezhnev's men?'

'You wouldn't if you'd been there,' I said, but rather mechanically. 'Anyway you're talking about pre-tax payments. How much change will we get out of it?'

He waved carelessly. 'We'll make it up somehow, leave it to a professional swindler. I didn't spend two years studying accountancy for nothing.'

At a glance you might have put Tom down as an accountant even then, after his fifteen years in newspapers. With his diffident manner, bony pale face and thick glasses that all but hid his eyes he belonged behind a desk somewhere. Perhaps because he knew this he seemed to have cultivated a hesitant and uncertain approach that masked the agility of his mind, an agility that was sometimes startling. Our profits from the invasion of Czechoslovakia were the newest proof of it.

'Just a feeling,' he had said before packing me off to Prague four days earlier. 'Just a feeling I've got that the fuse has burnt too short. It's one of those things no-one really expects to happen. Go and drink some of that Czech beer and keep your eyes open.'

I knew enough about Tom, after running Newsflash Ltd with him for four years, not to argue. I had been trained as a cameraman, which gives you an eye for situations rather than a nose for news. Tom did the writing part of our business and I trusted his judgment. He had a sixth sense that told him when and where things were going to happen, a sixth sense reinforced, admittedly, over discreet lunches with friends he had made in some of the embassies and in places like Whitehall. On the whole he kept these friends to himself; he wanted it that way and I'd never been curious. But by chance and otherwise I'd met one or two of them; from one in particular I'd earned a few grudging pounds for the company on the basis of returning favours.

I doubted whether the friends had had anything to do with Tom's hunch about Czechoslovakia. After all, it had taken everyone in the West by surprise. To me the only thing that mattered was that for Newsflash (the name had started as a joke and stuck, somehow) it had been a winner. I was at Ruzyne airport within ten minutes of the first Tupolev disgorging its troops; in the suburbs when the tanks started rolling in; in the centre of the capital when civilians began to hurl defiance at the invaders and out of it, at sunrise, before the secret police had started stripping film out of cameras. I'd met a German fashion model and we found a lot in common, including a hotel room. She was easily convinced that she and I and her Karmann Ghia were best out of it. From Munich I had an open-dated return air ticket; I made the plane with six minutes to spare and I was home almost before the first foggy radio pictures from our competitors had reached London. We were able to offer a full range of pictures to the evening and national papers and – what was much more important – we caught the deadlines of nearly all the glossy weeklies in Europe and America, which hardly any other freelancers had done. *Paris Match* had already bought one for their cover, *Life* had taken a whole batch and the agencies had snapped up rights on another dozen. After developing and printing since midday, packaging and dispatching second-priority pictures to the weeklies, the smaller agencies and the London offices of the provincials, the job was over. We were relaxing as fast as the level of the Scotch went down. And Tom's glasses were already misty.

'Oracle Blakeney,' I said, tilting my chair back against the crumbling plaster of the wall. 'You could have put Old Moore out of business years ago.'

His hand made a deprecating gesture on its way back to the bottle. 'I've told you before,' he said. 'With my brains and your work .... But listen – I haven't said it once yet – great pictures, Michael, really great.'

He said it in the low-key way that journalists have; it is meant to imply a grudging indulgence of sentiment. From him it was unqualified praise.

Yvonne, perched on the edge of a chair, uncrossed her legs and tugged ineffectually downwards at her skirt. She looked at me in a special simpering way and said, 'Don't you think you can afford a rise for Yvonne now, Mr Mannis?'

She only called me 'Mr' to make me feel old. 'Payment in kind,' I said. She pretended to be embarrassed.

'I think it's Nathan's turn,' Tom said. 'Or shall we let them fight it out? First one to get the other's knickers off wins.'

The ribaldry was part of our working cohesion and we all played our little parts. Nathan had a spontaneous blush, however, which now appeared. In a seventeen-year-old from a different background this might have been normal but in a boy from Bethnal Green it was worth noting. I liked Nathan and sometimes caught myself being paternal towards him. He reminded me of myself at his age, the best part of twenty years before. When Tom and I found him he'd been working as what was called a runner boy at one of the picture agencies near Fleet Street. This meant that he spent the day running – literally – from one newspaper office to another delivering packets of prints. It was just how I had started, and I knew how it felt to begin with the cards stacked against you. Even the seven-pounds-a-week-and-lunch-vouchers they gave him weren't that much more than I'd been paid in postwar London. And Nathan, like me, had had the handicap of being a kind of foreigner in the rough-and-tumble of working-class life. He was Jewish and Bethnal Green, I was Greek and Camden Town (even if my sandy hair and untypically light complexion didn't give me away the accent that took years to disappear invariably did).

I liked to watch how Nathan worked, conscientiously and never overreaching himself. I could imagine him riding the taunts of petty dictators in a dispatch room and the hostility of the hard-case Cockney kids; I remembered it all myself. And I could see him watching and learning, as I had, because even the simple sort of higher education you could pick up going at a fast trot round the fringes of EC4 was an added protection. Officially he would never be allowed into the darkrooms or drying rooms, but while the other youths spent their idle minutes playing pontoon for pennies Nathan was becoming a competent darkroom assistant. He was that when he came to us. A few months later he was carrying a modest Japanese camera round with him. It wouldn't be long before we lost him and I would be glad for helping him on his way. One day he was quite likely to be a better photographer than I was.

'Don't worry about me, Mr Mannis,' he said now as the blush receded. 'I'd work here for nothink, truly.'

'Tell you what,' said Tom, digging in his trouser pocket, 'while we're feeling philanthropic we'll toss for it. Five quid a week for whoever makes the right call. Or would you rather split it between you?' He balanced the half-crown on his finger and prepared to flip it, looking slyly from one to the other of them. Yvonne pouted uncertainly but Nathan's eyes brightened. He was a gambler. 'Flip it,' he said.

Yvonne frowned and said, 'I don't ... '

The telephone rang.

It was our only phone. Tom was nearest and he got up with a mechanical curse to answer it.

'Should have disconnected the bloody thing,' he said.

'If it's work,' I said, 'tell them we've gone into liquidation.'

I turned my attention to pouring another round while Tom quoted our number into the phone and said guardedly, 'Oh, hello.' Yvonne crossed her legs again, composed another frown and said, 'He isn't really going to flip a coin over our rises?'

'You ought to know anything can happen in this office. Listen, we're going to have to put a height limit on those skirts of yours.'

'I don't see why you shouldn't learn some self-control instead.'

I sometimes felt that if I showed the merest flicker of interest Yvonne would be tugging her knickers down off her pert little bottom. But there's an insidious myth about office affairs being bad for business, and I suppose I had fallen victim to it.

'Are you going to buy the new darkroom gear now?' asked Nathan, steering us back to shop talk.

'Maybe. We've still a few bills to pay off. What we *should* do' – I surveyed the peeling walls – 'is move to a posher office. This one won't do much longer for a swinging outfit like us. It depends on how much Blakeney is prepared to shell out.'

On the strength of being a failed student of accountancy Tom looked after all our finances; had done since the earliest days when we'd regularly had to pawn our watches to pay the rent. That was before we could afford salaries for ourselves, let alone two employees. What we had lived on in those first few months together I still couldn't think. For Tom, with a wife and baby, it had been worse than for me.

The telephone tinkled as he put the receiver down. 'Swinging?' Yvonne was saying to Nathan. 'It's years since I heard anyone use that word.'

'Joe Goodwin,' said Tom, settling back behind the bottle. 'He wanted you.'

'Oh God. What for?'

'A favour. What else?'

'And so? What kind of favour?'

Tom shrugged. 'He wouldn't tell me. Anyway, I told him we'd shut up shop till the day after tomorrow. Which,' he added with emphasis, 'we have.'

'Maybe there's something in it for us,' I said. 'Have you gone off Joe Goodwin?'

'Forget it.' He waved a bony hand at me. 'Look, I'm tired of your giving these guys your time in return for a twenty-quid cheque. And you'd think they had to pawn the Crown Jewels to pay us. We're beyond that now, Michael. This time it's no.'

'Yes, *sir*,' I said. Once in a while we'd have a real set-to over who gave orders to whom. Now, of all times, it wasn't worth an argument. 'But we haven't heard the last of him. You know what he's like.'

'Never mind. If he wants us he'll have to come and get us. Drink up.'

The subject fizzled out. Nathan and Yvonne agreed to share the extra five pounds and soon began to worry about last buses and trains. Tom dug out two pound notes and told them to take cabs and they left, both giggly from the whisky. I looked at Tom. It was the first time I'd got him on his own since I came back.

'Well, you old bastard,' I said. 'How did you know?'

'Know what?'

'You know what I mean. Czechoslovakia.'

'I didn't.' He studied the two inches left in the bottle. 'I didn't know, God's truth. Nobody could have known. It was the wildest guess I'd ever made and it came off. You brought it off, that's the important thing. Your health, you ugly Greek.'

'That story has a singularly unsound ring,' I said, but it hadn't really. Tom had no reason not to tell me the truth, but he'd often amuse himself by evading a subject so as to leave a margin of doubt. He smiled slowly. 'We're not going to cut our celebrations so short?' he said.

'I don't know, I'm pretty knocked out.'

'Go on, you're getting your second wind. Just a nightcap – or two – at the Press Club and I'll drive you home.'

My arm was easily twisted. 'Prop me up against something if I fall asleep,' I said. In fact the whisky had dissolved some of my tiredness. And outside, where summer rain had damped down the petrol fumes, the air was clear and crisp. We picked our way through the maze of alleys and courts to Fleet Street and across to Salisbury Square.

The Press Club has generous licensing hours. It is usually full of newspapermen talking about other newspapermen. For half an hour we gossiped with a crowd from the *Daily Telegraph*, then they left and we had the bar almost to ourselves. We indulged in dreams of expanding our empire: the new premises we would take, the staff we would hire, the stories that had never been written, the fortunes we were going to make. And we were entitled to a dream or two. In the past twelve months we had grossed over fifteen thousand pounds and every month the bank balance was gaining weight.

Hector, the barman, leaning on his elbows over the counter, was getting a glassy look in his eye. Sitting against the wall opposite me Tom was in the middle of a jerky, animated description of a new office he had in mind when he closed his eyes – switched them off, almost, behind the window-frames of his spectacles – and groaned. 'I can't look,' he said. I turned and looked at the doorway.

Joe Goodwin had found us. He stood there giving us a tight, triumphant smile, then walked over to our table.

'You're not a member,' I said.

'I'm sure one of you will sign me in. What will you have?'

'Scotch,' said Tom. 'Doubles.'

Goodwin strode over to the counter, a tall figure with a bronze face and a shock of grey curls above his impeccably-cut dark suit. Hector hesitated but served him at a nod from me.

When he came back I said loudly, 'You haven't come to drink our health, Joe. What does MI5 want?'

Pleasantly enough he said, 'Shut up, will you? Anyway, I wish you'd get the name right.'

2

Joe Goodwin was linked in my mind with events of contemporary history. He would appear in their vicinity like an art gallery attendant, unobtrusive but watchful. In the same way his presence was overshadowed by his surroundings but somehow you were always conscious of it.

I first met him lurking around the corner from one of these events three days after it had arrived in the gallery. It was a minor work, Rhodesia's seizure of independence from Britain. To be accurate I should not say that I met Joe Goodwin on that day in November 1965. I was taken to a room in a cheap boarding house off Jameson Avenue in Salisbury and introduced to a man with straight dark hair and a pale complexion, an ugly cauliflower ear and a pronounced limp. He was presented to me as Samuel Siedel, a visiting British businessman who had lost his passport and was being urgently issued with a new one so that he could catch his plane to London that evening. Tom and I had arrived the day before on an assignment to do a colour feature for one of what we called the 'stiff' Sunday papers. Tom had bumped into an old Whitehall contact who had asked if I could take, develop and print a passport photograph of Mr. Siedel.

At first I wondered what his objection was to putting half a crown in a photo machine. But the Whitehall man was gently

14

insistent. I took my pictures, developed them in the darkroom of one of the Salisbury newspapers and drove back with them to the boarding house. Then I saw that the passport, into which the photograph was pasted there and then, was not a new one. It was frayed at the edges and even had stamps covering a dozen pages. What reason there was for creating a well-travelled man named Siedel in place of the man – without the hair dye, the skin toner, the limp and the rubber ear – who had entered the country under another name I never found out.

In the normal way Goodwin's life was less melodramatic. He put in a nine-to-five day in Whitehall on the staff of something called 3 Committee, Research, Projects (Tactical), Ministry of Defence. He was available on the telephone under his own name. It was almost a year after Salisbury that he presented himself at our office, and of course I didn't believe at first that he was the same man. Only his eyes finally convinced me: there couldn't have been two pairs with the same dark brown, almost black, liquid quality, flashing with intelligence but giving away very little of what went on behind them. The eyebrows, which had been shaved and dyed in Rhodesia, had grown back to their shaggy greying thickness. He looked much less English than he had with the name of Siedel. He carried his forty-odd years well in spite of the grey hair; the skin was deep brown, with a texture as leathery as a fisherman's, and there was a certain Arab quality about his strong beaky nose and thin lips. On the waterfront at Marseilles or sipping coffee in Alexandria he wouldn't have been out of place. The public-school tie, the slightly pedantic manner and the deep English voice sorted strangely with it all.

It wasn't a social call, this visit in the autumn of 1966. I came not to expect that of him. George Blake had escaped from Wormwood Scrubs and Goodwin was one of the men looking for him. In some way he was now assigned, like a specialist reporter, to matters affecting the Balkans and the Middle East, and he was following a lead that suggested Blake might try to get through Yugoslavia into Hungary. He'd heard I was going to Yugoslavia to do a piece on the recovery of Skopje from the great earthquake; could I do him a favour on the way? Because Tom said he was worth keeping in with I spent three days photographing tourists and peasants along the road from Zagreb to Varazdin. Three months later we were paid twenty pounds for this service. If I'd caught George Blake and returned him to custody I might have got fifty.

We'd done Goodwin and his masters three or four more services, at the same rate of pay, but they had hardly bothered us since the 1967 war between Israel and the Arabs. With the freedom accorded to pressmen, but not foreign agents, to inspect the Sinai battle-grounds I had photographed in minute detail the gun mountings of wrecked and abandoned Arab armour on Goodwin's behalf, thereby missing a deadline I had to meet for *Der Spiegel.*

Hence our reluctance to meet Joe Goodwin. Or rather Tom's reluctance, which had infected me. I had vaguely hoped that Goodwin would one day give us more profitable work.

Now he had us trapped, obligated by the price of two drinks.

He came round the table and sat next to Tom. He took a swallow of his drink as if he needed it, then looked round the room and with secret amusement at us. There was something in his manner that suggested an officer visiting the sergeants' mess. Finally he said, 'You know I've been wanting to see you, Michael?'

There was no apology for the intrusion. The officer was pulling his rank, perhaps needing to impress us with the authority of 3 Committee. It was, so Tom said, an arm of the Ministry of Defence's Joint Intelligence Agency. Like good sergeants Tom and I summoned up indifference through the mist of alcohol; in the curiously classless world of newspapermen Goodwin choosing to be superior was definitely not on. I dropped a blob of ash on the table and worried it with a matchstick till it fell over the edge. Tom's eyes seemed to withdraw deep into his head.

'I thought I could put a little business your way,' Goodwin said.

Tom's voice rasped from too many cigarettes. He said, 'We're on holiday, Joe, as I told you. We're not making any trips.'

'And besides,' I put in, 'you know what we think of your payments.'

He waited testily, like a schoolteacher, for silence. 'I admit we haven't been over-generous in the past,' he said. 'Would a thousand pounds interest you? Tax-free, of course.'

Goodwin had our sense of values weighed up, at any rate. Tom and I exchanged glances.

16

'I thought you'd sit up,' Goodwin said, assuming control of the discussion. He allowed himself a smile. 'Get things on a business footing, eh? You've done rather well out of the Czechs, haven't you?'

'That's one way of putting it,' Tom said.

'Amazing bit of luck that, having Michael right on the spot.' He went through a peculiar ritual of unsealing a packet of Players and transferring the cigarettes, one by one, into an ostrich-skin case before offering them to us. 'And initiative,' he went on. 'A nice bit of old-fashioned initiative. Don't you think journalists on the whole lack it these days? The free access to information you used to demand — well, you've got it and it's taking its revenge. Your standards are being set for you by public relations men.'

We stared at him. I said, 'You were talking about a thousand quid.'

'Yes, indeed. And since I had to trail through every grotty journalists' pub in London to offer it to you, you can't object if I build up the suspense a little. I want to borrow you for a few days again, that's all. A week at the most.'

'Oh yes? What's the catch?'

'There's no catch.' Now he was speaking quietly enough not to be overheard by Hector. 'It's a little more complicated than before, naturally. The details will be for you and me to sort out. Later. I need a photographer, and for certain reasons you're the one I need.'

'Nobody could accuse you of giving away too much,' I said. 'In the past I've done jobs for you because I happened to be going to some place you were interested in. Is this different?'

'Yes.'

'Then why not use one of your own photographers? You've got plenty, haven't you?'

Goodwin sighed. 'It's no use asking me for details. What I want is the answer to one question. In principle, are you interested in making a thousand pounds or not?'

I looked at Tom again. He'd been untypically silent for a while and was staring at nothing. 'All right,' I said to Goodwin. 'I'm interested, in principle and every other way.'

'Good.'

All our glasses were empty. Tom made no move to buy a round

so I went to the counter. 'The last one,' I promised Hector. 'Have one yourself, it'll stop you fidgeting.'

I was keeping Hector up and Goodwin was keeping me. At any other time the offer of a thousand pounds for a week's work would have doubled my pulse rate, but now I was wishing he'd left it till the next day. My watch said nearly two o'clock and I was conscious again that I hadn't slept for nearly forty hours.

Apparently there had been silence while I was away from the table. Tom sat rigidly upright and Goodwin had his strong profile tilted back, looking at the ceiling. I wondered again whether they'd fallen out.

Without looking round Tom said, 'I'm still waiting to hear what the catch is, Joe.'

'I've told you there isn't a catch.'

Turning to Goodwin with the remote, eyeless look he got when he was being obtuse Tom said, 'You haven't used your personal charm to persuade the Treasury that Michael's worth a thousand pounds a session instead of twenty. Let's have the rest of the story.'

Goodwin's mouth made a white-edged line of anger for a moment. 'When I discuss this,' he said, 'with *Michael*, I'll make it quite clear what the risks are.'

'Risks,' Tom snapped. 'Ah, now we're getting to the small print. These sods are very strong on the small print, you know,' he said to me. It suddenly struck me that he was drunker than he'd seemed. 'You know what he said just now? For *certain reasons* he wanted to use you and not one of his own people. You should find out what that means. It could mean you're more expendable than they are.'

'Balls,' said Goodwin softly.

'And I'll tell you what else it could mean.' Tom went on. 'They don't want you because your camera work is such poetry, no sir, don't kid yourself. Have you seen some of the Box Brownie stuff that lot turn out? If Uncle Tom were to hazard a guess, he'd say that from their point of view the only thing that makes you different is that you're a Greek and they're not. Isn't that right, Joe?'

From the uncomfortable glance Goodwin gave me I knew that it was true. Then he retaliated. 'What makes you so curious?' he demanded.

'I'm not curious,' Tom said. 'I'm not the least bit curious. I just

18

don't want to see Michael buying more than he's bargained for, that's all. Michael is the kind of guy who'll sign papers without reading them. So don't you go round telling him this is the same old snapshot routine when I know it isn't. This is serious. You're going to send him to Greece and Papa Dop-Papadopoulos will stand him up in front of a firing squad.'

'You're pissed and patronizing,' I said.

Tom turned to me again as if I still didn't understand. 'Look, this man is a spy. S-P-Y. He recruits other people to do his S-P-Ying for him and he does it by trickery, chicanery, thieving, blackmail and knavery ...'

'Is there any point in continuing this discussion?' Goodwin asked coldly. I stepped into the breach. Only the thought of money was keeping me awake.

'Shut up, Tom,' I said. 'And look, Joe, if what he says about your wanting a Greek is right ... is it?'

'Yes,' Goodwin admitted.

'Well, you've got the wrong number then. I'm Greek only in the sense that I was born there, in Athens. I was brought to England as a kid of five before the war, and I've only been back on odd visits since. I'm English. I *feel* English, you understand?'

The shaggy eyebrows went up. 'But you still speak the language? Fluently?'

'Of course. My mother tongue.'

'So there's no problem.' Goodwin smiled sarcastically at Tom. 'You see, you were way off the mark. All I want is a plausible Greek.'

'That doesn't answer any of my objections,' Tom said. 'Not one.' He was at his argumentative worst.

'For Christ's sake,' I said, 'you know we can use a thousand quid. We can re-equip the darkroom and buy the television camera we want. The least you can do is listen to him.'

'I say Joe Goodwin puts all his cards on the table before he spirits my partner off anywhere.'

Goodwin said pleasantly, 'What made you think I was going to tell *you* about it anyway? This is between Michael and me.'

'Are you going to listen to this crap?' Tom demanded, swivelling to me.

I was barely listening as it was. My brain was swimming with fatigue and I resented having to exert myself to reply.

'I'll listen to anything but your bloody bitching,' I said. I was having trouble with my esses. Anger was turning Tom paler than ever and he gesticulated nervously.

'You're a bloody fool, Michael Mannis. This whole thing smells and if you take my advice you'll have nothing to do with it. It's for your sake I'm trying to put up a fight, don't you realize?'

'I can look after myself,' I said. 'I've done it before, you know. You're very good at getting me in the firing line and giving advice from behind your typewriter.'

This was a bitterly unjust remark but it came out, the way these things do, and I was too irritated to retract it. Goodwin by now was uncomfortably silent, like a third party at a husband-and-wife squabble.

Tom stood up slowly. He had a way of enfolding anger into himself like clenching a fist. 'All right,' he said, 'do it your way. And leave me right out of it. If you do earn your thousand pounds you can stick it, d'you hear? Stick it right up where it belongs. I don't want a penny of it.'

He stamped out of the room, knocking over a barstool near the door. Goodwin released the breath he had been holding, looked at me and muttered, 'Thank God.' I said, rather foolishly as if Tom had caused the whole scene on his own, 'Never mind him, he'll get over it.'

Goodwin swirled the melting ice round in the bottom of his glass. 'I wanted to talk to you alone in the first place,' he said.

'But not now.'

He thought about that and nodded. 'You look exhausted. Can I give you a lift home?'

'I'd appreciate it.'

Hazily I followed him down the stairs of the club and out into the early-morning chill. In Bouverie Street the UPI bureau threw down snatches of chattering telex music, and vans were backing and jostling to collect their loads of papers from the lighted citadel of the *Daily Mail*. We approached a Mini-Cooper parked with two wheels on the kerb and a curious mark on its numberplate, KKK.

'Is this yours?' I asked.

20

'No, I'm down on the Embankment.'

'Ku Klux Klan,' I said.

'What's that?'

'Nothing. I'm light-headed, that's all.'

I should have expected better of Goodwin. He had an Aston Martin DB5 that carried us westward through the swathes of fluorescent lighting. The only late walkers were tourists wondering where all the things they'd read about London actually happened. It was three o'clock when we drew up outside my flat in the shadow of the Brompton Oratory.

'How early can we meet tomorrow?' Goodwin asked.

'Not before five. I intend to sleep at least once round the clock.'

'It's rather urgent,' he said tactfully.

'Oh hell, I refuse to make any decisions. Ring when you want to and take a chance on getting your head bitten off. I'm in the directory.'

He drove off flicking his lights. I tramped up the narrow staircase of the mews flat and was asleep, half-clothed, five minutes later.

3

Hackney Marshes must once have been mainly marshes. Now it is mainly football fields, a great plain of them fitted together like a patchwork quilt. At weekends in winter half the male population of East London seems to descend on them in soccer boots, and even at two-thirty on a Thursday afternoon in summer they were not empty. Half a dozen boys were having bangs at goal on a field next to Eastway, the road that crosses the Marshes. Beyond that the landscape of rich green grass, faintly segmented by whitewashed lines and goalposts, stretched for a mile to the gasworks and power station at the northern end.

'I see the season has started,' Goodwin said absently. He was staring into the rear-view mirror, with his fist still around the handbrake of the Aston Martin. 'This game is never played away from the sight of smokestacks, have you noticed? Afraid I'm a rugger man myself. Come on.'

He was waiting for me to ask the questions but I wasn't playing. I'd sat in the car while he drove at a leisurely pace on the Ring Road past the City, through Islington and Clapton. He had phoned to wake me at one and picked me up at a quarter to two and we had barely exchanged a dozen words.

We walked out on to the fields. Pigeons and seagulls paraded across them in orderly rows and men were cutting chunks out of the turf with hired five-irons. *Members of the public,* said a notice, *are warned of the risk of being struck by golf balls.* Goodwin had brought a heavy pair of binoculars from the car. We had passed the second set of goalposts before he spoke.

'Everything must be between us,' he said abruptly. 'I meant what I said last night.'

'I can't really see your point,' I said. I didn't want the wedge between me and Tom driven any further. 'You've confided in both of us before. And we're partners, after all, we make the decisions between us.'

'Even after last night?'

Last night seemed a long time ago. I was refreshed by ten hours' sleep; Goodwin had changed his clothes but otherwise showed every sign of having spent the night up. The dark eyes were tinged with red and in two places he had cut himself shaving. 'That was unfortunate,' I said. 'But we're both pig-headed and we rarely get through a week without a row. There's still a business to run. It's got to be done on a basis of trust.'

Goodwin grunted. 'That's just the point, I suppose.'

I turned to him sharply. 'What do you mean?'

'Nothing you can't work out for yourself. How did he know about Czechoslovakia?'

Goodwin was holding my gaze and involuntarily I turned back to look at the boys banging at goal. For no reason I could think of my mouth had gone dry. 'He guessed,' I said. 'Guesses are sometimes right, you have to accept that.'

'Of course guesses are sometimes right. But I can't afford to accept it, don't you see? Tom's gone to a lot of trouble making friends in the right places. Including the embassies at Kensington Palace Gardens.'

'And in Whitehall,' I said. 'Don't forget that. Some of his best contacts are in the Ministries there. And at the American Embassy.' I was over-justifying, and both of us knew it. Hadn't I wondered myself, and tried to avoid wondering, where Tom got some of his brilliant inspirations for stories? Goodwin might have been following my thought processes.

'You're a trusting soul, Michael, that's all I'm really saying. You're a trusting soul and I'm not. You've never gone in much for speculating about things that don't seem to concern you, aren't I right? And why not? You've made a good living out of depending on Tom's judgment. I'm not accusing him of a damned thing. He's a shrewd reporter, he picks up hints here and there and acts on them. Among his various friends he exchanges bits of rewarding gossip ... '

'And that's all perfectly legitimate journalism,' I said.

'Of course. But what I want to tell you — it's not for his ears, that's all. Incomplete knowledge is tempting, I know how bloody easy it is.' Goodwin was struck by a thought. 'Do you remember Jerusalem? That German chap?'

'Yes.'

'Mm. Messy.' He glanced at me. 'Let's move on.'

We swung round and started walking again. The shouts of the boys back at the goalmouth receded; the sun was coming and going among gathering clouds. I thought that Goodwin's eyes were protruding a little more than they once had, and that the dark patches around them had spread. Even with his obvious good health he couldn't hide the signs of strain. He wasn't doing very well at hiding his basic distrust of Tom, either, and this made me curious as well as annoying me. Goodwin must have thought I knew more about Jerusalem than I actually did: all I remembered from June of the year before was that he'd been staying in the same seedy hotel in Beth Hakanem as Tom and I. It might have been by chance, and then again, it might not have been. We simply discovered him at breakfast one morning, complaining that his boiled egg was overdone. Naturally we talked about the war and I mentioned that I was going on a facilities trip into the Sinai that day. By some remarkable coincidence Goodwin had been wondering ... I took some pictures he wanted, delivered them late that night and found that he no longer seemed very interested. He was having a drink with a swarthy man who wasn't introduced to me, but who complained bitterly that the war had caused him to miss his flight to Hamburg. The next morning we found Goodwin had left the hotel. Later, the *concierge* told us, a man from the military police had been round asking for him. There were things in Joe Goodwin's life that I would rather not know about.

I said, 'So you want me to promise not to tell Tom anything?'

'Yes.'

'What's a promise worth?'

He smiled, rather tiredly. 'Sometimes a point is reached where even I have to take people on trust. Not very often, mind.'

'All right,' I said. 'But I listen to you without obligation.'

'Certainly. Just a minute.'

Goodwin had the binoculars slung round his neck. He raised them to his eyes, adjusted the focus and made a sweep along Eastway and Ruckholt Road, which we had left behind us. Then he made a half-turn and studied the council flats and factories that formed the western boundary of the Marshes, another turn to the north-east for a sweep from the gasworks to Leyton station. He seemed to see nothing of interest.

'I'll save you asking,' he said with a grin. 'If in various parts of London you saw the same man in your vicinity three times in two days, what would you think?'

'I'd think it was an odd coincidence, nothing more. But you wouldn't, of course. Is that why you came all the way out here, to draw them into the open?'

'And drove slowly enough to make sure they didn't lose me. They might just be curious enough to know what we're doing in the middle of Hackney Marshes to come to the edge for a look.'

'Who are they, Joe?'

He shrugged, perhaps a little too carelessly. 'Any one of a dozen interested parties. It gets to a point where it doesn't matter much. I'm suffering from over-exposure, you see, it's bound to happen. Following me around once in a while, apart from being a complete waste of time, is supposed to remind me that I'm blown – a brilliant idea, whoever thought of it. There's no-one there anyway. And in case I'm giving you the jitters it's got nothing to do with what we've come to talk about. That concerns you, not me.'

'And what is it?'

'Yes.' He kicked impulsively at a scuffed piece of turf. 'You've been to most of the Iron Curtain countries, haven't you? Ever tried Albania?'

'No.'

'That's not surprising. It's difficult to get into. In the normal way they wouldn't let a journalist within a hundred miles of the place. But I can get you in. I want you to go in and take some photographs for us. Your entry would be, well – approximately legal. No difficulties. The photography, frankly, would be anything but legal.'

'Albania.' Even the name was unfamiliar on my tongue. I coupled it with the one or two facts in the wastepaper-basket of my memory.

'That's why it's no good going on an official trip with your movements restricted. That's why you'll have to become a Greek again.'

An unmemorable country. I remembered its outline on a school geography map I had drawn, an oval shape squeezed up against the Adriatic coastline by the bulk of Greece and Yugoslavia. And there was only one other thing I really knew about it, something of more recent vintage. Albania was hardline Chinese communist, the only communist country in Europe to come out on China's side in the ideological dispute.

'I'm beginning to have Blakeney-type reservations,' I said.

Goodwin flapped his hand at me. 'Don't be hasty,' he said. 'Let me tell you a few things. What do you know about Albania? Nothing. I'll bet. It has borders with Yugoslavia and Greece – the Greek one's the one that interests us. Been closed for a long time. Technically Albania and Greece are still at war. But there were people there before there were borders. In the southern part of the country there's a fair-sized community of Greeks. Some of them still have close family ties with people across the frontier.

'Now' – Goodwin assumed a lecturer's manner – 'if you were the Albanians what would you do with those Greeks? If you cut off all their contact with outsiders there'd be an increase in clandestine contacts, refugees, smuggling, that sort of thing. It would make the border situation tenser than it is already. So they do the wise thing. They allow these people to have very limited visits from their relatives. It keeps them happy and it helps the authorities keep an eye on them. Neither side would admit it but there's quite a regular flow of unofficial traffic between Epirus and Albania. It goes via the northern Ionian islands: the mainland frontier is closed and guarded so the only approach is by sea. There are boats that take these relatives across, among other things. There's even a small barter trade and a certain amount of smuggling. Simple needs are being met in practical ways as they are everywhere, regardless of political barriers. Are you with me?'

I was more than that. I was intrigued by the plan I could see emerging. 'So I suddenly have relatives in Albania,' I said. 'Is that right?'

'An uncle and aunt and several cousins, I gather. All waiting to welcome you with open arms. You'll travel under your own name, a false identity is more risk than it's worth. So it comes down to a couple of white lies about your background, really. Like the idea?'

'White lies,' I repeated. 'It can't be that simple, surely?'

Goodwin held up a cautionary finger. 'It *is* that simple — so far. But that's only stage one, the approximately legal part, remember. Stage two is where you start earning your money. There's something that 3 Committee very badly want you to find and photograph. Something that may not even exist. If it does exist it's of vital importance. If not, well, you'll get your thousand anyway. You'll have some local assistance.'

We had crossed a bridge over the sluggish River Lea and were near the north-eastern boundary of the Marshes. Goodwin stopped and inspected the perimeter again through his binoculars, then we turned and started back towards the car. He was waiting for my question.

'I don't want to sound like Tom,' I said, 'but there are obviously risks. What are they?'

He gave me his tired smile. 'If I could honestly tell you I would. As yet I know too little about the subject. If you'd settle for my opinion in the meantime I'd say the only risk will be at the time you're taking photographs. The subject is likely to be under military guard, but I'm hoping that won't be a major obstacle.'

'The *subject*,' I said, hinting, 'is sensitive?'

26

'Very. So much so that you're not going to know anything about it till shortly before you enter Albania. I have to be firm about that, I'm afraid.'

It was hard to reconcile the discussion with the little blob of land obscured beneath my schoolboy's drawing of the Balkan Mountains — a herringbone pattern in brown crayon, I suddenly remembered.

'I can tell you this much,' Goodwin said. 'It's sensitive because it's big. Perhaps big enough to threaten the security of this country. *If* it exists, I must emphasize.'

He was altogether too calm and reasonable. I stopped walking and said, 'Do you mean that seriously?'

'Yes.'

'You're not just trying to get me to say yes?'

'I can't afford to,' he said, sighing. 'We've got to trust each other, Michael. I'm being as frank as I can be.'

'But God, this must be some kind of top-level operation. You can't ask me to take part in it, with no training in that kind of thing. I'm just — just what we said I was last night, a photographer who speaks Greek.'

Goodwin's eyes were steady and serious. 'It's not a big operation,' he said. 'It might become one, but its scope at the moment is limited to securing these photographs. I'm responsible for getting them. And I need you for the job.'

'Isn't there anyone else?'

He shrugged. 'There probably is, if we could find him, screen him, be sure he's trustworthy. It all takes time and we haven't got time. You happen to be made for the part.'

A weight seemed to have landed on my shoulders. Remembering a wartime upbringing in a fiercely patriotic family — their patriotism all the stronger for being adopted, and from this distance seeming absurd among the Greek and Latin ghettoes of Camden — I suppose I had been left with some guilty notions of duty. I thought I'd worked them off doing my national service in Cyprus (an extra pound a week for interpreter's duties) but here they were again, looking at me through Goodwin's anxious Levantine face. He had always treated my past services as a right, not a favour. 'I don't know,' I said. 'I don't know whether I'm made for the part at all.'

27

'I'm afraid you are, though.' He looked away, brushing an imaginary speck off the shoulder of his navy-blue pinstripe suit. 'You're a versatile photographer, you've done risky work before, your nerves seem all right — better than mine, I should say. And don't forget the money's good.' That was sensible. It supported the idea of a buyer-seller relationship.

'How long do I get to make up my mind?'

'Let's say till we reach the car. That's about five minutes.'

I didn't laugh. We walked on in silence, stopping only for Goodwin to peer once more through the binoculars and lower them with a shake of his head. I was no nearer deciding when we went through the gate on to the road and he glanced at me; he was afraid the genie was going to go back into his lamp.

Most important decisions in people's lives are made, I believe, impulsively. Marriages and careers, if you take them back to the first critical moment, are made at the blink of an eye. That was how, between pressing the door-handle button on the car and tugging the door open, I decided.

'Yes.' I said.

Goodwin smiled quickly and groped in the inside pocket of his jacket, producing a small white envelope, unaddressed.

'That's for you,' he said.

I tore it open. Inside was the usual crossed cheque, drawn by the Ministry of Social Security. It was made out in neat round handwriting for five hundred pounds. To me.

'You bastard,' I said. 'You knew all along I'd say yes.'

'I had to get the bumf out of the way,' Goodwin said shortly, 'before the real work started. That's the first payment and there'll be another when you've secured the photographs. Or if you've got a good excuse for not having secured them.'

'Such as being dead. You realize this is going into Newsflash's account, whatever Blakeney says?'

Goodwin eased himself in behind the wheel and drummed on it with his fingers. 'That's something I hadn't considered,' he said. 'Can you keep it somewhere safe till you get back? I'll want you to sign a receipt before I drop you, by the way.'

We drove back through Stratford and Bow, with Goodwin's eyes darting frequently to the mirror. 'What's next on the programme?' I asked.

'Nothing till we meet at West London Air Terminal tomorrow. Midday.'

'You aren't coming too?' I said incredulously.

'Of course.' He had an odd way of assuming omniscience in the listener. 'You don't think I'm going to let you run loose on your own, do you?'

'I thought you would sort of run things from this end.'

'Oh no, I shall sit around getting bored waiting for you to come out of Albania. Things are being set up in Greece for our arrival. Let's talk about what you should bring with you.'

I told him what gear I had, we discussed the merits of various cameras and lenses and settled on the items I should bring. We reached Trafalgar Square as the traffic was starting to thicken towards rush-hour, and stopped outside the National Gallery. Goodwin gave me the receipt to sign and scribbled down a phone number where I could contact him.

'There shouldn't be any need for it,' he said. 'They can put you through to me at home if necessary, but don't talk to anyone else.'

'Urgent calls only, then. How urgent is that?'

'Use your discretion. Remember what I said about Tom — and of course, not a word to anyone else either. If you have to tell people you'll be out of town say you're going anywhere but Greece.'

He drove off. I stood for a few seconds watching the Aston Martin round the square towards Whitehall, and wondering for the first time quite how much I'd been talked into.

It was a fortunate pause. I had started across Duncannon Street on my way to the tube station when I recognized the car that was following Goodwin.

I shouldn't pretend that there was anything intuitive about this, unless it came from spending most of my life in London. Two ideas had somehow fallen into place and meshed. The first was that in a city of three million cars you don't see an olive-green Mini-Cooper with the same KKK number twice in less than twenty-four hours. The second was that no-one who drives a Cooper avoids taking a gap if he gets the chance. This one stayed in the same lane as the Aston Martin, keeping a steady fifty yards and two cars between them as they went round the square.

29

A lady with an armful of parcels had flagged down a taxi outside South Africa House. I vaulted over the crush barrier, leapt into the cab ahead of her and slammed the door behind me. 'Get after that Mini,' I said, but the cabbie hadn't seen the right films.

'What?' He screwed up his face behind the partition. 'Here, are you a copper?'

'No, but I've got good friends who are,' I said. I pulled out my Scotland Yard press pass and waved it at him. The card gave me no special privileges but sometimes it impressed people. 'Will you follow that car or do I report you for refusing a fare?'

'All right, old love, only asking.' He swung out into the traffic stream.

The Cooper had gone round into Whitehall by now and for a minute I thought we'd lost it. Then I saw it just ahead, pulling up next to the kerb opposite the War Office. Of course, I realized anticlimatically, Goodwin had gone straight back to work and the people following him would wait till he came out again. But I had an idea, and the delay might just give me time to put it into effect. The taxi driver gave me a sceptical look.

'Pull in about fifty yards ahead of them,' I said. 'By the phone box in front of that van, where they won't see me. And wait.'

The taxi was an ideal tail car and I didn't want to lose it. We cruised past the Cooper, and from the corner of my eye I saw there was only one man in it, sitting staring straight ahead. The cab's tinted back window obscured me from his view as we drove on and stopped in front of a Royal Mail van next to the phone box. I slipped across the pavement, shut myself into the cubicle and dialled Claire Conway's number.

It was a number I knew but pretended to forget now and then, for which a lot of men would consider me ungrateful. Claire and I had what I suppose was a curious relationship: too sensual to be friendship and too casual to be an affair. Claire, I suspected, wanted it to be less casual. She'd started to accuse me of having bachelor's habits, and that was one warning signal. She'd also recently moved to a place only three minutes away from my flat, to which she had a key.

She was at home. I said, 'Can you grab a cab on my account, nip round to my place and bring a few things down to me in Whitehall?

It's important,' I added when she started to interrupt. I told her where to find me. 'I can't do it myself and I need the stuff urgently.'

'What do I bring?' she asked.

'Two black Leicas and two lenses – fifty-mil and hundred-mil telephoto. Four 36-spools of black-and-white Plus-X film. It's all in the camera cupboard in my sitting room. Got it?'

'Yes.' She enjoyed reminding me that she knew a bit about cameras. 'Got caught with your cameras off, did you? I thought you were the one who never went anywhere without them?'

I could hardly explain that Joe Goodwin, secret agent, wouldn't have liked a man with a bag full of cameras walking about with him. And this led me to wonder, as I went back and took my seat in the cab, whether he'd like me doing what I was doing now. Perhaps I was taking on too much: I should have consulted him before trying to sneak pictures of the man who was following him.

Then I thought of something else. By asking Claire to help me I'd indirectly broken my promise to keep everything to myself. Idiot. Best to shut up about Claire, I decided, carry on as I'd planned and talk to Goodwin later. I managed to convince myself that he'd appreciate what I did as long as I did it professionally. He *had* to be worried about being watched, more worried than he let on. Even if it had nothing to do with the Albanian mission, even if Goodwin believed it wasn't important, the man in the Cooper was persistent enough to suggest it was important to him. Why was there only one man, I wondered.

The taxi-driver must have decided I was a nut case with an expense account. He sat studying greyhound selections with the meter ticking while I prayed for Claire to arrive and kept an eye on the Cooper. It was only partly hidden by the Royal Mail van and I could see half of the driver, a bulky-looking man, probably in his thirties, with glasses, plump cheeks and thin hair of an indeterminate light colour. He had a strong face in spite of its flabbiness; he looked like Rip Kirby run to fat, and if he was a foreigner there was nothing in his appearance to suggest where he came from. Like the taxi-driver, he had the patience of a man used to waiting.

Big Ben down the road chimed five o'clock, then a quarter past. The news-stand posters were full of Czechoslovakia. Defiance in the streets, Assembly in Session, flag-waving: it could all have been

31

happening on another planet. Now the bowler hats were spilling out of the ministries but Goodwin wouldn't necessarily be among them. He was putting in overtime, after all.

When I wait a long time for things to happen they usually take me by surprise. Big Ben's hands were edging towards five-thirty when the Aston Martin came by in the wrong direction, going fast against the traffic stream towards Trafalgar Square. 'Get going,' I said to the cabbie and glanced back. The Cooper was frantically trying to nudge its way out into a U-turn. Another taxi, co-operating against the common enemy, held up a line of cars to let my driver make a turn and we shuddered off behind Goodwin.

Altogether I was having a lucky afternoon. In front of the Horse Guards barracks I saw Claire trotting down the pavement with my black camera bag. We stopped and bundled her aboard, breathless.

'Couldn't find a taxi,' she said as we halted at the first set of lights, three cars behind Goodwin. 'I came by tube. Is my lipstick on straight?'

'Perfect,' I said without looking. I'd watched the Cooper untangling itself from the traffic and moving into place behind us.

The teams were all in position.

4

'What car do you want me to follow now?' the taxi-driver asked politely.

'The same one. Let him overtake you,' I said and closed the sliding panel in the partition. Claire watched me curiously as I loaded the Leicas. We were crawling behind the Aston Martin up Regent Street.

'What's it all about?' Claire asked.

'We're tailing a car that's tailing another car. Don't ask me how it started, I've just taken it on myself to do someone a favour. I hope he sees it in the same light.'

What I really needed was for the Cooper to stop and the driver to get out so that I could take passable pictures of him. But that wasn't going to happen until Goodwin himself stopped, and soon the light would be going. As we joined another queue of traffic in Park Crescent I remembered Goodwin once mentioning that he lived in Chislehurst: this route certainly wasn't taking him home. I'd begun to realize that the more I interfered the less he was going to like it; I should have phoned to tip him off about the Mini and left it at that. But having started my bit of freelance tailing, I had to see it through.

'A favour,' Claire repeated mockingly. 'Don't tell me Michael Mannis is deigning to touch a camera without charging somebody up to the back teeth for it.'

'For once, yes. Well, not quite,' I said, remembering the cheque for five hundred pounds in my pocket. I ran my eye over her generous figure. 'Are you accusing me of greed?'

'Concupiscence,' she said, smoothing down her dress. It was a shift-style thing in light red corduroy, and under it she was big-breasted and broad-hipped, a late nineteen-fifties shape. That had been her decade, and mine too, if youth had something to do with it. Personally I liked her as she was, mature and dignified, with a faintly Latin sultriness to the broad dark face and the black hair that swung loosely around it.

We'd driven into Regent's Park. The driver entered the spirit of the thing, let the Cooper overtake us on the Outer Circle and then gunned the taxi as hard as he could to keep up with it. Maybe it gave him some amusement.

'How did you get back from Prague so quickly?' Claire said.

'I had a ticket from Munich. I got a friend to drive me there.'

'What was her name?'

'Helga, since you ask. Blonde, to save you another question.'

'I didn't need to ask that,' she said sardonically. 'I know how bad your taste is.'

Hidden jealousy too, I reflected — another bad sign.

We caught sight of Goodwin's car turning out of the park into Avenue Road. The Cooper followed and so did we. Goodwin couldn't have known they were behind him, unless by some fluke he too remembered the curious triple-K index I'd noticed near the Press Club the night before. It seemed unlikely – only my kind of grasshopper brain retained things like that in it. He might guess somebody was still following him, but if so he was taking no trouble to shake him off.

About halfway up Avenue Road the two cars turned sharply left. Our driver went after them at the right distance and then suddenly slowed down and rapped a warning on the partition. It was a narrow road with a dog's leg bend in it and across the next intersection the Cooper was pulling in by the kerb. So Goodwin must have stopped. I glanced at the light and made speed and aperture settings on the Leica with the 100mm. lens.

'Go left here at the normal speed and stop just round the corner,' I told the driver. Claire, falsely sensing a social encounter, had her compact out.

There was a pub on the corner. We turned past it into a street lined with young chestnut trees and opulent neo-Georgian houses, in time to see Goodwin walk up to the saloon-bar entrance, adjust his tie in the window pane and go in. Almost immediately Rip Kirby appeared at the opposite corner, crossed the road and went in after him. My palms were sweating as I turned the focusing ring, and, resting the camera on Claire's shoulder, got two shots of him through the side window of the cab.

'That's our man,' I said. 'Jesus, who'd have thought he'd get that close?'

'Close to what?' Claire said vaguely. She was frowning into her compact mirror.

'Come on, we've arrived.' I opened her door and pushed her gently out. Something was worrying me. Goodwin hadn't come all this way to quench his thirst. He was bound to be meeting someone, or collecting or leaving a message in this pub, and without his knowing it Rip Kirby was practically breathing down his neck. I wished once again that I'd let Goodwin know about the Cooper.

I paid the driver and he swung away, shaking his head. It takes all sorts, he'd be thinking, and I suppose it does. I did a quick reconnoitre. Goodwin had parked his car about forty yards down the turning. Opposite the saloon-bar entrance there was a row of houses with basements and area fences. The Cooper was round the corner and to reach it Rip Kirby would have to cross the road: I could do with a close shot of him, preferably full-face instead of profile. I hurried Claire across the road, looked round to make sure no-one was paying us any attention, then chose a basement flat that looked deserted and took her down six steps till our heads were at pavement level. Through the railings we had a view of the pub entrance without being obtrusive ourselves.

Claire had been on picture-snatching expeditions with me before. She said, 'You still haven't told me the story.'

'Did you see the man who was being followed?'

'No. Is he the friend you're doing a favour?'

'Yes.'

'Does he know he's being followed?'

'No.'

'Why not tell him then?'

Why not? Goodwin had been in the pub about a minute. The more I thought about him meeting an important contact in there with Rip Kirby listening in, the more uneasy I felt. I'd taken on too much by assuming that 3 Committee's boffins would be able to identify a foreign agent from my pictures. Very likely there was no record of Rip Kirby so my work would leave them with nothing but a car registration number and two profile views of an unidentifiable man. The obvious move was to go in, contact Goodwin in some way and point Rip Kirby out to him. It would make up for my earlier mistake.

I rested the camera on the pavement with the lens peeping out between two railings. 'Can you handle this?' I asked.

'I think so,' said Claire. 'You'd better set it for me.'

I opened the shutter a couple of stops to compensate for the failing light. The black Leica was designed to be inconspicuous for press work, with no shiny surfaces, but the secret of snatching lies in the cameraman's ability to blend with the scenery. I focused on the pub doorway. The place was called the Horse and Hounds.

'Did you see the guy I shot just now?'

'No,' said Claire.

'Don't you notice anything, for God's sake? Thick-set, thin hair, glasses, dark suit.'

'I was powdering my nose. Your descriptive powers aren't what

I'd call startling anyway. That description fits about one man out of every three in London.'

'All right,' I said. 'I can't afford to miss this shot. Stay here and take a picture of every man who walks out of that door till I come back. Let them take two steps till they're out of the shadow and then click. Okay? Keep down low.'

'What do I get out of all this?'

'Dinner,' I said, 'later.' I went up the steps, across the road and into the Horse and Hounds.

It was one of those townsmen's pubs with a countrified decor. Perhaps bow windows, plastic coachlamps and hunting prints, all *circa* 1955, struck some wistful chord among the St Johns Wood urban rich. The place was crowded, anyway, and the air thick with smoke and noise. A man said, 'Pardon' and brushed past me on his way out, a man I could have sworn for a second I knew. Then I caught sight of Goodwin's grey mop across the heads of the crowd. He was making for a door with the silhouette of a man in riding gear on it. I picked my way after him. He balanced his drink and cigarette on a ledge next to the door and went in.

Moving through the wall of people involved some displacement. I elbowed aside a director investing drinks in his secretary and spilt half a Dubonnet over a youth who was talking about call options; the ink on his degree wasn't even dry. Somewhere among them would be Rip Kirby but for the moment he didn't matter. I reached the lavatory door, opened it and knew in a moment that Goodwin was no longer there. The two cubicles were vacant and there was only an old man at the pissoir. To the left was a door leading to the car park. With a surge of excitement I knew what Goodwin was up to. I flung the door open in time to see him disappearing round the dog's-leg bend towards St Johns Wood station.

Very neat. I hadn't given him enough credit for knowing – or guessing – that he was still being watched. He did have an appointment, but it wasn't at the Horse and Hounds and he wasn't having Rip Kirby around to monitor it. I almost laughed out loud as I went round the building and joined Claire in the basement foxhole.

'I've taken six men,' she said. 'But I don't think the one you wanted has come out yet.'

'He'll be here in a minute, as soon as he realizes he's been had.' I took the camera off her. Sure enough, Rip Kirby appeared round the corner from the car park. He'd realized too late that Goodwin was spending a little too long in the gents. I brought him into magnified clarity in the viewfinder and took three pictures, full and three-quarter face, as he crossed the road.

At some point it was inevitable that my luck should run out, though in the context of the evening's work what happened didn't seem too important. A twilight hush had fallen and the click of a shutter can be quite a penetrating sound. It was the third one that he heard, when he was closest to me. He stopped and looked straight at the camera and at my head behind the railings. He stared the way any innocent citizen would stare, but unlike an ordinary citizen he didn't demand to know what I was doing. He hurried on round the corner, and a few moments later the Cooper started and roared away.

'So he's the one,' Claire said. 'He looks the kind to be skulking in a doorway. Why is he doing it?'

'I don't know. I daresay Joe Goodwin could tell you, but he wouldn't.'

'Goodwin — he's the one with the fancy car, is he?'

Absently I looked along the street to where Goodwin had parked his DB5. I was still preoccupied with Rip Kirby and it took me a second to register the fact that the car was gone.

'Good God,' I said. 'Did you see who took it?'

'What, the car? Your friend — at least I assume it was him. He came out of the pub just after you'd gone in.'

'No, he didn't.' I was confused. Then I remembered that Claire hadn't actually seen Goodwin going into the Horse and Hounds. 'Start at the beginning. Who came out of the pub?'

'A little dark man. He went down the street and drove off in the car. What sort of childish antics are all these people up to, anyway?'

A little dark man had brushed past me on his way out of the pub, a little dark man that I thought I knew from somewhere but couldn't place now if my life depended on it. He'd had some connection with Joe Goodwin, too. Joe Goodwin's ploy had been even cleverer than I thought; the dark man was without doubt the one he'd set out to meet. Goodwin's arrival in the saloon bar, drawing his tail in after him, had been the signal for him to depart.

And using a duplicate key he'd driven off in the Aston Martin while the man from the Cooper was stuck inside the pub. Later, when Goodwin had spent an hour or so switching trains on the Underground, they'd meet somewhere else.

'You've just learnt how to make two men and a car escape from observation all at once,' I said. 'Try to remember the trick: it could be useful.'

'You're obviously not telling me what it's all about,' said Claire, 'so you'll pardon me for getting bored.'

'All right,' I said. 'You've earned the dinner I promised you. But there's one more chore first. I've got to develop this film.'

'Do you have to do that now?'

'Our office is on the way home and it'll take about twenty minutes, no more. Come and watch the master at work.'

We climbed up out of the basement and went looking for a cab.

5

It was partly by chance, partly to do with Claire and partly through a stupid act of carelessness almost too embarrassing to write about that I never developed that spool of film. I've told myself since, and I'd suggested as much to Goodwin that afternoon, that I wasn't a trained agent and couldn't be expected to act like one. But there was no excuse, really. By following that Cooper I was trying to compete with the professionals, and I should have learnt the rules first. I should have been warned the minute that I knew Rip Kirby had seen me photographing him. The trouble perhaps was that my own job was too much like fun, too much of a game in which I stood to lose nothing of importance. It had taught me a certain amount of discretion but nothing about the humdrum sense of discipline that ought to go with it.

A small, unforeseeable annoyance started it off. When Claire and I reached the Newsflash office I found we'd run out of photographic fixer. Apparently we had used every drop developing the dozens of films I'd brought back from Prague.

'Now what?' Claire demanded. It was after seven; the shops were shut.

'I may be able to get some from the all-night chemist in Piccadilly. I can be down there and back in twenty minutes.'

'Forty would be more like it,' she said.

'Why don't you go home and let me pick you up later?'

'Because you'll never get there. You know you underestimate everything. Forty minutes to get down to Piccadilly and back, another forty developing and printing. It'll take you half and hour to get home' — she was counting off the hours on her fingers — 'And you're going to change, aren't you?' I was wearing a linen suit I'd had tailored in Hong Kong five years before; I couldn't see anything wrong with it. 'That's another half-hour,' Claire said. 'And you've got to pack if you're going away tomorrow. You'll be lucky if you make it by ten o'clock.'

She was right, of course. She was an artist living on precarious earnings and she wasn't letting me wriggle out of a promise of dinner. Besides, no matter how soon I developed my pictures I wouldn't be able to tell Goodwin about them till later that evening. He would be tied up with the man from the Horse and Hounds.

I decided the film could wait until later. That was my first mistake, reducing its urgency and therefore its importance. After that it was easy enough to wonder whether I really needed to carry it about with me the whole evening. I hated doing that with exposed film, it was so easy to lose or forget. Once I'd lost some to a pickpocket, and another time I'd sent a whole feature on old steam engines to the dry cleaners in a coat pocket. I looked round the office for a safe place to leave it and settled on one of the filing cabinets, bottom drawer. The bottom drawers of filing cabinets are always full of junk. I locked it with the key on my own ring and we left.

A taxi dropped us at Claire's flat in Ennismore Gardens and I walked home from there. I changed into a dark suit and then threw out the soiled clothes from the small suitcase I had taken to Prague, and repacked it. It held the kind of things I would have taken on a summer weekend: two pairs of slacks, a couple of shirts, underwear and a pair of plimsolls that were the badge of Mannis on Holiday. I packed my camera bag, which usually accounted for any excess weight I had on an air trip, lightly as well. Joe Goodwin and I had settled simply on the best camera I owned and was ever likely to, a Rolleiflex SL66. Single-lens reflex, 2¼-inch square format, it was to a photographer what a Rolls Royce is to a motorist. An auxiliary viewing prism, a couple of other accessories and a dozen spools each of colour and black-and-white film went into the bag with it. The immense 500-mm telephoto lens would be carried separately in its cylindrical leather case.

'Is that all?' I had asked Goodwin. 'Don't your own lads use cross-hatched film for gauging distances and infra-red stuff for night work?'

'This is most likely to be straightforward daylight photography,' he had said, 'and you'd best use the gear you're accustomed to. Besides, you can only smuggle so much through the Albanian customs.'

Smuggling and entering a country under false pretences – well, I'd done worse things in the course of newspaper work. It gives you a sense of impunity by which the worst that can possibly happen is to have the film stripped out of your camera.

At eight o'clock I collected Claire and walked her through the soft summer air down the Old Brompton Road to a restaurant where they knew us. We drank a bottle of Chablis with the *moules poulette* and a bottle of red Bordeaux with the braised beef. I didn't know whether it was the extra Kirsch in the fruit cup that did it, but at ten o'clock Claire was licking my ear in a way that was bound to be embarrassing, even in a French restaurant.

'Why can't you do this in private?' I said, so we went back to her flat and she did. She made love with easy, voluptuous enjoyment – rather like the way she painted, only better. I fell asleep hugging her big Rubensesque body.

It was nearly one o'clock when I woke up and remembered with dismay the film I hadn't developed. I was tempted just to forget about it but it nagged my conscience; it had been nagging vaguely ever since I'd put off developing it. I got up and dressed quietly.

Claire lay sleeping with her black hair splayed across the pillow and a corner of the sheet trapped between her breasts. I wrote her a quick note, put it in the same place and left.

There was a light on in the Newsflash office. I saw it and felt my pulse quicken as the taxi dropped me at the corner of Grays Inn Road. Nobody had been at work that day and certainly no-one had any business being there now. Carrying the bottle of fixer I'd bought, I went as quietly as I could up the rickety stairs and stopped outside the door.

The person inside was moving about and making no attempt to keep quiet. And I knew only one person who worked to the tune of 'Summertime' rendered in a harsh East End whistle. Nathan started back a couple of paces as I flung the door open. 'Hello, Mr Mannis,' he said lamely.

'What the hell are you doing here?' I said.

He looked uncomfortable. 'I come in to do some of me own stuff, Mr Mannis.'

'What stuff?'

He was edging back towards the darkroom door. 'Just some printing. It's the firm's paper but I replace it every week out of me wages .... '

I pushed past him. A dozen eight-by-ten prints were curled up in the tray where they'd come off the drum of the glazer. Several studies of a cat yawning, a surrealistic bomb-site landscape, trees reflected in water. The ones of the cat were quite good, but heavily grained and printed with strong contrast.

'Arty stuff,' I said. 'Are you doing a coffee-table book?'

'I'm trying to learn, Mr Mannis.' Nathan was miserable. 'I come in now because I don't get time when I'm working.'

'That's not the reason,' I said. 'It's because you don't want us to see it. You're embarrassed, aren't you?' I got an abject nod out of him as he followed me from the darkroom. 'You won't learn unless you show people what you've done and find out what's wrong with it. My advice is forget the *art nouveau* and take pictures of people .... ' I was going to add, 'People make pictures come to life,' but thought I was overdoing the father-figure bit.

'But you've got to experiment, ain't you, Mr Mannis? I mean I've got to, not you. I mean, I've learnt enough to know you've got to

41

play around a bit. Have you lost something, Mr Mannis?'

I had lost something. But I couldn't quite believe that among the three-point plugs, bits of string, flashbulbs and paper clips in the bottom drawer of the filing cabinet, there was no film cassette. I stood looking at the heap of stuff before whirling on Nathan.

'Have you been at this drawer?'

'Me? No, Mr Mannis.'

'Has anyone else been up here tonight?'

'Only Mr Blakeney.'

'Tom!' I stared at Nathan's silly formless Jewish face. For a moment it seemed that the whole thing was some elaborate practical joke in which he had a part, but he looked back at me guilelessly, anxious to please. I felt the first clutching of fear. Was it conceivable that Tom was helping the other side – one of the other sides, whatever they were? Yes, I had to admit for the first time that it was. Goodwin was suspicious and this would confirm his suspicions when he found out. And he had to find out; I had to tell him because I'd made the most ghastly botch-up of the whole thing. I said, 'When was Mr Blakeney here?'

'I seen him leaving when I arrived,' Nathan said. 'About eleven o'clock. I nearly bumped into him down the front door, but I didn't want him to know I was here ....'

Did he have to be so bloody blatant about it? Did he have to leave me no alternative but to tell Goodwin who'd have MI5 or the Special Branch or whoever they were landing on him like a ton of bricks? I realized my hands were shaking as I lit a cigarette. Keep your cool, I told myself, explore the other possibilities first.

'There's a spool of 35-mil Plus-X gone from this drawer,' I said to Nathan. 'Maybe Mr Blakeney's put it somewhere else. Help me look for it, will you?'

We searched every corner of the office. In thirty minutes I knew we weren't going to find it and I'd also decided what to do. I would talk to Tom, ask him bluntly whether he'd taken the film and give him the chance to return it. Perhaps it wasn't wise, perhaps it wasn't what they'd call 'secure,' but there were ten years of friendship and four years of business partnership at stake. They couldn't be forgotten. I shooed Nathan off home and dialled the number; I knew Tom's wife and child were on holiday in Spain, so we could talk without causing any curiosity.

'Tom Blakeney,' said a seductive voice suddenly and loudly in the earpiece, 'is out of town from Thursday night until Sunday. If you have a business matter to discuss, please call his office number during normal working hours .... '

The tricky bastard, I thought – he had never used an answering machine before and it seemed more than a coincidence that he should have installed it today.

'If you wish to leave a message,' the voice purred synthetically, 'please speak now.' I said something obscene and slammed the receiver down, feeling annoyed with Tom as if he were refusing to be serious. I thought of taking a cab to his home in Richmond but I knew it wouldn't work. If he had made up his mind to avoid me then I couldn't change it. He was making things difficult for me, and ultimately for himself as well.

I had smoked two cigarettes and paced about a good deal before I found the courage to phone Goodwin. I would tell him the truth, basically, but for the moment I was going to leave Tom out of it. I couldn't bring myself to do otherwise. As it turned out, Goodwin took a guess that was disconcertingly near the mark.

A woman answered his office number noncommittally. 'Hello.'

'I want Mr Goodwin of 3 Committee,' I said.

'Who's calling?'

'My name is Mannis,' I said, and waited for her to get it wrong.

'Mr Manners? Hold on.'

There was a series of crackling noises and Goodwin came sharply on the line: 'Yes?' It was two-thirty but his voice told me I hadn't woken him up.

'Trouble,' I said, and started to tell him the story. I told him about noticing the Cooper the night before and following it after he had dropped me in Trafalgar Square that afternoon. When I got to the Horse and Hounds episode he interrupted.

'Just a minute.' His tone was very deliberate, very controlled; it almost made me shiver. 'You say you actually took photographs of this man with the glasses?'

'Yes. And then he saw me.'

'And you had this woman with you?'

'She knows nothing, Joe. Nothing at all.'

There was a pause. 'You saw the man who drove my car away as well?' he said carefully.

'For a second.'

'Had you ever seen him before?'

'I thought I had. I just couldn't place him.'

Perhaps I expected Goodwin to respond to that but he said nothing. The silence was furious. I carried on talking, and when I reached the end he released his anger in one short blast.

'Bloody fool! Bloody, bloody, *bloody* fool!' Then he said quickly, 'First things first. I could lose my temper very easily but I won't. You may well have caused some damage and I'll have to try and patch it up. Give me that car number.'

I quoted it to him. 'I've apologised, Joe,' I said. 'What more can I say?'

'Nothing much.' His voice was remote. 'So the film has gone. Who's been in your office tonight – Blakeney?'

'No. He's out of town, as far as I know.'

'He has a key to the door and a key to the filing cabinet, presumably?'

'Anybody could pick the outside lock, if that's what you're thinking,' I said, and added desperately, 'You know filing cabinet drawers, they're not all that secure.'

He laughed sarcastically. 'It was a brilliant place to leave the film then, wasn't it? Hadn't it occurred to you that if this stooge was following me last night he must have followed you as well? All the way from the Press Club to your flat? If he knows his business he'll have found out by this evening who you are, where you work and anything else about you that matters. Perhaps he's been through your flat for good measure. Where've you been this evening – on the nest?'

'You said it was you they were interested in, Joe, not me. Have you changed your mind?'

'God damn it, it doesn't matter *who* they're interested in. I've got to see that this thing stays secure and the last thing I want is an oaf following me round with a bloody great camera!'

'All right,' I said acidly. 'But you've got a description of the man who was following you and the number of the car he was driving, and you wouldn't have had that without me.'

44

'And what do you think that's worth, pray? He'll have covered his tracks. I'm willing to offer you very good odds that that car was hired by a Belgian tourist with impeccable bona fides. As for the film – well, if you'd managed to keep it in your sweaty grasp for just long enough to hand it over to me we would have had one more entry for a very large file called Operatives, Alien, Unidentified. If he wasn't in it already. Don't you think I *knew* they were after me? And after all my precautions the net result of your efforts is to let them know in a very large way that I'm on to them. Your stupidity staggers me, Michael.'

'Well, after all that, do I send your cheque back or don't I?'

'Michael,' he said, and sighed, 'just go home where you can do no more damage and stay there, will you? The trip is still on unless I tell you otherwise, and for your own sake I hope it *is* on. 3 Committee have some nasty and very private ways of kicking people who get under their feet. Understand?' He rang off without letting me reply. But I understood. I put down the phone and booted a wastepaper basket across the room, seething with anger at myself, at Goodwin and at Tom. Histrionics didn't achieve much without an audience so I sulked to myself in the back of a taxi on the way home.

If anyone had been in my flat during my absence there wasn't the slightest trace of it. Goodwin was over-reacting, I reckoned. The Social Security cheque, the only thing that had caused me any anxiety, was still in the bureau drawer. I was almost sure it was in the position I had left it in.

I went straight to bed. As I dozed off I found myself trying to remember once again where I had seen the small dark man who had kept his rendezvous with Goodwin at the Horse and Hounds. But it wouldn't come back to me.

6

The West London Air Terminal was a short walk from my flat, but I managed to be ten minutes late. Goodwin was fidgeting about opposite the Barclays Bank counter, where we had arranged to meet. He looked frayed around the edges and he greeted me sourly.

'I thought you'd done all the harm you could,' he said. 'But I'd forgotten you could still miss the plane if you tried hard enough.'

'Perpetual latecomers never actually miss things,' I said. 'We have a very fine sense of timing.' We hurried down the stairs and out into the bus station. 'I assume you've been up all night. I've told you I'm sorry, there's not much point in repeating it.'

'Yes, yes,' he said absently.

'Did you have any luck tracing that Cooper?'

'It was just as I said. Triple-K is a Kent index. It belongs to a car-hire firm in Maidstone and it was leased for a month, by a *Swede* for a change. Inexplicably phoned and asked them to collect it last night, when it had only been on hire three days. And gave a false home address. So much for your private-eye work.'

Goodwin in a foul mood was impossible to argue with, and I couldn't exactly blame him for his feelings towards me. They were part of a tension that was growing almost visibly, together with the dark shadows round his eyes and tightening lines splayed out from their corners. But in the bus bowling along the M4 he seemed more relaxed, nodding off a couple of times with a secret smile hovering on his lips. He looked like a City-battered businessman dreaming of his holiday. I was happy about one thing: he had shown very little curiosity about Tom and I wasn't going to provoke any more. I had phoned Richmond that morning and got the answering machine again.

At Heathrow when we checked in for our flight I realized I didn't even know our destination. The ticket that Goodwin handed me said London–Athens, Athens–Herakleion. 'Are we going to Crete?' I said, mystified. 'That's nowhere near .... '

'After you,' Goodwin said, ushering me towards the passport barrier. He deliberately waited for a couple of people to crowd in behind me before following himself. At the tail-end of the passenger queue we were compressed into the Comet, where I realized at last that he was travelling first-class and I was with the economy crowd. I found myself next to a Rotarian from Beverly Hills who was anxious to fill me in on his vicarious knowledge of film stars. For as much of the three-and-a-half-hour flight as I politely could I laboured through the pile of weeklies I had bought, and I met Goodwin again in the bar at Hellenikon airport. The free champagne had made him more genial.

'Sorry about the spot of apartheid,' he said. 'For reasons you can guess at 3 Committee decided to book us separately. I happened to get the first-class ticket, that's all. Have a drink.'

I ordered a Scotch. 'When do we leave for Crete?' I said.

'Ah, we don't leave for Crete. Nothing like strewing the trail with a bit of confusion. Give me your ticket.'

I handed him the BEA ticket and in return he produced an Olympic one. It said Athens–Kerkyra, which made sense of the trip. Kerkyra was Corfu, the biggest of the Ionian islands, separated by a narrow strip of water from Albania.

'It's not like 3 Committee to waste money on phoney air tickets,' I said.

'It's not like 3 Committe to have people interested in what tickets they buy.'

The DC–6 lifted us against the lowering sun above Mount Parnassus and the fertile Amphissian plain, over the wild mountains of Epirus, across a dark sliver of sea and down after little more than an hour on to a runway whose light-studded edges reached out across a shallow lagoon.

At some point we had lost an hour of the day. We stepped out into a warm indigo evening and found two men waiting for us under the wingtip, silhouetted against the light from the small airport building. One was slight and dapper and wore a pink sports shirt, white denims and sandals. The other showed a V of black chest hair above the neck of an olive-drab shirt and surveyed us blankly through dark glasses.

'Ah, Terry,' said Goodwin to the pink-and-white man, 'I see you've gone native.'

'This,' said Terry quickly, 'is Major Lagoudis of the *Asphalea*.'

Asphalea means security, and is used as a title in the same sense as *Seguridad* and *Sicherheit*. Which didn't explain where the Greek secret police came into this.

Major Lagoudis seemed to consider a moment before taking his hand from his pocket, then shook our proffered ones silently. The dark glasses lingered over me.

'And Michael Mannis. Captain Terry Wicks from our Embassy in Athens.'

'This way,' said Terry Wicks. He led us into the building, past a crowded bar counter and an animated throng of tourists waiting for the turn-around of our plane. In a cleared space in front of the baggage counter we stopped and Lagoudis, lighting a cheroot, studied me again by the indoor light. Goodwin cleaned his thumbnail nervously with the edge of his baggage ticket and watched him with tacit hostility.

Finally, as a porter humped the first row of suitcases on to the counter Lagoudis pulled a small brown envelope from his shirt pocket and handed it to me. I accepted it numbly.

'Hereté,' he said shortly and turned away. 'Be happy' – it sounded peculiar, coming from him.

'Goodbye,' Terry said. 'Thanks for your help.'

Goodwin watched Lagoudis leave through the main entrance, then seized his suitcase and said with quiet fury, 'Who the bloody hell invited him here?'

'He insisted.' Terry shrugged. 'The junta boys are touchy about Greek *emigrés*, he wanted to be sure we weren't smuggling some political refugee back into the country. We couldn't do without his help; I had to agree.' Terry spoke with a slight Lancashire accent. He had the taut, sharp manner of a fox-terrier.

'And this?' I said, still clutching the envelope.

'Your new passport. Have a look.'

I opened the envelope. Inside was a pale green card, about five inches by two and a half, sealed into plastic; in one corner a familiar face which it took a second to recognize as my own. Below it a long series of printed and written notes, and my name strangely spelt out in the Greek alphabet, ΜΑΝΝΗΣ ΜΙΧΑΗΛ.

'A Greek identity card,' I said. 'How did you manage it?'

'Pulled a few strings,' Terry said modestly.

'Keep it somewhere safe,' Goodwin said, and turning to Terry, 'how much does that Gestapo type know?'

'Nothing, sir,' said Terry with patient insubordination, 'except what his orders from Athens told him. It was the best I could do at two days' notice.'

'And how are the other arrangements?'

'In the same state but I think we'll muddle through. I've got most of the gear we need and your fellow came in this afternoon—Roth. You signalled this morning you'd had a bit of trouble in London?'

'Yes,' said Goodwin unhelpfully.

I was curious and I was trying to match up pieces of conversation like a child learning about sex. So far the picture I'd formed was still meaningless.

With our suitcases we came out into the forecourt of the airport where Terry had a white Volvo parked. He drove us down a narrow road onto a promenade that smelt of rotting seaweed.

Corfu town is a bit of an intruder on a Greek island. While most of Greece was sweating under the Turks it thrived on the patronage of Venice, and it retains a prosperous bourgeois air. We swept past the Italianate town square and busy pavement cafés nestling in an arched colonnade, then high narrow shuttered houses looking over a harbour dotted with lights.

'Into the backwoods,' Terry said two minutes later as the buildings suddenly stopped and the road was flanked by dark masses of olive trees. 'It's a pity I can't show you round the island. You feel at home, Michael?'

'If not you'd better start,' Goodwin said gloomily.

'I suppose I can afford to now,' I said. 'I was born in the Plaka — that's the rabbit warren up on the north slope of the Acropolis — and if we hadn't emigrated I'd be living there yet. Greece is a good place to come back to when you've made it somewhere else.'

The island was bigger than I had expected. The tarred road ended after half an hour's drive and I was sorry for the car as it lurched along a shale-strewn track carrying us north-eastward along the hilly coastline. Terry practised his Demotiki on me. In the black abyss of the sea to our right were the gleams of fishermen's carbide lamps. At a point on the road a hundred feet above the water Terry turned sharply onto an almost invisible track that made six hairpin bends down to the sea. He took them expertly, nudging the car round the outside edges and pulling up at the front door of the house which, until we turned the very last bend, had been quite invisible.

It was a fine house, crouched on the bottom but one of an incredibly steep series of olive terraces which I had mistaken for a sheer cliff-face. It was white and flat-roofed with dark shutters and two huge open verandas, upstairs and down, looking out over the black channel towards the mainland. Even in the dark I could see that the high twin arms of the cove directly in front would keep the house invisible from other points along the coast. On the starlit water in the centre of the cover a big power-boat lay moored.

'Do you like the place?' Terry asked. 'It belongs to an Athenian building contractor, a friend of mine. He's kindly let it to me for a week.'

Goodwin had been taking it all in, as I had. For the first time with something like approval of Terry in his tone he said, 'Perfect.'

We carried our luggage into a huge sitting room, opening at the front onto a panorama of starlit water and distant black hills. On one of two long couches built against the side walls a big hulk of a man in white shorts, white T-shirt and sandals had been sleeping and he started up when we came in, gathering his features into a silly grin.

'Johnny boy,' said Goodwin, going forward and grasping his limp hand. 'Hard at work as usual. How's business?'

'All right, Joe, all right,' the man said, his voice gravelly with sleep.

Goodwin was brisk and busy, falling automatically into the roles of host and leader. 'Meet the new arrival,' he said, 'Michael Mannis. This is Johnny Roth, our tame sea-captain.'

Johnny Roth nodded at me. He looked slow of thought and movement but his pale blue eyes roved over us quickly enough once he was fully awake. They were set in a square, hard face, so deeply tanned that the contrasting lightness of the eyes seemed to drift out of focus when you looked at them. He wasn't all that big, about my height and shape, heavy-shouldered and chunky, but he looked twice my size. He had immense biceps, forearms corded with veins and sinews, big calloused hands and legs like a billiard table's. I put him

50

at about my age, thirty-five. He had thinning brown hair and needed a shave.

A smell of cooking fish had been coming from the kitchen. From it also came a small wiry man wiping olive oil from his hands on an incongruous frilly apron tied round his waist. His features were sharp and with his short black crinkly hair and moustache unmistakably Greek. He might have been anything from forty to sixty years old.

'*Mihaili,*' he said, beaming and seizing my hand. 'Welcome.'

'This is Nikos Varthis,' Terry said, as if it explained everything, and to Goodwin it did. 'Glad to meet you at last,' he said.

'I suggest you two go up and change,' Terry said. 'Then we can have a drink and try out the nosh Nikos has been making.'

Instinctively I knew Goodwin hated the word 'nosh.' 'Straight after dinner,' he said with emphasis, 'I'll hold a full briefing.'

Each of us had a large and airy bedroom upstairs where we spent a few minutes changing into cool clothes. Nobody spoke much during Nikos' dinner, which turned out to be scorpion fish baked with a sauce of red peppers. With it went a cabbage salad and retsina.

Replete, we spread ourselves about the sitting room with coffee and Mastoris brandy. Goodwin, who wore shorts and sandals and looked more Mediterranean than ever, stood up to focus our attention. He strolled to the front of the room where the folding doors had been drawn right open.

'First of all,' he said, 'I want one thing clearly understood. This is a secret operation and I'm bloody well going to see that it stays secret. From now until the moment it's put into effect no-one is to leave the vicinity of this house. Except Nikos, who'll be going to the village up the road once or twice. Any comments?'

I would have liked to say yes, but I wouldn't have known what to say after that. It was just an uneasy reaction to the idea of having my movements restricted. We all shook our heads. Goodwin looked down at the flagstone floor and then out towards the line of hills across the channel. There were small points of light among them.

'Secondly,' he said, 'I want you to bear in mind that the situation I'm going to describe to you is all pure surmise, based on the most flimsy evidence. Right? The situation is this, then. Across that channel is Albania, the nearest point a little over two miles from here. In Albania the Chinese install a strategic missile system. When operational, it may be equipped with enough nuclear weapons to destroy every city in Europe. If that sounds a little hard to take simply remind yourselves of what happened in Cuba.'

7

Late the next afternoon I stood, naked, on the small concrete landing stage below the house where the fibreglass dinghy from Johnny Roth's boat had been hauled out of the water. Behind me the sun had sunk below the crags of Pantokrator, the island's highest mountain, but it still cast a soft glow on the tawny hills across the channel and gave them a flat impressionist look, as if they had been pasted on the horizon. Daylight had painted in their details, among them a gently curving bay directly opposite with white houses clinging to the slopes above it. Daylight had also shown us the misty, haunted mountains in the distance behind them, now partly obscured by threatening cloud. It was a world of Griegian fantasy, as out of place in this soft Mediterranean setting as the philosophy that had taken root there.

During the day a south-easterly wind had sprung up, making it doubtful whether the caique would leave for Albania the next morning. The flat blue Ionian water had wrinkled and turned grey-green, with racing white-caps out in the channel. In the sheltered cove it slapped and sucked at the rocks around the landing stage, and Johnny Roth's boat, fifty yards out, pitched rhythmically at its mooring, the supple new radio aerial at its masthead whipping back and forth.

The change in the weather was not enough to deter me from a swim. All day I had been going over and over the plan, rehearsing my role and limbering my tongue in conversation with Nikos into the harsh dialect of Epirus. Now there was time to relax.

52

I dived, surfaced tossing hair out of my eyes and swam hard and fast for a hundred yards out, enjoying the fight against the waves and the rush of warm water against my skin. For twenty minutes I burned up the energy that was suddenly brimming in me, then let myself drift in on the starboard side of Johnny's boat, caught a rung of the ladder he'd left in place there, and hauled myself aboard.

Through the window of the locked wheelhouse door I saw the radio, a gleaming new array of dials and knobs clamped to a fixed metal table aft of the wheel. It was, I gathered, the property of the Royal Corps of Signals, a newly approved model specially installed for this mission; twice a day Goodwin used it to transmit a coded report to the listening-post in Athens.

The rest of the boat was equipped as it normally was for its work off Gibraltar. It was a wooden-hulled workhorse sixty feet long with its wheelhouse well forward and a lot of room aft for cargo and for its three diesel engines. It was known as a general service pinnace, GSP for short, an innocuous boat of a kind I had seen doing harbour and coastal work for the armed forces. But this model was innocuous only until you saw how she sat heavily in the water with the weight of bigger engines and fuel tanks that Johnny had installed, and how every square inch of her from stem to stern was painted in neutral navy grey so that not a steel stanchion or a brass cleat glinted in the sunshine.

If the boat had a name no-one ever used it. Johnny referred to it and many other things obscurely as 'him,' which perhaps reflected the inverted order of things in his life. His business was smuggling, soundly organised, well-equipped and highly profitable. It was long-range stuff, cigarettes for Alicante or whisky for Toulon from Gibraltar's duty-free warehouses, and Johnny reckoned his boat could outrun most of the coastguard vessels in the western Mediterranean.

'And he'll get us to Malta in sum'ming like sixteen hours,' he had said with pride. Johnny was part German and part Australian, apparently, and his English was strangely stilted and unmodulated, as if he were reading aloud.

Only Terry had seemed unenthusiastic about this stage of the plan when we had discussed it the night before. It was the part that explained why Goodwin and I had arrived on one-way tickets.

'I know I've already put my case to 3 Committee,' Terry had said, 'but I'm still prepared to argue that you should fly straight from Athens to London. It would be far quicker.'

'Quicker, but not safer,' Goodwin parried, with the edge of impatience that seemed to come into his tone when he spoke to Terry. He said this as if it answered the objection completely, then added unpleasantly, 'I was the one who overruled you. I'm not taking the risk of crossing foreign territory with the film, this thing could blow up in our faces at any moment. But Johnny is here for another reason as well, in case anything goes wrong in Albania.'

'Goes wrong?' I said.

'If for any reason you can't take the caique back in the normal way. We may be able to come and pick you up.'

Terry said incredulously, 'You don't mean you'd enter their territorial waters?'

'I'm not afraid,' Goodwin said irrelevantly and, looking at Johnny, 'are you?'

'No,' Johnny had said folding his huge arms across his chest and giving Terry a flat-eyed stare.

A shout came to me over the slapping of water against the bow. On the landing stage was Terry's diminutive figure, naked and lightly tanned except for a white band across the middle. He couldn't have been taller than five feet four; I wondered how he had got into the Army in the first place, before he was switched to intelligence work. He dived in and ploughed his way towards the boat with a bobbing of white buttocks. I reached down and helped him slither under the rail.

'Lovely water,' he said, wiping some of it from his face with both small hands. 'You swim like a fish. I was watching you.'

'Not really,' I said with automatic deprecation. Secretly I agreed with him; swimming was the only exercise I really enjoyed and I could keep at it for hours. 'But I may have to if I miss the boat coming back here.'

He laughed meaningfully. 'We may all have to swim to Malta if we're depending on this hulk to get us there.'

'You feel strongly about it, don't you?' I was perversely interested in the antagonism between him and Goodwin.

'I just think it's an arse-about-face way of doing things.' Terry sat

54

down on the engine-room cowling behind the wheelhouse. 'Taking a boat to Malta and then relying on the good offices of the RAF ... I don't know.'

'It makes sense if there's a security risk,' I said.

'Who said there was a security risk?'

'Well, after what happened in London ... ' From the puzzled way Terry looked at me he couldn't have known, and I was putting my foot in it again.

'What happened in London?' he said.

If Goodwin hadn't told him there must be a reason. 'Joe was being watched, that's all,' I said. 'You'd better ask him about it.'

'Who was watching him? Does he know?'

'No. He says not, anyway. Look, I've already got a book full of black marks off Joe, it's no good asking me questions.'

Terry looked at me carefully. 'Black marks, yes – he's very good at handing those out.' He stood up, walked to the prow and watched the white-edged waves rolling past the boat. I started to wish for a cigarette.

'You'd better not tell him you mentioned this to me,' Terry called out. It may have been the fact that he had to shout against the wind, but his tone seemed a good deal less casual than it was meant to be. 'I'm just the leg-man around here, I don't get told very much.'

And I wondered why. I wondered as well, because my job had taught me that curiosity is as natural as breathing to most people, why Terry had suddenly lost his; unless people who worked for 3 Committee learned to turn curiosity on and off as required, like a light switch. At any rate his irony was rather heavy. I had learnt how Terry, working in Yugoslavia, Corfu and the province of Epirus, had revived part of an intelligence network in Albania that had worked behind the communist lines during the Greek civil war; how he had slipped Nikos and other men across among the unofficial traffic of relatives to bring back information from Albania; how Nikos, only a week before, had returned with a story that made Terry's heart miss a beat.

Nikos, unlike me, had a genuine relative in Albania, his brother Takis who was a part of the network. Nikos was allowed four visits a year, each of three days' duration, and he would spend this time at Takis' home in Koritsa, a hundred kilometres from the coast. Any

55

information that Takis had picked up between visits would go back via Nikos.

An hour before Nikos was due to leave the house on his last trip they were visited by a half-mad shepherd named Volni, a nomad who roamed the mountains and knew Takis from the days when he had not been quite so mad and they had fought as partisans together. He told a rambling, incoherent story about stumbling on a secret military base high in the wildest part of the mountains, where he had been seized by the soldiers and brought down to Koritsa to be interrogated for three days. Finally convinced that he was a harmless lunatic the military had released him with a warning that he would be shot if he repeated anything of what he had seen. Apparently they had not thought him quite mad enough to tell the whole story to the first two people he met, Takis and Nikos.

Nikos Varthis was a patient, painstaking man. By asking the right questions he had extracted from Volni finally a vivid description of what he had seen in the mountains before he was captured. Repeated to Terry, repeated again to a dozen different experts in London, the mad shepherd's vision had been transformed into a working strategic hypothesis. What he had seen was a half-completed launching site for ground-to-ground rockets. His description of the two objects already installed there could have only one interpretation: they were medium-range strategic missiles, weapons the Albanians could never have developed themselves, weapons that no-one believed China yet capable of producing.

'But they *have* produced them,' Terry said emphatically. 'Volni described them down to the last rivet, and he didn't pick up that sort of information reading the comics.'

'Let's keep our sense of perspective,' Goodwin had said archly. 'This is nothing more than one man's story, and a madman at that. It's a tale told by an idiot.' He had looked at us as if expecting someone to cap the line, but nobody could help him. 'Full of sound and fury,' he muttered, 'and signifying nothing but a bloody great hole in our own intelligence set-up.'

I could understand Terry's feeling resentful when the whole thing was lifted out of his hands by the people he would probably call 'the brass' and when Goodwin came in to supervise the field work. On

56

the other hand it was not, I supposed, the sort of responsibility to leave to a junior officer. Goodwin had brought the tension of a War Cabinet meeting to his informal briefing session and had produced a bewildering volume of information from all kinds of sources — considering, as he had said, that the idiot's tale remained nothing more than exactly that.

'We're calling it System V,' he said, 'after Volni. That's a working title until we get more information. We hope that by now Takis has seen the place and will be able to pinpoint it for you.'

Goodwin had been eloquent and encyclopaedic; had explained (perhaps with the help of a memorandum from the Foreign Office) how the ideological split with Russia was leading China towards asserting herself more firmly as a world power; had talked knowledgeably of China's nuclear capability and said it was commonly thought that she would not have either ICBMs or an effective medium-range missile ready for another four years.

'So we begin with the disadvantage that no-one really believes the story; no-one is prepared to accept that our assessments could have been that wrong. I'm giving you the whole picture so that your approach will be the positive one.'

He had spoken of how Albania — small, backward, never fully a part of Europe and its culture, surrounded by traditionally unfriendly neighbours — had sided with China over a purely ideological issue six or seven years before. Since then she had become increasingly dependent on the Chinese for aid of every kind. Now Russia, for a long time disturbed by Albania's waywardness, might be planning a Czech-style return to grace for her. The Albanians could be returning a favour and improving their own security by allowing their patrons to station rockets on Albanian soil which could be used with equal effort against Western or Eastern Europe.

'The situation is ideal, geographically,' he said and produced a map from somewhere. Tracing lines with a long brown finger from Tirana, the Albanian capital, he had read out the names and figures like a litany: London 1,100 miles, Paris 950, Berlin 750, Moscow no more than 800. In the north even Leningrad, Oslo, Stockholm, all with the likely range of 1,500 miles.

'But now look at it particularly from our own, the British point of view.' The finger went back to Albania and slowly drew a line straight through Trieste, clipping corners off Austria and Bavaria, across north-eastern France and over the Channel to London.

'Do you see where it enters British air space? Dover. It won't be news to you that our early-warning system is geared mainly to a possible attack from north or east. No-one yet has given me a straight answer when I've asked how effective it would be if the attack came from here – the direction of Luxembourg or Munich.'

He returned to China and her foreign policy, explaining how with operational missiles in Albania she could undermine the whole of NATO's strategy in Europe and reverse the American and Russian nuclear domination in one blow. He spoke of the gains she could make simply by using this as a holding position: pressure on Britain and the United States not to resist further encroachments on Indian territory, enhancement of prestige in Africa, perhaps even a forcing of America to choose between retaining her influence in Asia and rallying to Europe's support.

'And all this isn't just long-term prognostication. If System V exists then we are being caught – perhaps have been caught already – on the hop. We've known for some time that Albania was potentially a second Cuba but we've been depending on this idea that China wouldn't have a nuclear missile system – even a medium-range one – ready for another three or four years. It's likely that by then both the Yanks and the Russians will have antimissile systems good enough to make China's armoury useless. So they must act now or never.

'Of course' – Goodwin sat down, as if to bring himself back to earth – 'I'm taking this to the furthest possible lengths. I'm doing it to convince you, as I said earlier. By some tortuous reasoning process the official policy is to disbelieve the story and yet expect the worst. Until we can convince them that System V exists, and that it is what we think it might be, nothing can be done. Nikos and Michael, hopefully, will bring us the proof one way or another.

'We're not the only people concerned in this, of course, but for the moment we are the most important. There's no harm in telling you that we're keeping a watch on the two ports, Durazzo and Valona, further up the coast. Reports so far are negative. We don't have the satellites or the high-altitude recce planes we would need for aerial pictures but even if we did we have no idea where to start looking. And there are other unknown factors. Volni may have been exaggerating the size of the missiles, they could be just ground-to-air defensive weapons which we know the Albanians possess. So the only proof we are going to get will be from Michael's camera.

'I'll wind up in the proper lecturer fashion by throwing a couple of abstract conclusions at you. There are two elements of priority balancing each other out here, time and secrecy. For the Chinese secrecy is the most vital element. They've got to prepare bases, get their weapons in place and arm them in secrecy, then they will be able to present us with a *fait accompli*. They'll be working slowly, carefully; they can't afford to go off at half-cock the way the Russians did in Cuba. If the missiles are detected before they're operational they are worse than useless.

'For us, time is number one. We've got to find the missiles and do something about them before they are capable of being fired. For the present stage of the operation our time is limited to three days. In three days Nikos and Michael must find System V, photograph it and get the photographs back here.'

There had been silence for a long minute in the yellow-lit room. A hornet that had discovered the standard lamp buzzed like a bandsaw against its vellum shade. Then Johnny belched nonchalantly. I was the only one who asked any questions.

'Surely,' I said, 'this is a case for some kind of joint action by the countries that are threatened? Politics isn't my department but I shouldn't have thought we'd be keeping this to ourselves.'

'We won't be,' Goodwin said, 'once we have established what we want to know. It will go up to NATO level, I should think. But how would you set about selling the desk generals in Brussels a story that came second-hand from an illiterate madman? For the moment the job is ours alone, I'm afraid.'

'And if we find System V, find that it's as bad as you think, what then? What's the something that you said would be done, and who's going to do it?'

Goodwin sat staring across the dark water. 'How can I say? Transfer the Cuba situation into different hands several years later and ask yourself. Will one American President act the same way as another? Is Chairman Mao as sensible as Khrushchev was? Mount a blockade, invade Albania, bomb the sites? I just don't know. Or rather I'll borrow your phrase this time. It's not my department.'

I suppose I could have protested more at what Goodwin had dropped me into. When I had time to think about it I was frightened, and later, when he and I went over my part of the plan in more detail, I told him I'd no idea so much depended on me and repeated that I wasn't qualified for it. In the last resort he couldn't have stopped me leaving the house and catching the first plane back to London, but both of us knew I wouldn't. Morally he'd got me in a corner in which my co-operation was a *sine qua non*. Besides, I'd made some mistakes and Goodwin was very good at holding one to account for mistakes. He said, 'You want reassuring, do you? Then I'd better confess that it's my policy to see things in their worst possible light. One is disappointed much less often. I hope to have some new information before you leave, something that will make you feel easier. For you alone – all right?' And it did seem all right.

Now darkness was gathering over the channel. On the boat the wind explored my damp skin with chilly fingers and away to the south it was towing a bank of dark cloud towards us. Terry had come back and sat down next to me with his elbows resting on bony knees, preoccupied, I supposed, with his own strange resentments. Johnny had come to the landing-stage and was launching the dinghy. Goodwin strode down the path from the house, coming to make his routine seven o'clock call to Athens.

'Where did Joe dig up a character like Johnny Roth?' I asked Terry.

'I've no idea, really. They've worked together before but I hadn't met Johnny till yesterday. But I know a roughie when I see one .... ' Terry laughed. 'I mean nowt against him, he's just one of these blokes who can't stay away from trouble. You know the type? Foreign Legion, Congo mercenary, now he's in smuggling. I gather from his talk that he bought the boat last year with the proceeds of some fishy deal in the Middle East. That must have been about the time he met our Joe; they were talking about it. Still' – Terry came from a background of Northern thrift and was careful to offset his prejudice against easy money – 'He's reliable, a good man to have on your side, I should think.'

The dinghy bobbed crazily but Johnny rowed hard with a

rhythmic pulsing of his back muscles under the T-shirt, and in a minute they were alongside the boat. Goodwin scrambled up the ladder and Johnny came over the rail with a vault. Goodwin looked thoughtfully at our nakedness. 'You've found a lot to talk about out here. Or am I interrupting at a delicate moment?'

Johnny Roth laughed as he obviously would and said, 'I didn't think you were that way, Michael. Terry's a different matter, though, you'd better watch him.'

Terry, suddenly upset, said, 'What are you suggesting?' I opened my mouth to tell him it was just a bad joke but Goodwin said unexpectedly, 'Will you two leave the boat now, please? I've my call to make.'

Terry tried to summon up indignation, realized perhaps that his size and his nakedness made it impossible and said rather plaintively, 'I'm supposed to be 2IC here, you know.'

Inserting a key in the wheelhouse door Goodwin said, 'I make this call in private, all the same.'

'With him on board?' Terry's eyes flashed angrily to Johnny. 'He's not even a member of the Service.'

'It's Johnny's boat, I can't stop him. And he'll close his ears if I ask him to. You know, the longer you stay here the more you're destroying one of my illusions. I always thought small men had a compensating advantage down there, but Michael's got a definite edge on you.'

For a moment Terry gave Goodwin a look of pure hate, then brushed past him, clambered over the rail and dived awkwardly into the water. Johnny laughed again. With a smile to Goodwin that preserved my neutrality, I followed.

An hour later, when the four of us sat stiffly drinking ouzo on the veranda, Nikos returned from an expedition to Kouloura, the village up the road. His news was that the caique would not leave the next morning. If the wind had dropped it might go the following day, Monday.

Goodwin said to Terry, as if it were his fault, 'What's the matter with these damned Greek seamen? A capful of wind and they won't move out of harbour.'

'The caiques are built for coasting and island-hopping. They can't take much rough weather.'

61

'Rough weather my eye! A North Sea trawlerman would call that sea a millpond.'

'There aren't any North Sea trawlermen here, unfortunately.'

'Well, it's something you could have foreseen,' Goodwin said. 'London has been counting on our reaching Malta by Thursday.' He got up and left the room. A little later I happened to stroll into the garden and found him standing under an olive tree; he was smoking and staring across the dark channel.

'I'm surrounded by incompetence,' he said abruptly. 'Incompetence and bloody-mindedness. You've made your contribution too.'

'The pictures I took? Aren't you still insisting that they couldn't have anything to do with the Albanian thing?'

'They *couldn't* have. They couldn't have known anything about it. Unless ... no, it's too ridiculous to contemplate.' He flung his cigarette down the terraces towards the sea. 'You made a mess, but it was a purely incidental mess concerning me alone.'

'And Tom Blakeney?' I said. I'd been hoping to put out a feeler about Tom. 'You don't seriously think he took that film and gave it to the people who were following you about, do you?'

'I don't know.' Goodwin sounded preoccupied. 'There are a lot of things I don't know about. Most of them can wait till I get back to London. Did you tell Terry about the man in the Cooper?'

The question took me by surprise. 'I thought he already knew,' I said, 'and it slipped out. Just a mention, I told him almost nothing ... '

'Good. I thought you might.' Goodwin turned to me with a strange smile in the half-light. 'What was his reaction? Surprise?'

I had an odd instinct to cover up for Terry, I couldn't think why unless it was because he'd been humiliated. 'Sure, he was surprised,' I said.

'But he didn't press you for more information?'

'Not really,' I confessed.

'All right. Thanks. I got the information I told you about on my call this evening, and I hope this time you'll keep quiet about it. When you go across there' – he gestured towards Albania – 'you won't be entirely alone, you and Nikos. If things don't go according to plan there'll be someone there to help you.'

62

'Who?'

'I can't tell you that. You'll have no way of contacting him, he'll make it his business to get in touch with you. He'll be around, like a guardian angel, you might say.'

'He's not part of Terry's network?' I asked.

'No.' Goodwin smiled again. 'Terry's network does what it's supposed to do and does it very well. But networks are for the small fry. This one is too clever – and too valuable – for that. Terry's clearance isn't high enough to know about him, so consider yourself privileged. And remember it's between you and me.'

'Not Nikos as well?'

'Not Nikos. He may be going in and out of Albania again. If our man has to show his hand that'll be soon enough for Nikos to find out. For everybody's sake, I hope he doesn't have to show it.'

We went in to dinner. The atmosphere in the house was something like that of a seaside hotel full of mutually hostile guests on a wet weekend. Or rather, some of the guests formed hostile camps – Goodwin and Johnny in one, Terry in the other – and tried to recruit the two neutrals, Nikos and me, into joining them. The boredom, bickering and tension went on till Monday morning, redeemed only by the huge and varied meals that Nikos cooked. To complete the English holiday atmosphere it poured on Sunday morning, a cloying summer rainstorm so sudden and heavy that it blotted out even the view of Johnny's boat bucking in the cove. But when it was over the wind had gone, the damp grass sparkled in the sunlight and the sea lost the certainty of its thrusts at the shore.

Towards nightfall Nikos went to the village again and asked about the caique that was to sail discreetly to Albania. Yes, he reported, if the weather held she would go.

Nervousness spoilt my sleep but in a way I was glad to leave.

8

A trail of thin blue diesel smoke hung over the oily swell behind the caique. Cloud covered the summit of Pantokrator, which had come into spectacular relief above the shoreline of Corfu behind us, and the day was dull though without rain.

Nikos and I sat on the gunwale aft, next to where the leathery old skipper handled the wheel with casual deftness. He wore a battered sailor's cap and whistled tunelessly. I wondered how much he was paid to take the risk of a trip like this, a journey which historically would never have taken place. If he and his boat didn't come back from Albania no questions would ever be asked, for officially he had never gone there. No policeman or other official had supervised our departure; we went, an animated crowd of peasants, on a non-existent trip at our own risk. Only Major Lagoudis, silent and dark-spectacled, had driven into Kouloura in a black Mercedes and sat watching our boat cast off.

The skipper's boat was painted bright red, inside and out, and had a spray of purple heather like a figurehead over the cutwater. In the narrow deck space there was scarcely room to move, for the twenty-odd Epirites and one or two Corfiots were bringing abundance to their kinsmen among the bare hills. There were live chickens with their legs trussed under the thwarts, baskets of fruit, huge jars of wine, parcels of bloody meat, whole cooked lambs, rolls of cheap cloth, bags of salt and flour, barrels of oil. And for their stay of three days (they would have to leave Albania by the same caique at a specified time) the peasants took trunks, suitcases, kitbags, saddlebags, cardboard boxes, rolled blankets, pots, pans, kettles and crockery. Nikos and I had been the first aboard and with each new arrival I wondered how the tubby little boat could take any more.

We were peasants ourselves, of course. My normal middle-class presence would have been suspect immediately. Nikos, as the owner of a few olive trees and a share in a small cartage business in Epirus, belonged to a class of Greeks indistinguishable from those of peasant status. He wore a gay cloth cap and a woollen maroon shirt.

Fitting me out had needed more care. Dressed for an outing I wore a linen suit of a rather startling royal blue, a white shirt with the open collar-ends turned neatly outside the jacket, brown imitation-leather shoes, and underneath a baggy vest and drawers, all chosen by Terry and Nikos before my arrival. On a chain round my neck hung a cheap medallion of St. Michael and in my jacket pocket was my identity card, now treated with dirt and sweat to give it the appearance of age. It was dated, I had noticed, 1962.

Among the things in my cardboard suitcase was a large box of Turkish Delight, a gift for my supposed uncle and aunt. Beneath the top layer of sticky jelly, tightly wrapped in a plastic bag, were the square body of my Rolleiflex, its couple of small accessories and the twenty-four spools of film. The wicker covering of the six-litre demijohn that Nikos clutched had been unpicked, a hole had been cut in the glass bottom of the jar and the big 500mm lens in its leather case inserted into it.

'They'll never search us anyway,' Nikos had said. 'I've been over a dozen times and no-one has ever been searched. Strange, I suppose. But then we are only poor peasants.'

He said it with a sly smile, having a joke at my expense. I was just beginning to realize how much I depended on him and how little I knew him. I looked at his profile, skeletally sharp and high in the cheekbone. A smile played over his lips. I believe he was actually enjoying this adventure, and so in a perverse way was I.

Somebody nudged me from the other side. A nut-brown old man with bristling moustaches offered me his bottle of pungent amber wine. It was seven in the morning but I was in no state to be fussy. I had not shaved for two days and had eaten raw garlic to add to my authenticity. I took a pull at the wine, disguised a shudder and accepted cold fried whitebait from the old man's newspaper-wrapped package.

'From Kerkyra?' he asked conversationally.

'Ioannina,' I said.

'Ioanı.ina?' He nodded sagely. He was a mountaineer from Metsovon, we agreed that the islanders lived far too frivolously. But even he was affected by the excursional merriment in the air. We all sang and women laughed shrilly. I was glad of this short trip because it helped ease me back into the feeling of being Greek and this would be vital for the next three days. It is not easy to forget attitudes learnt from thirty years' living in an advanced society. Nikos, knowing this, all but forced me into a dozen conversations and arguments that were going to and fro along the length of the caique.

'Don't tell me about the good wines of Thessaly, my nephew and I have drunk them all. Tell them, nephew!'

'Careful how you stand up, girl, my nephew will have to jump overboard and rescue you.'

We were all comrades of a sort in the twenty minutes it took before the boat chugged into the small bay I had seen from the house. What had looked earlier like a few scattered dwellings at the waterside had emerged as quite a substantial little town. This was Yaliskari, a small port connected to the hillside village of Drimi, southernmost of a chain of settlements linked by road to Valona. At a glance it looked little different to a Greek fishing village. A stone jetty with a row of boats tied up along one side of it, a small square just behind the jetty with a few tables and chairs set out, a row of houses painted in pastel colours a little further along the front, an official-looking low, square building. Only the white tower of a small mosque in place of the flat rectangular belfry of a Greek village church struck a false note. For here Islam, never embraced by the Greeks in four hundred years of Turkish rule, held sway.

The throb of the engine died as our boat nosed in on the clear side of the jetty and there was a bustle of people and baggage.

I watched two men in green uniforms and leather pistol holsters striding down the jetty to meet us and I had my first sick pang of fear. It began somewhere in my stomach, a hand grasping at a bundle of nerve ends, and in a moment clutched at my throat and started me sweating. Then it passed and left me shaking slightly and wiping the liquid film from my brow. Nikos had been watching me as if he expected it and he said softly, 'Don't worry. Do what everyone else does, and remember not to argue.'

It was good advice to give to someone from England, where it is still not quite unheard-of to talk back to officials. But forget about England, I had to keep telling myself, you're a Greek.

We clambered ashore, handing our identity cards to one of the sallow-faced men who shuffled them into a little stack. He looked us

over without expression but tapped his foot as two women held up
the line, heaving a great sack of flour off the boat. Then everyone
assembled with our mountain of luggage on the jetty. The weight of
my suitcase felt doubled by the single camera.

The uniformed men were security police, members of something
called the SSSh that made me think of tonic-water ads. They were
para-military police, anyway, part of a force almost half the size of
the army, and guarding the frontiers was one of their more mundane
duties. One of them said something to the skipper of the caique and
he cast off and reversed slowly out of the harbour. There was no
going back now.

I knew what was to happen next. Nikos and I had been over it a
dozen times but facing its reality wasn't any easier. We were to be
checked in by the Albanian authorities. As a first-time visitor I could
expect to be interviewed at length.

The policemen marched us like a straggling Boy Scout troop from
the jetty along the front to the official-looking building. A couple of
dozen people stood along the way waiting to meet us but they
offered no greetings or embraces yet, as if we were in a quarantine of
silence. Our high spirits seemed to have gone back to Corfu in the
caique and we talked in low murmurs as we shuffled along under the
great weight of baggage.

The building was a long low shed of sorts with a wide doorway at
either end; it had perhaps once been a warehouse. There was nothing
to indicate its present function, only a row of tattered posters on the
wall facing us, from which Mehmet Shehu and Enver Hoxha
alternately stared, grim with socialist purpose. Inside the building we
were allowed to stand easy again while the man with the cards went
into one of a line of small austere offices partitioned off along one
side. We sat on our suitcases, smoking and waiting with peasant
docility for forty minutes while officials came and went. I was too
nervous to be impatient but finally I asked Nikos, 'Does it usually
take so long?'

'We have not even started yet. The interviews sometimes take
hours. I saw my brother outside so the message reached him.'

The message, the outline of the part he was to play, had been
passed to Takis, who for three days was to be my uncle, by a
complicated series of signals between a fishing fleet from one of the

more northerly villages and a fleet from Corfu. Every evening for years they had passed close to each other as they set off for their night's work and the Albanian fishermen would receive and deliver messages for Greek Albanians in exchange for oil or wine which would be dropped with floats where they could be picked up in the nets. I had wondered how long this and the other little bridges across the gulf of isolation would hold up if I succeeded in what I had come to do.

Eventually a man we hadn't seen before, wearing a similar green uniform, came to the door of one office and called out a name. The old man from Metsovon stood up and shambled in. The door of the office was left open; I could see the Greek standing facing a desk.

'That's a different officer to the usual one,' Nikos said quietly. 'I've never seen him before.'

'I hope he's no smarter than the other one you told me about; the old one that you could bribe with a bottle of brandy.'

The brown-faced old man was a veteran visitor, apparently. He was out in two minutes giving the rest of us a sly wink, victory over bureaucracy. But the other interviews dragged on. Several people who hadn't been across the channel before were kept in the office ten or fifteen minutes. Nikos, who was on the last of the four visits he was allowed that year, went in and came back with a reassuring smile that didn't reassure me. An hour and a half had gone by and I was wondering if there was a reason for keeping me till last when I heard 'Mannis!' called out and felt my hair roots prickle. I got up and walked into the room.

I realized at once that the young man behind the desk *was* smart. He had a long, vulpine face that gave unpleasant prominence to the nose and mouth. He wore no badges of rank but he took himself too seriously, at his age, to be anything but an officer. Black eyes roved quickly over me and he said, 'You have not been here before?'

'No, sir.'

'Whom do you wish to visit in the Popular Republic of Shqiperia?'

The Albanians' own name for their country; the pedantic title sounded strange in conversation. His Greek was excellent and I hoped he wouldn't pick up the Attic inflections in mine.

'My uncle, sir, Takis Varthis. He lives in Koritsa.'

'Takis Varthis,' he said to himself. He picked up my identity card and examined it. There was every personal detail on it that he could possibly want to know. For some reason I suddenly remembered that the photograph was the one I'd had in my last British passport.

The officer looked up sharply, as if he had detected an alien thought entering my head. 'You are thirty-five years old?'

'Yes, sir.'

'Then why,' he said, leaning back and looking straight into my face, 'have you suddenly decided to visit your uncle?'

There was no logical connection between the two questions but I thought I knew what he meant. Then I checked myself, sensing danger. I stared at him and said, 'Sir?'

'You are thirty-five,' he said impatiently. 'You have never bothered to visit your uncle before. Why do you want to now?'

I had got what I wanted, time to answer at my own pace. 'We were a close family, sir, but I have not seen him since I was too young to remember. For many years my people in Greece heard nothing from Takis. We thought he might have died. Only last year his brother Nikos had the first reply to all his letters and learned that it was possible to visit him.' I shrugged. 'The letters had not reached Takis. Nikos has been to see him two or three times: this was my first chance to come with him. I work hard, sir, I have little free time.'

The officer suspended me at the end of a long stare. Then he nodded, reluctantly satisfied, and turned to some papers on his desk. He had put me on the defensive, tried to trap me into thinking too quickly. Why? Or was it his standard approach? I could feel whole drops of sweat falling into my shirt under the armpits.

He found a long form of some kind and started firing questions at me, checking some of the answers against my identity card. My name was Michael Mannis. I worked as grocery shop assistant (this had been Nikos' suggestion; he had pointed out that my hands were too soft to have been an honest peasant's). I had lived near Ioannina all my life but had visited Athens once. I had never visited any other country. I recited the carefully-prepared genealogy that made me Nikos' and Takis' nephew: my parents' names had been Vassilios and Agathi; they had both been shot by the Germans for resistance activities during the war (a sympathetic aside, this was in fact what

69

had happened to Nikos' eldest sister and her husband, and a transposition of surnames made me their son). When he reached the end of the form I felt I had made a good showing. I was as impressively ordinary as I was meant to be. Then his next question froze me. 'Have you,' he said evenly, 'brought a camera with you?'

Could he have guessed? Surely he must have. I would have to admit it and try to pretend I had innocently brought one for snapshots. But then I remembered the careful concealment and the kind of camera it was, the kind that wasn't for beginners.

'No,' I said desperately.

'Or any radio equipment, petrol, electrical apparatus?'

I almost collapsed with relief. He was simply asking if I had any contraband, a routine question that Nikos had told me to expect. 'No,' I replied, I had only a few Greek cigarettes for my uncle.

The officer tapped the desk absently with his anachronistic fountain pen. 'You know, if I should search your luggage and find any of these things, what the consequences would be?'

'I understand, sir, I have brought nothing like that.'

'You know that you must not stay at any place other than your uncle's home, you must remain in the police district of Koritsa at all times until you come here on Thursday morning to collect your card and depart?'

'Yes, sir.'

'You may go.'

He pushed a slip of paper across to me, my three-day entry permit. I tried not to wobble as I left the office. When I sat down next to Nikos and lit a cigarette my hands shook so badly that I almost dropped the matches.

'You were a long time,' Nikos said casually. 'Did he suspect anything?'

'For a moment I thought he did. Now I can't be sure.'

'I understand. He is suspicious by nature and he gives nothing away. But if he had any real doubts he would have searched our luggage.'

There were a few other interviews which were soon over. Mine had been the longest of all, apparently, and I was an object of mild interest like a Catholic who has spent too long in the confessional.

Finally all the pilgrims had been questioned and the young officer

70

came out with a list, counted us and with a jerk of his head signified that we could go. The crowd rose with an end-of-term murmur of excitement. I happened to walk right past our interrogator who gave me a sardonic smile, the kind some people use to suggest they know more about you than you think.

'Enjoy your stay,' he said affably.

'Thank you.'

Released from the shed into the glare of a newly-appeared sun, we were fallen upon by demonstrative relations. My supposed uncle Takis seized Nikos and me and enveloped us both in a huge bear hug. 'Brother!' he shouted. 'How good to see you. And is this Michael at last? What a fine-looking young man!'

He kissed me lavishly on both cheeks. It couldn't have looked better if we had rehearsed it, which was just as well, because when we turned to walk back to the square the young officer had come out of the building and stood there with his hands in his pockets. He watched us out of sight down the road.

Takis was fairly prosperous, about as prosperous as one could get in southern Albania, I gathered, although as with many Greeks in Greece itself I was never quite sure how he earned a living. At any rate he had a car, an old bullnosed Skoda, into which he swept us and our suitcases and set off driving crazily up a steep road through Drimi and into the hills. He was a big man with a heavy, humourous face, not at all like Nikos, and he went into an enthusiastic monologue about family affairs until, when we were clear of the village, he said suddenly, 'I didn't want you to come. Did you have trouble getting through?'

I told him about the questions of the young officer and Takis scratched his unshaven chin and grunted.

'I'll tell you who that is,' he said. 'His name is Jemel Kish, a lieutenant in the SSSh, one of the Gheg fanatics from the north. He was stationed in my district until last week, then suddenly he was moved down here.'

'That sounds ominous,' I said 'He *knows* you?'

'Knows me and doesn't like me. He has it down on Greeks for a start, thinks we do nothing but plot against the Government. I've just got the feeling he thinks I am up to something. Be warned, Niko, our network may have to close down.'

71

'But he let us through, so he knows nothing definite. I may have to stop coming after this visit anyway. What happened with Volni?'

'He took me to his place in the mountains,' Takis said carefully. 'It was just as he described it.'

9

Takis' home in Koritsa (he pronounced it Kor-cha, I noticed) was a drive from the coast of more than a hundred kilometres over unbelievably tortuous and ill-made roads and he used the Skoda to fight them rather than ride them. But once we had exchanged our news about System V we had a cheerful time of it with Takis singing at the top of his voice, telling us stories and laughing in great bursts that set the car rocking. We were three Greeks on a joyride; Goodwin and the desperate seriousness of our task were forgotten in the heady clean air of the mountains and the ready intimacy of Takis and Nikos. Neither of them, I believe, really understood the implications of mad Volni's discovery and their ignorance was a kind of reassurance to me.

We talked, I about London (which was now far enough away to sound exciting, even to me) and they about their lives. Takis had lived in Albania since the days of King Zog's dictatorship, had fled into the hills when the Italians invaded the country and spent an incredible five years among the partisan bands of wild mountain men on both sides of the frontier, harassing the ambushing Germans and Italians with indiscriminate relish. When the war ended he and some of his comrades kept their primitive intelligence network going and during the Greek Civil War they had helped to keep the Royalists, the British and the Americans informed of Greek communist movements behind the frontier.

In Epirus his brother had been similarly occupied and in the civil war he was among the commando raiders who crossed the border to destroy communist installations. Amazingly enough neither of them had since been marked as a suspect in Albania, though they belonged to the Greek minority which had been suffering for its dual loyalties ever since.

'Pah!' Takis snorted and removed both hands from the wheel to make a gesture of contempt. 'They have a method for running this country, the Albanians and their Chinese friends, a hard, stupid method. I have a method too, one that is better than theirs. Fifteen years ago they took my land from me and made it a communal farm, divided it among twelve people. None of the twelve could make a living on it so the Government had to make me the manager of the farm. Today the people are better off and so am I but they accuse me of being bourgeois. And I am. Do you know how many private cars there are in Albania? Perhaps two hundred. And I have one of them. Pah!' He expelled air from his mouth with a little explosive sound.

'But I don't forgive them, Michael, for other things they have done to me. They turn my church into a barn, teach my children to hate the Greeks, perhaps they will force the girls to marry Muslims. And I fight back in the only way I can, by betraying them. Oh, Jemel Kish would like to know about some of the things I have done. But he won't. My method has kept me safe for twenty years against stupid Ghegs like him.'

I said, 'Aren't you risking a lot? Things would be even worse for the Greeks here if we were caught.'

'They can't get much worse. Our only hope is that someone who is sane will take over this country, and I do what I can to encourage that. These are the people who call Volni mad. Pah!'

In darkness Volni had taken Takis to the place where he had had his vision, finding his way unerringly among the mountains. It turned out to be closer than Takis had expected, a matter of a short drive and a three-hour hike. From what he could see by starlight he knew the shepherd's description had been accurate.

'It's all there, rockets, things for launching them ... but you'll see for yourself. Tonight, if you wish. Volni has gone on his way, back into the mountains, but I have the place pinned down in my mind.'

The road climbed and fell steeply over one barren mountain after another giving us, at unexpected turns, breathtaking views of the stark purple and ochre landscape, never a foot of it level. Here and there a huddle of uniformly white and square buildings betrayed a farm or village, but never enough to destroy the sense of utter wildness and desolation. It wasn't difficult to imagine that fierce clansmen, dressed in sheepskins and led by men of Takis' mould, still prowled the slopes in a state of total war against authority. Here – and even more so further north, where the Gheg tribesmen lived – were the most militantly primitive pockets of Europe. Slowly the tentacles of order were reaching into them from the seat of government in Tirana. But the iron discipline of the Party and the watchfulness of its Chinese patrons still hadn't eradicated much of the old anarchy.

Only a large-scale ordnance map would show the series of roads and tracks by which we reached Koritsa from the coast. Takis had driven this way often, but he was a wild driver and several times he misjudged the sharpness of a bend and almost took us plunging into a chasm. We passed only three or four other vehicles, two of them army lorries, and when that happened we had to come to a complete halt and crawl past each other. Eventually we wound down one long descent to the town, a place of Ottoman antiquity thinly spread over the floor of a valley between two great arms of the Dinaric Alps.

'Just over there are the big lakes and the Yugoslav border,' Takis said. 'And the Greek frontier, further south over the mountains. A useful escape route if you could get over the minefields.'

In four hours we had crossed from one side of the country to the other.

We did not enter the town but turned left onto a road that skirted its western side. In a few minutes we stopped outside a cluster of houses, bright with their whitewashed walls and green shutters against the clayey drabness of the town's architecture. This was the little Greek colony of Koritsa, Takis' home and the base for our operation. In the flinty mountain soil of their gardens a few fig trees struggled for survival.

Takis' wife was diffident and quiet: with a husband like that she couldn't be much else She and their six children had been cued to treat me as the long-lost cousin from Epirus, though apparently they had no idea what I was there for. In return I pretended an avuncular interest in the children, of whom the eldest was a girl of eighteen called Aliki. She had a pert oval face and her father's teasing dark eyes. And my interest wasn't avuncular enough to escape Takis' notice. He dug me in the ribs.

'Now there, Michael, you haven't seen our Aliki when she's in a temper. That's when you want to start thinking what a nice girl she is! Come now, food, wine and sleep!'

We lunched late in the Greek summer style, though without olives or oil, which were constantly scarce here. Then Takis showed the two of us to the small room we were to share.

'You'll go tonight, Niko?' he asked, lingering in the doorway. Nikos nodded.

'When you have slept I'll show you the way on your map. I can't go myself.'

'Can't go!' Nikos said incredulously. 'But you are the only one who knows where it is.'

'I can mark out the route easily enough. I would rather not risk being away from home too long, you see. I am suspect, as I told you. If there would be inquiries I can at least be here to make excuses for your absence. If not .... Besides, there is room for only two in the foxhole that Volni found.'

'If you prefer it,' Nikos said, shrugging. 'I thought it would be easier if you came.'

'Have you forgotten Takis' slogan during the war?' Takis said. 'The easy way is the way to the firing squad.'

Nikos and I had a long siesta in preparation for the night ahead. At seven Takis woke us, when the mountains to the west were silhouetted before the setting sun. First we changed from our outing clothes to the things Takis had scrounged up for us, workmen's dark denim overall suits, tough but pliable boots and sheepskin jackets; the nights were cold in the mountains. I gingerly removed my camera and film from the box of Turkish delight and the huge lens from the demijohn, and managed to get them all into an old British Army rucksack, one of those ubiquitous objects that turn up all over the world. It still had its date of manufacture, 1943, inside the flap and a name in marking ink, CPL B.D. BILLINGS. I wondered by what routes it had travelled into Takis' hands. I was buckling down the flap when Nikos said quietly, 'I'm taking this with me, by the way.'

Sitting on his bed he was pressing the last of a series of fat copper-nosed 9 mm cartridges into the magazine of a pistol which lay on his knee. It was a Spanish Astra automatic. He put down the magazine, picked up the gun and cocked the action twice, loaded it, put it on safety and slipped it into his jacket pocket.

I felt slightly betrayed. 'Goodwin didn't tell me you were bringing that,' I said.

'Goodwin doesn't know.'

'And if we're caught with it?'

'If we're caught it won't make any difference. That camera of yours will tell them everything they want to know. I feel safer with this, that's all. Like during the war.'

He smiled reassuringly. I didn't like it, it made everything that much more serious, more professional, and I wanted desperately to believe it was just another skylark. But there was nothing I could do; by seniority if not by appointment Nikos was the leader of our expedition.

In our heavy boots we clumped into the living room where Takis awaited us with a bottle of black wine and a plate of sheep's-milk cheese. The rest of the family were discreetly absent. We sat down at the rough deal table, nibbled on the cheese, touched glasses and drank before anyone spoke. It was a silent toast to success.

'The position,' Nikos said, producing the ordnance map he had been given in Corfu. 'Let's get the position right first.'

We spread out the map in a pool of yellow light from a small electric lamp and Takis ran a brown finger familiarly over the contours west of Koritsa. He didn't look for place names, I noticed. He was back in the mountains showing an illiterate raiding party the route to an Italian petrol dump.

'Here.' Takis' finger left a smudge on the paper. I leaned across and saw that the mark covered a small bulge in the nine-hundred-metre contour a little way south of a wrinkled line marked RIVER DEVOLL.

'This is the place, a small plateau, the only level ground for many kilometres.'

Nikos found a pencil and made an X on the spot, then ran a finger down and across the map, silently mouthing the longitude and latitude as he checked them.

'Forty-forty north, twenty-forty-two east,' he said finally, looking up at me. 'Will you keep that in your head, Michael, while I keep it on the map?'

I asked 'Why?' and realized why the moment I had said it. The hand inside my stomach clutched at something again. As matter-of-factly as he could Nikos said, 'In case I don't get back, that's all. Taki, let's look at your route to the place.'

They marked out the route, Nikos making scribbled notes on the margin of the map to help him locate the three or four nocturnal landmarks we would need. Already something had been achieved, the pinpointing of System V. Logically, Goodwin had said, there would be three or four similar bases in preparation further north.

'I'll start by driving you to this spot,' Takis said, making a mark a little to the north-west of Koritsa. 'There is a road all the way up to the base but we daren't drive any closer to it. You need daylight for your photographs, Michael?'

'Almost certainly.'

'Then I will show you exactly how to reach Volni's foxhole. It's a small rock crevice in the little slope above the base, perfect cover, no risk of being seen. But it will mean that you must spend the whole day hiding there tomorrow and come out again in darkness.'

'If there is no other way to do it,' I said.

He shook his head. 'None that I can think of. Leave the place at midnight tomorrow and you will reach our rendezvous point by four o'clock. Let's call the point Zita' – he made a Greek Z on the spot near Koritsa – 'where I will meet you to drive you back here.'

'Are there guards outside the base?' Nikos asked. 'On the surrounding plateau?'

'I saw none. But there must be at certain points. Follow the route that I will draw you to the foxhole and you should be safe.'

Takis drew a sketch of the plateau and we spent an hour discussing the finding of the foxhole and the alternative routes back. Then we ate a light supper and Takis packed us a bag with bread, dried meat, two bottles of water and one of wine. At ten o'clock we went silently out to his car and set off on the five-mile trip to our rendezvous point in the foothills. He stopped the car and doused the lights on a deserted stretch of track a hundred yards short of an abandoned shepherd's hut. The night was warm and filled with the song of crickets. Nikos and I got out and closed the doors quietly behind us.

'Thank you,' I said to the white moon of Takis' face framed in the car window.

'Till Wednesday morning, four o'clock;' he said. 'Good luck.'

'And to you. Take care.'

Nothing more needed saying. Takis swung the Skoda's blunt nose around and vanished down the track towards the town. Nikos said, 'Come on,' and led me off the track on to an almost invisible footpath meandering towards the black mass of mountain.

There was no moon and we used Nikos' torch sparingly, hooding it to examine the map with a tiny pinpoint of light now and again. But Nikos found his way like a nocturnal animal, leading me along a series of footpaths that wandered up stony hillsides, down into silent deserted valleys, along the dry courses of winter streams and past occasional co-operative farms where patches of tobacco and wheat ripened precariously. He chose from among the dozens of diverging and tributary paths those which skirted round villages, farmhouses and shepherds' huts.

We moved gradually but inexorably upwards. On the high ground there were pine forests and the going became harder and the paths fewer. The mountainsides were steep and uncultivable; we more or less left human habitation behind. I felt the weight of my camera and lens increasing gradually; I breathed harder than Nikos but was determined that he should not slacken the pace for me. Every hour we paused for five minutes and sat smoking behind cupped hands and when we moved again I would feel my thigh muscles stiffening. With familiar skill Nikos used his small compass to take bearings on the peaks around us, faintly outlined against the starlit sky.

I had temporarily exchanged my automatic watch for a cheap one more in keeping with my Greek identity. Its greenly luminous hands said two-fifteen when we reached the base, coming on it abruptly as we crossed a steep ridge. I saw it at first as a rectangle of light in the centre of the plateau and it materialized in a few seconds into a fence of high barbed wire lit right around the perimeter with electric lamps. A few other lights were scattered round inside and a soft humming noise, probably made by a generator, drifted across the still plateau. The sound of my heartbeats was suddenly there as well, growing swiftly to an excited crescendo. Here it was, the thing even I had only half-believed in, System V.

Nikos touched my arm and turned me round. We went back behind the line of the ridge so that we would not be silhouetted against the sky. With Nikos silently counting his paces we walked for about a quarter-mile parallel to the long side of the enclosure facing east, then he stopped and motioned to me and we got down on our bellies and crawled over the ridge.

We dragged ourselves down for about forty yards and I stopped while Nikos manoeuvred around us, back and forth along the slope. Finally he found what he was looking for and waited for me to move over to him.

It was precisely where Takis had said it would be. In the darkness it looked like a clump of bushes, which in fact it was, but I did not see the large boulder beneath them until Nikos parted the branches. Feeling around I discovered the neat vertical cleft, about four feet wide, in what was otherwise a solid single rock ten feet across.

I finally understood the signs Nikos was making and I got down and slithered feet-first into the cleft. He followed me in and there was just enough room for us to lie full-length, side by side, facing outwards. We rearranged the long fronds of bushes hanging over the opening and we were completely sealed in. Nikos settled himself more comfortably on the leafmould floor of our hideout and gave a grunt of satisfaction.

In the army I'd been an infantry section leader and learnt a bit about camouflage. From what I remembered of it I knew our hiding place was perfect. Volni, the mad shepherd, would have had an instinctive knowledge of fieldcraft. An impenetrable growth of prickly-leaved ilex smothered most of the outer surface of the rock. From beneath it thick broom and a kind of leafy bramble spread their vines across the front opening to make it invisible, even from a few yards away. The boulder would look round and solid. And while remaining hidden we had only to part the fronds in front of us slightly and nose the camera out between them. When the sun rose we would remain completely in shadow.

We lay waiting for daylight.

10

As the blackness of the plateau below us softened into grey the circles of light from the perimeter lamps folded into themselves like closing flowers. In the morning mist the scene behind them was at first a geometrical nightmare of blurred rectangles, cubes, spheres and lines, then it sharpened slowly as if a lens were drawing it by tiny degrees into focus. Colours crept into it from the edges, the yellow of stunted mountain grass and the washed-out blue of the sky. At the instant it was focused precisely it came to life.

The lights went out and a series of long harsh sounds came from an electric buzzer. Nikos and I lay in our little cave about a quarter of a mile from the site on a gentle rise that formed the eastern boundary of the plateau. Over the ridge behind us the ground fell away steeply. Our position was in line with a point about halfway down the long eastern fence and we had an even view over the whole area.

To the right, parallel to the shorter northern fence of the rectangle, were four long huts of corrugated iron painted a drab yellow to blend with the grass. From these sleepy men now came shambling out to a field latrine and ablution block next to the fence. One of the huts seemed to house soldiers and the others workmen who wore uniform grey overall suits.

Against the western fence, on the side away from us, a dozen troop carriers were lined up with a water tanker and two command cars with radio aerials at one end. At the southern end building materials and equipment were scattered in untidy contrast to the military neatness of the rest of the base. Six huge concrete mixers gaped with black mouths at stacks of cement bags; a fleet of wheelbarrows lay at rest around each of them. A self-propelled crane was parked in one corner near a heap of metal girders and scaffolding. Steel reinforcing rods were bunched elsewhere at intervals among sheds and lean-to's, buckets and barrows, with lengths of timber strewn everywhere in a handily muddled way. The ground was patched with spilt, hardened cement.

And down the centre of the site, dominating it, ran a broad

platform of concrete raised two feet from the ground, perhaps six hundred feet long and two hundred wide. It was not yet complete; at the northern end a wooden framework was dug into the ground, ready to receive a new pouring.

Along the completed length of the platform were six objects, in two rows of three and in ordered stages of construction. The two nearest the north end were simply saucer-shaped indentations twenty feet across, ringed by the protruding ends of H-iron lengths and reinforcing rods set in the concrete. The next two were structures of metal bridgework, adjustable ramps of a sort, about thirty feet high and built on circular and apparently rotative bases. The ramps were supported by what must have been powerful hydraulic lifts which had one of them raised to about thirty and the other to sixty degrees. They looked almost ready for use.

The two southernmost ones were the completed article. The ramps were lowered to the horizontal and had both been swung to face due north. They looked like very sophisticated emplacements for large cannon. But instead of the barrels of guns, immense silver-grey rockets, lightly shrouded by the mesh of brown-and-yellow-speckled camouflage netting, rested on them. They were over a hundred feet long, supported in a grotesque illusion of imbalance by the ramps, looking as if they would uproot them and drop nose-first to the ground at any moment.

The morning sun cast a pattern of fine chequered shadow on them through the netting. In this state there was nothing that looked menacing about them except their anonymous simplicity. They looked the way I expected rockets to look, slender, needle-nosed, with fins at the tail jutting past the bridgework of the ramps and another set of fins halfway along them.

Nikos and I looked at each other. In a few hours our perch had become uncomfortably cramped; the ventilation was bad. The prospect of spending another eighteen hours there was one I preferred not to think about.

'System V,' I said softly. 'If my opinion was worth anything I'd say they were the genuine article, uncle.'

He nodded. 'There are still only two of them in place, as Volni told me. But the next two are ready, do you see?'

I hadn't noticed them among the builders' equipment but just off the platform on the southern side two long flatbed trailers were parked with canvas-covered cylinders on them. The rockets were apparently brought here fully assembled and not piecemeal for assembly on the site. Risky from the security point of view, but I supposed there must be no alternative; and it lent weight to the proof we were going to provide.

Both of us felt jittery, I think, but since Takis' news the day before, confirming Volni's story, we had spent too long anticipating the vision to be awed by it. Even Goodwin had been able to tell us what to expect, from the camouflage netting that would make photography difficult to the launching ramps that looked rather old-fashioned but were designed for speed and versatility in selecting targets; they could be swung to any point of the compass and raised to any elevation in a couple of minutes. Underground silos would have taken too long to build. And now, having taken it in, there was not much left to say about it. We lay waiting for the light to strengthen so that the camera could be used to best effect, and occupied ourselves making notes about the day's routine, recording as Goodwin had told us to as many facts as we could, however insignificant they seemed. Any one of them might turn out later to be important.

I could see no sentries outside the enclosure but they patrolled constantly inside the fence, more as if they were meant to keep their comrades and the workmen in than to keep intruders out. Who would expect spies to get as close as we had? But Nikos agreed with Takis in thinking there must be guards tucked away at commanding points around the site, certainly on the hilltop at the other side of the plateau. This hill overlooked the rough newly-made road from Koritsa which led to the main gate on the southern side; it would have to be a reasonable road for the missile-laden trucks.

Two vehicles arrived in the first hour after sunrise, the first a supply lorry that offloaded crates of food at a section of one hut that seemed to serve as a kitchen, the second an army command car like the other two, containing an Albanian officer and a Chinese civilian. Both went into a door at the end of one hut, probably a guardroom of some kind.

Fitting my long lens to the camera and using it as a telescope I picked out several other Chinese among the men moving about the site. They were not in workmen's overalls but wore high-buttoned Chinese drill suits, Mao-style and supposedly proletarian. They also did not join the teams of Albanian workmen who were being formed up to start their day; the centre of their activities seemed to be yet another section of a hut that might have been a site engineer's office. These would be the engineers, consultants and specialist technicians who really ran things.

Two groups of workmen were formed. The first was marched in military formation to the southern end where the concrete mixers ground into activity. The others were set to continue digging a series of rectangular trenches in the north-west corner next to the iron huts.

'What do you think they're going to build there?' Nikos asked.

'Some kind of permanent building, I suppose. Someone has to remain in control of the base once it's complete. Keep the missiles polished − and fire them, I suppose, if the need arises.'

'I suppose so,' said Nikos, who seemed slightly out of his depth.

It wasn't for another couple of minutes that the significance of what I had said dawned on me. From the little I knew about strategic missiles I had some notion that they were aimed, primed and launched with the aid of complex electronic devices. These would hardly be housed in the metal huts, they needed a permanent home of some kind. If work had barely started on a building here then the two missiles already in place couldn't be ready for launching, and wouldn't be for some time. Or could the button be pressed in Tirana, or even Peking? Suddenly I remembered, almost with a sense of glee, the hum of the generator that had gone on right through the night. This place was providing its own electricity, at least for the moment. No cable from outside meant no remote-control launching. No control centre here meant no launching at all, so the missiles were still harmless, as we had hoped, and if our side moved quickly enough they would remain so. We had tipped in our favour the balance between time and secrecy. But perhaps I had it all wrong. I scribbled down some notes on the blank side of Nikos' ordnance map.

At nine o'clock I loaded the first film in my camera. I wished I had an even stronger telephoto and a series of filters that would increase contrasts and heighten the value of each colour in turn. But

I would make do – I had one of the world's best lenses working for me and I had made a selection of fast and slow films which, with a bit of mental arithmetic and some juggling, I could use to make pictures with contrast.

The camouflage over the two fully installed missiles worried me. It was easy enough for us to see the rockets beneath it but with the diminished perspective on film their definition would become vaguer; the experts might have trouble deciding what sort of weapons they were. And the netting was an anti-aircraft camouflage. When all the rockets had been installed and covered with it detection would be almost impossible from the air in the surrounding jumble of mountains. I felt a new anxiety at the thought of how vital my pictures were going to be.

Holding and aiming the camera was a clumsy business in these circumstances. And with a lens that size there was no question of taking general views, the bulge of a single rocket practically filled the viewfinder. I went over the whole base, section by section, missile by missile, hut by hut, so that all could be fused together if necessary into a gigantic composite print. I used up ten spools of colour and ten of black-and-white, keeping back four for no particular reason. The work took a little over an hour and I thought I had done as good a job as I could.

I withdrew the camera from the opening, dismantled it and put the parts in the rucksack at my feet. Nikos had watched my drill with cautious interest and now he said, 'Do you think the photos will come out?'

It had been so long since anyone had been innocent enough to ask me this that I laughed. 'They've got a fair chance,' I said. 'What about breaking out some of that food?'

Takis had packed us generous portions and we chased the bread and meat down with gulps of wine which had kept cool in the shade. Now that there was really nothing else to do I suggested that we finish the bottle, but Nikos said, 'You have not spent much time in dugouts, *Mihaili*. What are you going to do when you want to make a pee?'

That was something I hadn't thought of and when it came I just had to sit on it. There wasn't room in our hideout.

We arranged that Nikos should get some sleep while I stayed on

84

watch. He settled down on the leaf mould and seemed to doze off quite comfortably while I steadily got bored watching the antlike activities on the base. Labourers pushed a steady stream of wheelbarrows back and forth, north and south, and on the two almost completed launching ramps Chinese technicians tinkered. Others moved between the office hut and various parts of the site, self-important with their clipboards under their arms. The industrious clank and clatter echoed strangely across the plateau. The day grew hotter, the poor ventilation of our hideout worse. I caught myself nodding off.

When I actually went to sleep for five minutes, shortly after two o'clock, I was startled awake by the alien sound of a car engine. Two closed vehicles similar to jeeps were swinging in through the main gate. At the same time, I realized, there was activity around one of the flatbed trailers on which rested the unmounted rockets. In growing excitement I reached for my camera.

The official party seemed to have two VIPs at its head, one a Chinese civilian and one an Albanian in uniform with a good deal of red at the shoulders. With a small escort of site officials they walked along the concrete platform and inspected the two vacant launching ramps and the two mounted rockets. Then they stood back expectantly while workmen stripped the canvas covering from one of the new missiles. They might have been opening a flower show.

A tractor had been coupled to the trailer carrying the missile and it manoeuvred out among the builders' gear and backed its load up the gentle slope on to the platform at the southern end. It manoeuvred again to get the rocket's tail lined up with the ramp nearest me.

This was the luckiest break we could have had. I would photograph every stage of the mounting and give the experts an unimpeded view of the missile.

It was backed slowly on to the ramp, which had been lowered horizontally to receive it, then it was fastened in place in some way I could not see clearly. I was using my camera as fast as a street photographer, concentrating on reloading as rapidly as possible. The Chinese civilian was no innocent guest of honour; he offered advice several times on points of mounting the rocket. Perhaps he was a leading weapons engineer, perhaps the man who had made all this possible. His small drill-suited figure looked insignificant against the mountain backdrop.

A ragged cheer went up from the workmen, reaching me a second or two later, as the rocket was lifted by the ramp mechanism to the forty-five-degree angle. Immediately it was lowered again to the horizontal, and I took the last picture of the four spools of film which had recorded the whole operation. The boffins couldn't ask for anything better. Shortly afterwards camouflage was drawn over the new addition to the arsenal and at half-past three, as the jeeps wheeled out of the gate again, I woke Nikos and went to sleep myself.

I slept patchily, frequently waking to shift away from a sharp stone or to rub life into an arm or leg that had gone to sleep too. When Nikos nudged me awake I was aware of two things at once. The light had faded and he lay rigid with concentration, staring through the curtain of bramble. I knew something was wrong. Parting the bushes carefully I looked.

Along the line of the escarpment across the plateau a pink glow marked the recent departure of the sun. There was enough light left by which to see the unusual activity on the missile base.

Four trucks had been started up and were backing into line just inside the secondary gate of the base on the western side. From the barracks a body of troops was raggedly falling in. There were two or three officers urging them on, awkward-looking in their calf-length boots and high-waisted grey-green uniforms. Along at the southern end the concrete mixers were silent; the workmen's day being over, the soldiery seemed to be taking up the noise.

'What's happening?' I asked softly.

Nikos shook his head slowly, his eyes fixed on the scene. 'Something has alarmed them in the last two or three minutes. I can't tell what.'

'They aren't just changing the guard?'

'They did that while you were asleep. This is an emergency of some kind.'

Our tension mounted as we watched the soldiers scramble in platoons to the trucks. They mounted and were driven out of the western gate where two vehicles turned left and the other two right. Rocking over the scrub of the plateau they headed out to its four corners, two of which were on the ridge that ran behind us, and began slowly to drive round the perimeter, each truck offloading one soldier every fifty yards. He would take up station where he was dropped, slouching with an assault rifle over his shoulder and facing inwards towards the base. The vehicle that came closest to us drove along the edge of the plateau just behind us, so near that we heard the long squeak of brakes as it slowed for long enough to let a guard jump over the tailgate. As the engine whine faded away to the south Nikos and I turned to look at each other, a long look of incredulous dismay. While we had watched helplessly we had been surrounded, probably cut off from our escape route. Nikos signalled to me to whisper close to his ear before I spoke.

'How?' I demanded. 'How do they know we're here?'

He shook his head gently. 'They don't. They only think we might be. You see' – he indicated the weak light filtering through our curtain of bush – 'there's not enough light left for a full-scale search. So they have scattered as many men as they could afford round the perimeter in the hope of trapping us if we are here. We could only be somewhere on the plateau. Then they will find some way of getting us out of our hideout.'

'But who has told them?' In anger and tension my voice became louder; Nikos put a warning finger to his lips. 'Who, God damn it, who?'

He shrugged noncommittally and returned to his peephole. His calmness seemed indecent, for I assumed the first thought that had entered my mind must be burning in his as well: that Takis had betrayed us. At once I knew, though, that it couldn't be Takis; he had been here himself, he could have led them to the exact spot where we lay. Helpless frustration gnawed at me: it suddenly seemed that the plan we had thought so clever was toppling over on us. Something had gone completely wrong, something Goodwin hadn't foreseen or hadn't chosen to. Where the hell was the guardian angel he'd told me about? He probably didn't exist. How absurd it was, after all, that so much should depend on us, two men lying on a hillside with a camera.

Nikos seemed to channel all his concentration into the darkening view outside the hideout. He was rigid, balanced on his elbows and toecaps, knuckly thumb and forefinger held three inches apart to separate the bramble branches. I said, 'We're a pair of fools, Niko.'

He looked faintly surprised, as if he had just remembered I was there. His face was sharp with animal intelligence, its strong vertical creases set with purpose. This was Nikos as he must have been twenty years before, a ruthless and intuitive guerrilla; this ability to concentrate on the immediate had kept him alive. And I knew now that my own life depended on him.

'We'll talk about that later,' he said. 'Look outside, you'll see how they hope to capture us.'

Numbly I turned to make my own peephole. Night was falling rapidly. In a straight even line projecting southwards from the main gate were twenty-five or thirty bobbing points of light which cast larger white circles on the ground below them. As I watched the line began to move slowly eastward, the lights playing out all around their pinpoint sources, towards the south-eastern corner of the base.

'A lamplight search,' Nikos said. 'A platoon of troops with lamps. They will sweep right round between the fence and the edge of the plateau where the guards are, looking into every hole and every bush that could possibly hide a man. The stationary guards will see anyone who tries to slip out.'

I had a quaking, empty feeling, as if I'd suddenly realized I was starving. 'What are we going to do?' I said.

'We *will* slip out,' said Nikos. He shook his head thoughtfully. 'If they'd got that alarm an hour earlier ... we are very lucky.'

If that was luck I'd rather have done without it.

11

Slowly and methodically the line of soldiers came on, picking with their lamps and bayonets at the bushes and broken ground between the base fence and the edge of the plateau, certain to find us if we stayed in the hideout. The little cave was perfect cover but it would not survive a systematic search.

We had estimated that there were four or five platoons, not much over a hundred troops, garrisoned at the base. All of these except the ones who still patrolled inside the fence were engaged in the search and they were making the best possible use of their numbers. The site of System V was not ideal because it was overlooked from three sides by the gentle upward slope of the plateau but, as Takis had said, it was probably the only extensive piece of nearly-flat ground for miles. Now we were sealed into it by a ring of guards while others moved round inside the cordoned area like game beaters to flush us out. There was a certainty about their method that told me they knew we were here somewhere and again I asked in senseless repetition how, how, how? I felt the beginnings of the terror that is peculiar to unknown things and with a deliberate effort I slammed a door on it.

'We must wait a few minutes,' Nikos had said, 'until it is darker.' Now it was almost as dark as it was ever going to be. The last faint haze of light had vanished from the western horizon but the starlight which had helped to guide us the night before was menacing. We had gathered our equipment together and lay watching the approach of the lamps. Faintly in the still air we heard the sounds of the search as well, the crunch of a boot on the flinty ground and the slap of a rifle-butt swinging against some other accoutrement, part of the inevitable clatter of troops on the move; it didn't matter how much noise they made. They rounded the south-eastern corner and swung towards us and in front of the lights we saw dark limbs moving and the prod of bayonets into the low bushes. They were a little over three hundred yards away when Nikos nudged me and began to ease his way out through the opening. He moved swiftly and silently, writhing through the clutching brambles like a snake, and soon the patterned rubber of his boot soles vanished among them.

I followed, dragging my way forward on elbows and toes, clutching to my chest the camera bag, which I had stuffed with leaves to stop it rattling. Twice the tiny thorns caught in my trouser-legs and freed themselves with a whipping sound that seemed to echo across the hillside. Finally my head came out into the crisp air and I found Nikos, lying still as a rock, facing up the slope towards the ridge, beyond which lay the welcoming mountain darkness. There were only fifty yards or less to the crest but crossing them would be perilous. We had no way of knowing where the nearest guards were stationed. We might have to slip past within a few yards of them, or they might surprise us in the dark. But the searchers' lamps were coming closer, we couldn't afford to wait.

With infinite, agonizing slowness we began to inch our way upwards, moving in the leopard-crawl motion on our elbows, dragged forward by shoulder muscles so that our heads and backs were never more than eighteen inches off the ground. Before we had gone ten yards my lungs screamed for more air and I almost fainted with the effort of keeping my breathing normal. Already bruised and cramped from eighteen hours in the hideout my muscles quaked with the strain; every six inches of forward movement was the equivalent of one pressup. But there was no time to rest. The lights and the clanking of the search moved closer, and on the ridges all around us a hundred men watched for our approach.

Still, when we were halfway up the slope, there was no sign of a guard above us. If we were lucky our course would take us between two of them, with a maximum of twenty-five yards from the nearest man. On a clear starlit night, on a hillside almost bare of cover, that was no distance at all.

Nikos, ahead of me, moved unflaggingly forward in swift jerks, pausing for a second between each one and once in a while raising his head very slightly like an animal testing the wind, his eyes trying to pierce the darkness ahead and his ears to pick up sounds through the strangely distant chirping of crickets and the noises of the search party. Seeing him on one of these halts, with the food bag slung across his back, I felt a warm glow of comradeship for him. You couldn't spend eighteen hours in a hole with someone without either loving or hating him at the end, I supposed.

The strain of moving in total silence and by infinitesimal degrees is incredible. Impatience and pain reduced themselves finally, in the knowledge that there was no alleviation till we crossed the ridge, into a dull and sullen ache in every muscle.

The ridge loomed before us when the search party were about a hundred yards away to our right, a dark horizon against the star-freckled sky. And still we could not see a guard.

90

Between every advance of six inches now Nikos was peering and listening all around him, as if he sensed the hunter close by. Very slowly he reared and craned his head. Along the slope we heard distinctly the soft, uneven shuffling tread of the search party, never speaking but often clattering with their lamps and loose pieces of equipment. A whisper now, the touch of a boot on a brittle patch of stone, might have given us away. Even if one of the soldiers had carelessly cast the beam of his lamp further along the rise our two dark, diagonal forms might have been picked out against the scrub.

Nikos pulled himself forward with two quick movements, then froze into total stillness. I heard the soft footfall across the ridge as well, and a second later the soldier's silhouette came up against the sky, right in front of us and ten yards away. He was close enough for me to see the ovals of his eye sockets in the white mould of his face, the blob of a badge above the short peak of his forage cap. He stopped when he was fully visible, turning his head slightly to look down at the advancing line of lamps, then eased his weight on to one foot and hitched the Kalashnikov rifle higher on his shoulder. Unbelievably, he still hadn't seen us.

The three of us made a still tableau on the ridge. Jesus God, I thought, we would pick a route that brought us right up against a sentry. He had left his post for a few minutes, perhaps to go behind the ridge and relieve himself, and now he was back and practically standing on our fingers. We couldn't go on. If we tried to withdraw and cross the ridge further on he would certainly see us moving, and anyway there wasn't time. Without turning my head, without even shifting my riveted gaze one millimetre, I knew that the nearest of the search party was no more than fifty yards to my right. In the furthest corner of my eye I saw the beam of a light prancing about on the ground. They would be on top of us in one minute at the most.

The soldier cleared his throat and spat, the spittle white in the starlight as it arced out and landed in front of Nikos' face. The guard seemed to watch its trajectory and then half-turned back to the lamp line. At that moment the shape of Nikos suddenly mushroomed from the ground. He came up in one swift motion and went in a silent, crouching run at the guard.

At the limit of his field of vision the Albanian must have caught the movement. The white face flashed around and I saw the eye sockets again in the instant before the face vanished behind the angle of Nikos' left shoulder. The beginnings of a shout bubbled softly and died in his throat. Then their two bodies were locked together in a swaying dark mass. No limbs flailed, no fists or boots thudded into flesh, but the mass quivered with electrical energy. It lasted for seven or eight seconds before there was a sound – partly a tear and partly a snap, as if a juicy sapling were being broken – and one of the figures went limp and was supported by the other. The rifle, which had remained slung over the guard's shoulder, went down like a lowered standard.

Fearing I could not run as silently as Nikos I went up the slope on all fours, trying to choose hand and footholds that would not give under me. When I reached him Nikos already had the guard's rifle slung over his own shoulder and he gestured at me frantically. The nearest lamp by now was not more than twenty-five yards away, moving in a methodical zig-zag across the line of the search. A glance showed me a face above it, glowing yellow by its light and intent upon the ground.

The soldier lay on his back. Understanding Nikos' signals I picked up the feet while Nikos seized the man under the armpits and began to back away towards the descent over the ridge. Once as we moved my foot crunched on a splintered stone and sent a tiny avalanche of pebbles tinkling into the darkness. And then we were over the crest, running with our heavy burden in a nightmarish and awkward slalom down the steep slope around rocks and bushes, our bodies threatening to overtake our legs and send us plunging nose-first into the valley. We made a lot of noise but we were safe now in the deep shadow of the escarpment.

We ran and stumbled for half a mile, not because we needed to go so far but because we were elated by our escape. I hardly felt the weight of the soldier which almost dragged my arms out of their sockets. Reaching a dry river bed below the water-shed of the ridge we turned south-east along it and soon stopped in the shadow of a small cliff where willow trees hid us even from the starlight. Nikos squatted on the ground. I stood resting my hands on my knees, hanging my head, breathing in deep gasps and feeling nauseous. When I had recovered some breath I looked at the limp soldier where we had laid him down in the sand of the river bed. Only then did I see how his head lay at a grotesque angle to his body. He had a young, swarthy peasant's face. The eyes were closed, the mouth gaped pinkly; by the hooded light of the torch two drops of blood glistened in his nostrils.

'He's dead?' I asked.

'Yes,' Nikos said tersely. 'I couldn't do anything else, Michael. You know I couldn't.'

'I know, Niko.'

I felt a strange detachment, the sense of dreaming and yet knowing you are dreaming. 'This makes things different,' I said. 'It won't be long before they know he's missing.'

'A missing man is better than a confirmed dead one. Come on, we must find a place to hide him.'

Nikos stood up, took the torch and walked to the base of the cliff. I followed and found him flicking the light along the rock face where it came down to meet the little dunes of river sand. He soon found what he wanted, a pattern of hollows ground out of the rock by year after year of rushing water. He chose the largest of these and I helped him drag the body to the foot of the cliff. With some difficulty we bent the Albanian double, bringing his knees up to his chest, and forced him into the tiny tomb. Nikos used his handkerchief to wipe all the fingerprints off the rifle and jammed it in alongside him. From a jumble of water-smoothed rocks a short way upstream, where during the winter rains rapids would churn, we brought half a dozen large ones and blocked up the entrance as naturally as we could, building up the sand around them to suggest they had been there a long time, and scattering a few more about in the area. Then with two small willow branches we erased our tracks, the drag-marks of the body and every other sign of the disturbance we had made. With a last sweep of the sand behind us we stepped upon the hard shale of the river bank and looked at each other as if something needed to be said.

Nikos turned away quickly and crossed himself in the Greek manner.

'The poor bastard's better off wherever he is,' I said.

'He was a Muslim,' Nikos said. 'Allah will look after him.'

It was a hell of a funeral service, I thought as we walked rapidly away. I knew that the reality of the killing had not yet reached me. Once in Stepney I interviewed a little boy who described enthusiastically how he had just seen his father shoot his mother and then himself; it took almost an hour for the grief and horror to settle into him. It happened to me as well. We soon located the path by which we had approached the missile site and hurried along it through the cool Balkan night. When we had gone a couple of miles I had to stop and let the nausea that had been building up overwhelm me.

Retching and empty I looked up through water-filled eyes and said, 'Oh *Christ*, Nikos ... '

He was silent with cautious sympathy and suddenly I felt melodramatic. He had done his share of puking in disgust many years ago and had outlived it. He had done the killing after all, done what he must have hoped he would never need do again.

He helped me up and I followed him weakly along the myriad mountain paths. Up to that moment a kind of facile confidence had underlaid my attitude to this mission. Now the confidence was brutally torn away. Like a schoolboy's game of chicken the risky tantalizing business had inexplicably turned to murder. Because that was the only word for it.

12

We had left the base much earlier than we'd planned and now did not want to get back to point Zita too soon for our four o'clock rendezvous with Takis. So after walking for two hours we stopped at the edge of a pine forest, ate some more of our rations, drank the villainous remains of the wine and took turns sleeping for an hour and a half. This time I did not feel the discomfort of the hard ground and slept dreamlessly under the sheepskin jacket.

'You realize,' said Nikos as we packed up to move on, 'that our whole strategy must change now?'

'Because of the ...soldier?'

'Because of that and because they started to search for us in the first place. It is plain that they know we were up there.'

'I've been trying to tell *you* that, uncle,' I said. 'But it doesn't mean that they knew we, Varthis and Mannis, were the ones. Some peasant probably saw us heading towards System V and simply reported that he saw two strange men. So there was a routine search, they found no-one and went home happy.'

I wasn't making a very good job of convincing myself. Nikos said, 'Except that one of their troops vanished while the search was on He would not desert in a place like that, he would have a dozen better opportunities, and he would be reported missing as soon as the search was over. If they are determined to find him they will, very soon. Perhaps they have already. I prefer not to be an optimist.'

A small chill ran through me. I said, 'What do you suggest?'

'We must abandon the idea of going back to Kerkyra on the caique. We will get Takis to drive us to the coast, this morning, and use the alternative escape route, Johnny's boat.'

'But,' I objected, 'that's a plan for emergencies only. It means we'd have to stop being visitors and become ... outlaws. And think of the risks involved in bringing that boat into Albanian waters.'

Nikos stood up, slinging the bag of provisions over his shoulder. 'They need not be too great. I think it is worth the risk. There is something about all this that we do not understand. But even if they do not suspect the two of us and we take the caique back do you realize how powerless we are with your cameras and the film? If Jemel Kish were to search your luggage thoroughly ... '

'Jemel Kish!' I said. 'He can't connect us with this. He suspects Takis of plotting against the Government, that's all. He's a junior police officer, he wouldn't even know that System V existed.'

'But he might know about a missing soldier – or a dead one, especially one who was based at a secret installation. It happened in the Koritsa area and we were in the Koritsa area, two Greeks who are relatives of Takis. For a man like Kish that is enough to make him suspicious.'

'All right,' I said. I was not able to disagree with Nikos, simply reluctant to turn away from the last pretence of legality. 'So we'll go on the run. But there are dangers in being too cautious as well.'

'I kept myself alive for eight years by being too cautious,' he said, experimenting with a smile.

'The trouble is that this plan was top-heavy to start with. Your network wasn't built for handling a thing this size.'

'Perhaps. But we have got what we came for, *Mihaili.*'

We seemed to have the world to ourselves as we strode over the starlit heights. Only the alarmingly close hoot of an owl and an occasional rustling in the grass at our feet reminded me that there was life around us and would startle me out of a series of reveries about the dead Albanian. The memory of the body in its tomb lingered with me and I didn't seem able, as Nikos was, to think ahead to the consequences of the killing. The incident seemed like some ghastly mistake that had no relevance to what we were doing in Albania.

At half past three we halted on the slope a hundred yards above the shepherd's hut at point Zita. Across the valley scattered lights marked the western edge of Koritsa. If all went well we could be at the coast a couple of hours after sunrise, within sight of Corfu. The thought of getting that close to home so quickly made me certain that Nikos was right. We sat on the dew-damp grass and waited for Takis.

'There is one man in Drimi who will hide us for the day,' Nikos said. 'George Milios, a member of our group. His house looks right across the channel.'

'When we don't take the caique back Takis will have some explaining to do,' I said. 'You're forgetting about that.'

He looked at me evenly. 'Takis will think of something. There is his method that he always talks about. But even if he does not we must not expose the films to risk for his sake. They are the most important thing.'

'But ... '

'Yes, Michael, you know they are. Takis is my brother but they are more important than he is, more important than all of us together. They are the only proof that System V exists, and if they do not get to Goodwin it will be too late to start searching for more proof. They must get there even if we do not.'

96

From anyone but Nikos the remark might have sounded like empty heroics, but he somehow had a sense of duty that did not need to smother itself with understatement. And disconcertingly he assumed it in me as well.

Waiting on the damp hillside I felt time beginning to drag. I thought of the ever-widening search behind us and I wanted to be moving, to use up the nervous energy I was generating. There were moving lights in Koritsa, the lights of sparse traffic along the main road that led to the north and the capital, but no sign of a car approaching us. I deliberately avoided looking at my watch; when I finally did it said five past four. It was another ten minutes before either of us dared to say the thing.

'He's late,' I said.

'Yes.'

We played it down, pretending it was no more important than if he were late to a party. I comforted myself with a list of obvious, harmless reasons, a flat tyre, a flat battery, a faulty alarm clock, and refused to face the one ghastly conclusion.

At four-thirty Nikos said, 'Takis is a man you can trust, Michael.'

'I know.'

'He would get word to us somehow if anything had gone wrong.'

'Give him a while longer. There could be a dozen reasons.'

At five o'clock, when the rising sun threw shafts of orange over the mountain opposite, we turned to face each other and the blunt fact: Takis wasn't coming.

'What are we going to do?' I asked.

'We must not go to his house.' Nikos said slowly. 'There is nothing we can do but wait longer.'

He was right, and once again I fumed inwardly at our help-lessness. Each stage of this plan depended on the successful conclusion of the previous stage. Except in the matter of leaving Albania there was no flexibility at all, and if Takis did not turn up we had no way of even reaching the coast. If he hadn't turned up for the reason that was every minute becoming more feasible .... I turned away from the thought.

I played a childishly fanciful game of closing my eyes for ten seconds, trusting that when I opened them Takis' red Skoda would have appeared on the road from Koritsa. It hadn't, of course, but all the same I traced the route it would take, turning off the northbound road on to the bumpy track that would bring it right to that spot at the foot of this hill. Point Zita.

Then, absently gazing at that very spot I saw something that should not have been there. It wasn't Takis's car, it was a hunched figure in black lying in the bushes at the side of the road. In the darkness it had been invisible. It was either dead or asleep and hidden mostly by the bushes, but identifiably human because of the white hand with its fingers splayed out on the grass.

I opened my camera bag, sorted the camera body and the long lens out from among the wilting leaves, fitted them together and had a look.

'What are you looking at?' Nikos demanded.

'Nothing special. What's the name of Takis's daughter again, the eldest one?'

'Aliki. Why?'

'And she has black hair usually tied with a white ribbon. Is that right?'

'Yes, yes, but what are you ... ?'

'I think that's her down there, that's all.'

Unable to restrain himself longer Nikos seized the camera two-handed from me and squinted with furious and clumsy concentration into the viewfinder.

'It is her,' he said. 'Asleep. She must have brought a message for us ... I told you Takis would send one somehow.'

I stood up. 'Just a moment.' Nikos cautioned me with his hand. 'I'll go down alone. It may be a trap.'

'A trap ... how?'

'You know what I mean. You have been thinking the same thing as I have for the last hour. I'll take the pistol, you stay up here.'

Nikos chose a route that would give him as much cover as possible and set off down the slope. By turns I watched his progress and examined the scrub patches of the neighbouring hillsides for any sign of movement. Just as difficult as it would have been to see us in our hideout at the System V base, I supposed.

Silently Nikos crept up to the girl. I had started to think she was dead, not asleep, but she awoke in startled confusion when he touched her arm. A minute later he was helping her up to our perch.

98

Something she had told him had hardened the lines in his face and turned down the ends of his mouth and moustache. He was angry.

'Cousin Michael,' Aliki said with a quick preoccupied smile. I had forgotten we were supposed to be related. Her calf-length striped skirt and black high-shouldered tunic, an adaptation of Albanian peasant dress, were damp with dew.

'How long have you been down there?' I asked.

'Since last night. I only dozed off in the last two hours, I'd meant to call out when I heard you coming ... '

Nikos cut across her sharply. 'Jemel Kish has arrested Takis.'

He said it savagely, as if the words were knives thrusting into my tautened nerves. It was this that I had been half expecting since four o'clock, that had disturbed me the day before when the search began, that had sounded some tiny alarm in me at the moment when Jemel Kish first looked me over with his quick eyes. And because I had not wanted to believe it I had shut it out of my mind. I found that I had been shaking my head mechanically for some time.

'How did it happen girl?' Nikos asked, more gently.

'Luckily I was out of the house.' Aliki brushed a strand of dark hair from her forehead. She was awake enough to be composed but not enough to hide the tension beneath the composure. 'It was about six o'clock when I came back from the shops and saw the police car outside the house. I hid behind a lorry parked a little way along the street and saw Jemel Kish and another policeman come out of the house with father and drive him away. They would certainly have left another man inside the house and if I had gone inside I would not have been allowed to leave. So I came straight here.'

'Six o'clock,' Nikos said bitterly. 'The search began just before seven. They didn't waste much time finding out why we were here.'

'Father hasn't told them,' Aliki said with sudden fierceness. 'I know he hasn't.'

'He wouldn't have to.' I said. 'Kish would guess soon enough. But your father had told you where he was going to meet us?'

She gave a small sigh. Dishevelled hair and tired eyes detracted very little from her prettiness. 'He told me more than that. I've known all about it from the beginning, why you are here and who you are doing this for. Father told me so that you would not be left helpless when they took him away.'

Nikos and I exchanged an incredulous glance. 'You mean he knew he was going to be arrested?'

'It was only a matter of time. When Kish was transferred down to Drimi he knew that the network would soon be uncovered. Kish could only have been waiting for the right people to come through the frontier.'

'Then why did he wait so long?' I said. 'He could have picked us up when we arrived.'

'He hoped to catch us in the act, perhaps,' Nikos said. 'Who can account for the way these Albanians think? Why didn't Takis *tell* me?' he asked desperately.

'Guess, uncle.' There was slight reproach in Aliki's tone. 'You would have abandoned the thing and gone back to Greece to protect him. He knew how important this was. It was the last chance to see Volni's place.'

'The fool,' Nikos murmured, confused between anger and pride. 'The fool, to sacrifice himself. So Jemel Kish has got something on him at last. I don't understand why he waited either, but he will make up for the lost time. You see, they checked at the base as soon as they knew we were missing from Takis' place. But they did not know where to find us, so he hadn't told them yet. By now they will have been at work on him ... '

Aliki bit her lip to stop its sudden quivering. Remorsefully Nikos put his arm around her shoulders and I changed my mind about telling her of the soldier we had killed.

'I'm sorry, niece,' Nikos said. 'You know how much Michael and I depend on your father's courage. More now than ever.'

Her self-control was good. She said, 'I know their methods, Uncle Niko. There have been other brave men who could not hold out against them. Sooner or later he will tell them the names of the other people in his network, the way you intend to escape, everything. Now the important thing is to get you quickly out of the country.'

I almost laughed. The haphazardness of the whole plan, the idiocy of thinking in the first place that we could casually wander in and out of a country with a highly-organised counter-espionage system, stealing secrets from under their noses – it had all settled into me with a kind of irony. And now we were depending on the resources of a girl of eighteen.

Nikos, who didn't seem to find it incongruous, said, 'Your father's car will have been impounded?'

'Of course.'

'Then we must find some other way of getting to Drimi. As soon as possible, before the search covers the whole country. There will be roadblocks out already, perhaps. You know of George Milios down there, a member of the network?'

Aliki nodded. 'He is the only one there, he will hide you until you are able to go back to Kerkyra. If it is not too late already.'

If her father had not already confessed, she meant. I had a sudden vision of what Takis might look like after twelve hours of interrogation, the kind of treatment aimed at getting quick results. None of the long-term psychological breakdown stuff, this was a job for boots, fists and electrodes. How much can you ask of a man? Because he would have been the one to arrange an emergency escape for us he knew every detail of our plan; every detail except one, I realized, and that only because we hadn't mentioned it — the signal that would bring Johnny's boat across the channel to pick us up. Much use that was to us standing on a hillside a hundred kilometres from the sea. And what kind of reprisals would men like Jemel Kish be dreaming up for the rest of the Greek community, the ones who wouldn't conform to the doctrines of Tirana and Peking? We were holding them all to ransom.

I remembered again the man Goodwin had told me about, the guardian angel. Where the hell was he? And what had been the good of telling me unless there was some way of contacting him? He couldn't possibly know where we were or what kind of trouble we were in. It crossed my mind to tell Nikos about him, but there was no point in raising false hopes. Aliki was saying something.

'There is a way to get you to Drimi.'

'That's our only way out,' Nikos said. 'I know the mainland frontiers, they are too well guarded. Drimi is where we entered the country so they will be expecting us. But we must rely on Goodwin's help.'

'Very well,' she said. 'But first you must rely on me. You will travel in an army lorry.'

101

'An army lorry? Don't be an idiot, girl ... '

'Listen to me, uncle, I've done it many times myself.'

Was I right in thinking that through the strain, the tiredness and the threat of tears there was a mischievous twinkle in her eyes, the look of her father, the man who had a method?

'There are many army lorries travelling between here and Drimi,' she said. 'In a country without cars the need of people to get from place to place is understood.'

'But you must understand that we are wanted men,' I said. 'We can't go begging for lifts.'

'You won't have to,' she said, 'I will.'

'Are army lorries allowed to pick up passengers?'

'It is not allowed. It happens all the same, especially if the passenger is a girl. Do you follow?'

I'd got used to thinking of Aliki as a little girl. But suddenly her small breasts seemed high and inviting and her hip, as she sat sideways on the ground, curved provocatively. Nikos and I stared at her.

13

Two hours later the two of us sat in shadow behind a ruined house next to the westbound road from Koritsa. The risk of detection was high but there was no alternative. Behind us the endless mountains rose tawny in the sunlight with peasant cottages dotted on the lower slopes, the nearest of them barely two hundred yards away. The ruin had once been a cottage too, probably abandoned when the road was built. It had long ago lost its whitewash and the sagging, splitting walls had gone back to the dun colour of the earth.

On one of the side walls was a row of identical posters facing the road, each surmounted by a red star and the title, in the curious

Albanian language that is spoken by almost no-one outside the country, RINISE KOMUNISTE SHQIPTARE. Below it was a group of youthful faces illuminated by a kind of heavenly light. I hated the faces with their handsome, mindless determination, hated the stupidity of their confidence. The youth on the right had a rifle slung over his shoulder, a guerrilla in the new folk-hero style; I couldn't help comparing him to the peasant boy jammed in a hole in the mountains behind us.

Around us the ground was bare of cover and only the wall and the shadow hid us from the sight of people passing along the road.

It was difficult trying to gauge how much Jemel Kish and the authorities already knew about us. If they had found nothing to confirm their suspicions at the System V base they weren't giving up easily. As we crept from Point Zita in a wide arc round the town to this spot on the main road we had seen two light reconnaissance planes skimming over the mountaintops towards the base. We had to race across a new narrow road which we guessed was the one leading to System V. Along it four troop-carriers packed with green-uniformed militiamen had moved towards the mountains. It was something, at least, to know that they thought we were still well away from the town. A scout car had gone by with a cadaverous Chinese officer standing in the turret, perhaps on his way to direct the Albanians in their search.

By now Aliki would be doing her stuff with the army drivers in Koritsa. She was taking a risk even by going into the town – which was only just big enough to be inconspicuous in – for Jemel Kish knew her as Takis's daughter and if she was recognised she would no doubt be held and questioned about where she had been the whole night. And there was a chance that the current scare would alarm the drivers into refusing to give her a ride. But then what randy soldier would be able to resist the expectation in her eyes and the suggestive way her moist lip would come out in a pout? She would have no trouble recruiting a driver from among the many whose trucks were moving about the streets of Koritsa. Her only problem would be finding an excuse to make him stop at this exact point, giving us time to scramble into the back of his lorry.

We deduced from what she had told us that the army garrison at Drimi had recently been placed under the regional command at

Koritsa, which meant there was a regular traffic of supplies and so on between them. We had asked her to try and find a lorry with a bulky cargo among which we could find a place to hide. A tall order and a crazy scheme, but the more we thought about it the more we realized it was our only real chance of reaching the coast. A military vehicle would not be stopped at roadblocks, or if it was would be given only a cursory examination. If any officious superior spotted Aliki riding in the cab the worst that could happen was for her to be ordered out and the driver chastised. The lorry, with us and the films in it, would go through.

Nikos squatted at one end of the wall watching for the approach of lorries. There would be no way of telling which one Aliki was in until it actually stopped, and then we might have only a few seconds in which to break cover, get out into the road and leap into the back, so we couldn't relax at all. Nikos looked battered by the news of his brother's arrest and by two nights of roughing it and I knew my appearance wasn't much better. His denim overalls were filthy with overlapping streaks of sweat and sand, and under the four days' growth of beard his face was unhealthily pale with the skin drawn tight over the cheekbones. Around us both there hung a rank odour of sweat.

I was supposed to keep a cursory watch in all other directions in case anyone approached, but I spent most of the time waiting for Nikos to stiffen with recognition and give me the signal to move. We were on the right side of the road, so the driver on the left of the cab would have a limited view in our direction.

Army trucks came and went, rattling heavily over the potholes. They were big six-wheelers with ugly snouts, red star badges and canvas canopies over the back. As in most authoritarian countries the presence of the military was conspicuous; there was virtually no private traffic. Once a bright red van went past with a loudspeaker blaring some announcement among the empty hills.

Another hour went by with both of us becoming nervously restive. We were horribly exposed; anything more than a casual glance from a lorry window would have picked us out. Koritsa was only two miles away. Had Aliki been arrested or had she already gone past, unable to make the driver stop? If we had known that she had it would probably have carried us over the brink of endurance.

I was expecting the sound of a slow deceleration, so when yet another lorry came speeding towards us I gave it no attention. The screech of brakes made me jerk up in alarm, thinking a group of searchers had arrived. The lorry slithered to a stop, turning on to the shoulder in a cloud of dust, about twenty yards past our hiding place.

'That's it,' said Nikos. We leapt up and, keeping the ruined house, the blindly staring faces on the posters, between us and the lorry we came out to the edge of the road.

A quick glance showed us no other traffic. No-one got out of the cab and the dark opening under the canopy gaped invitingly. We went to it at a quick trot, keeping to the right to stay out of the driver's wing mirror. I heard Aliki's voice, childishly shrill, for a second. Nikos got his boot against the tailgate and swung himself swiftly over, reached down for my camera bag and then helped me up.

The lorry was stacked with roughly sawn wooden crates but there was a space wide enough for us to lie flat between them and the tailgate. Everything around us vibrated with the throb of the engine but the vehicle didn't move. I heard Aliki give another little shriek, as if of alarm, a man's voice said something and the door on the driver's side opened, slamming shut a second later. Then there was a crash of gears and we moved off.

Once we were moving Nikos and I eased our way further forward among the crates so that we would not be seen by anyone looking in from the back. Eventually I was lying right forward, just below a small window in the back of the cab that was meant to give the driver a limited view into the rear. There was no interior mirror in the cab so we were safe enough as long as the driver kept his eyes on the road — or on Aliki. Nikos lay facing forward and I was hunched in sideways. Our faces almost touched. In the half-light he looked up at me and his features creased in a grin. We had made it.

Later I found out how Aliki had managed to stop the lorry so effectively. While she was walking around the town looking for suitable transport she had captured a big wasp and tied it up in three layers of her handkerchief. As the lorry approached our rendezvous she surreptitiously undid the knot, took the wasp in her hand and deliberately let it sting her. The shriek that she let out and the buzzing of the insect round the cab did all that was needed. The driver braked, pulled off the road and squashed the wasp against the windscreen. She wept briefly and the soldier solicitously removed the sting from her palm. When she was quite sure we had had enough time to get aboard she announced bravely that she was all right. She had worked on the assumption that nothing would preoccupy a man as much as herself in distress.

The smooth road along the valley floor soon gave way to the tortuous tracks over the mountains. There were roadblocks all right, one soon after we started and one near a village that clung to a mountainside against a backdrop of sparkling blue sky. They were a mere formality, though. We sensed a guard taking a glance over the tailgate at the cargo and heard another make a crude joke about the driver's travelling companion. The soldiers were easy-going country fellows in spite of the severity of their system; they weren't going to deprive a comrade of a lay by making officious demands for the travel permit that Aliki needed to go from one area to another. She had it all weighed up beforehand.

I felt secure in my dark corner, surrounded by boxes. All the danger of our situation seemed to belong outside the walls of the lurching truck and I actually enjoyed the ride, even with my ribs being jarred by the vibrating steel floor. The sense that we were winning, so far, renewed my hope. But from time to time I thought of Takis and wondered how long he would last.

In the cab desultory conversation went on between Aliki and the driver. Her occasional laughter came to us over the crashing and roaring of the truck. I thought she was making the soldier, who sounded middle-aged, feel twenty again. Somehow she would have to talk her way out of the payoff he would demand.

The lorry's size forced it to take the mountain tracks slowly, sometimes having to reverse once or twice to get round the sharp bends. The longer the journey took the better, for it brought us that much closer to the relative safety of nightfall. Still, it was barely two o'clock when we sensed that we were near the coast. A sharp turn gave us a view of the sea through the rear opening and we edged our way to the back to be ready to jump out. We were within a mile or two of Drimi.

Leaving the truck was going to be even riskier than boarding it

106

had been. We had no specific plan and had decided just to watch for the best opportunity of bailing out. But we couldn't be sure what might be in front of us when we did and who might see us. Delaying it too long, on the other hand, might trap us in the truck as it went through the village and into the army garrison that manned the Greek mainland frontier a short way further down the coast.

Nikos raised his head above the tailgate and peered cautiously forward. A casual glance to the rear and the driver would spot him, but he had to look for a suitable place to jump. Fortunately we had the topography of the country on our side; there were many steep gradients and blind corners as the road wound down towards the sea and these would hide us from the moving truck a second after we tumbled out. They also kept the speed down to a safe level for jumping.

He kept glancing out with quick movements and ducking back behind the tailgate, shaking his head at me. I started to think that we would be in the village at any minute. Then, as the truck rocked over one rough patch he looked again and did not withdraw, but swung himself over the back, hung on to the tailgate by his fingertips for a second and dived off to the right. I followed; the truck was making a sharp right turn at a corner where a thicket of brambles grew and I plunged full-length into it. As I let go of the tailgate my camera bag swung forward and hit it with a terrible clang that echoed after me.

I lay flat, somehow managing to keep dead still and suppress the agony of tiny thorns piercing my skin in a hundred places, until the sound of the truck had died away. Then there was a rustling in the bushes behind me and Nikos' head popped up.

'Are you all right?' he asked.

'Apart from being skewered on thorns, yes. By God, Nikos, we've done it.'

'Don't be too excited, the worst is not over.'

In a minute I was sitting in a tiny clearing among the brambles plucking thorns out of my arms while Nikos lit cigarettes for us. In spite of his caution we were both quietly elated. The hunt for us was concentrated a hundred kilometres away and if our luck held we could be out of the country on Johnny's boat before the Albanians even knew we had reached the coast. And always depending on Takis.

We couldn't risk trying to contact George Milios until nightfall but in the meantime we were safe enough where we were. Moving to his house in the village would be extremely dangerous if Takis had already cracked, but we had realized that we had to do it. We needed equipment for our escape, a lamp to signal with and, since we were likely to have to go out in the water to meet the boat, a waterproof wrapping of some kind for the films. Takis would have supplied these things. Once again the emergency plan had failed. From where we lay, in a shallow depression in the hills above the village, we could not see the channel but I kept imagining its blue expanse, with the hills of Corfu opposite and so close you could practically touch them. In half an hour Aliki appeared, ambling up the road from the village and singing a high soulful song. I waited until she was right opposite the thicket and softly called out her name.

She stopped singing and came casually over to the bushes, reaching down to pluck a sprig of wild thyme. Idly she looked up and down the road and picked her way into the clearing where we sat. Kneeling beside us she broke into a quick, excited laugh. The three of us embraced, chuckling softly at our cleverness. Then she settled back, businesslike.

'I must hide with you until you are safely away,' she said. 'If I should be asked for my travel permit or if anyone recognizes me ... they will know you are in the area.'

'It would be best,' Nikos said. 'You didn't see George's house, I suppose?'

'No, it's on the other side of the village. I walked back here as quickly as I could after promising to meet that driver tonight. Pah!' She made the same contemptuous gesture as her father had. 'I hope he waits all night. But, uncle, I am not at all sure that George's house is safe.'

'You think he has been arrested already?'

Aliki looked away from us, across the interfolding flanks of the hills. 'They are not waiting for father to confess, they are taking many innocent people. A purge has begun, the driver told me so.'

'*He* told you that?' I said sceptically.

'He knows a little. Enough. He did not take me for a Greek because I speak Albanian fluently. He told me' — she continued to look away, at the clouds on the eastern horizon — 'that two Greeks had murdered an Albanian soldier in the mountains near Koritsa last night. This morning an order came from Tirana to arrest all the Greeks in the south of the country who have ever been under suspicion of disloyalty to the state. You may be sure that many will be taken to the labour camps.'

She spoke with a sleepy sort of detachment. Between her thumb and forefinger the thyme had been crushed to a fragrant pulp.

Nikos cleared his throat. 'We did that, Aliki, to the soldier. I did it, rather. I did not want you to know.'

Her frown was painful, her eyes dry because tears would have been trivial. 'There may be as many as a thousand people, uncle. Is it worth the freedom of a thousand people, what you came here to get?'

'I am afraid it is,' he said gently.

So they had found the body. We were wanted now for espionage and murder and a thousand lives were hanging round our necks. Our own lives depended on the resilience of one man to the persuasions of professional torturers.

14

Banks of dark cloud had been building up behind us during our ride to the coast and in the late afternoon they spread right above us. With dismal certainty we knew that sometime in the next few hours we were going to get soaked. But more alarming was the thought that heavy rain might obscure the exchange of signals with Corfu and we rather hoped the storm would break soon and disperse during the evening.

All afternoon we had lolled around the clearing in the bramble patch, having little to say and no energy for conversation. With exhaustion shredding at our nerves a listless depression had settled on us. The killing of the soldier, the arrest of Takis, our own slender hopes of escape, were all the substance of it but for me none of them so telling as the thought of a mass round-up of disaffected people. At that range there was no comfort in thinking that we might be helping to save many more from a similar fate. I damned Goodwin and Terry for imposing the responsibility on me, damned Nikos and myself for stupidly accepting it. My bitterness was enhanced by physical strain, the lack of sleep and food and above all the fear that had been working on me like a slow debilitating poison.

I tried to share my guilt with Nikos and was annoyed when he would not accept it.

'It can't be helped,' he snapped. Aliki had fallen into a restless sleep and we talked in low voices. 'I knew there was that risk, I was prepared to take it. Takis knew it too.'

'Well I didn't. If I had I would never have come here.'

He looked at me resignedly. Tiredness made him look older, a little more sour. 'But you did come. And don't think that you and I can talk it over and agree that it was not our fault. It was, entirely. But something more important is at stake and my conscience is clear.'

'The greatest good for the greatest number. You're on the wrong side, uncle, you should be with the Chinese and Albanians.'

'Tcha!' He snorted in disgust. 'You talk in slogans, fancy phrases. It is an Englishman's way of talking when he does not understand. You are too English, you take your freedom for granted, you have not learnt that one man's life means everything and nothing at once. I saw, I actually watched, a whole village being machine-gunned to pay for what I had done, blowing up a German convoy. If I had given myself up I could have saved them. Don't you think that hurt me, deciding not to surrender? I was more use alive than the old men and children of that village were, and before the war was over I had killed three Germans for every one of them. It hurt me but it did not stop me because I knew what I was fighting for, freedom. It is just a word to you; to a Greek it was a new and precious thing.'

He shifted himself on the ground and was silent again. His sudden vehemence was disconcerting, like a display of temper in a placid child. It gave me no comfort but it left me with nothing to say.

Darkness came. Clouds obscured the stars and thunder rolled

along the eastern peaks but still it did not rain. In the whole afternoon only two vehicles had crawled down the road past us, both army lorries, both containing only a driver and cargo. That was a good sign, no unusual activity in the area of the village. Yet it seemed incredible that Takis had not yet cracked.

At nine o'clock I looked at Nikos. 'Well, is it George Milios' house or not?'

'There is no other place,' he said, 'no-one we can trust. But if he has been arrested and there is a guard on his house ...'

He left the sentence unfinished. We all knew the unspoken part. It meant that there was no way of leaving Albania unless we swam to Corfu or tried to cross the mainland frontier. Both would be suicidal.

'The house is ideal,' Nikos said. 'It is out of sight of the rest of the village and looks straight across the channel. We must at least try it.'

We got up stiffly and picked our way through the brambles again, crossed the road and went about fifty yards up the slope on the other side before turning to walk parallel to the road. It led into the village but we stayed well away from it, keeping behind the line of the hilltops. After walking for twenty minutes we came round an outcrop of rock and I saw, with a leap of excitement, the low black valley of the sea. It was difficult at first to distinguish it from the velvety darkness of everything around us but I knew it was there because I suddenly had a sense of perspective before me. It finally emerged as a patch faintly darker than the rest and at the very limit I saw a few tiny lights twinkling on the coast of Corfu.

At that moment the rain finally came. We had heard the thunder reaching out to us from the east and seen the lightning play along the mountaintops. A few fat warm drops hit us and then it fell in icy sheets that enclosed us in a little cube and hid everything outside it. My instinct was to run somewhere, anywhere, but over the slippery limestone ground it was difficult enough to walk. Becoming rapidly drenched we stumbled on, finding our way by the flashes of lightning.

In another ten minutes when the storm had eased into a steady drizzle Nikos stopped us at the summit of a hill with George Milios' house a hundred yards below us. It was a square whitewashed two-storeyed building which stood, as Nikos had said, at the southernmost tip of the village, out of sight of the port and all other houses. The hillside ran steeply down from it for two hundred yards to the seashore. It was shuttered and silent.

We stood there hesitantly. Water ran down my back, into my crotch and into my boots. A series of lightning flashes caught us all looking at each other speculatively. Aliki's hair clung to her wet cheeks and she frowned and blinked against the rain. Nikos let water drip from an eyelid, expressionless as an ox.

'It looks deserted,' I said.

'Stay here,' Nikos said. 'I'm going to have a look.'

His pistol was in his right hand and cocked. He moved away to the left, looking for a route down the slope that would give him some cover, and I didn't see him again for twenty minutes. He appeared as a dim shadow creeping round the building, peering and listening through the shutter slats. Then he vanished and ten minutes later emerged, silent as a snake, from the darkness on our right.

'No-one there,' he said, his voice a whisper through the hissing of rain. 'And no-one watching it. I've been up the slope, down the slope and out for two hundred metres in every direction.'

'What do you make of that?'

'There's only George and his wife now. Either they are away on a visit or they have been taken as part of the general roundup. There would be no need to guard the house unless we were expected.'

Were we both trying to convince ourselves that Takis had held out? 'We'll risk it then?' I said.

'I don't like it but we'll have to. *Ela*, let's go.'

Nikos turned and led us down. It was muddied ground criss-crossed with streams of rushing water, and we slithered and slipped down so that we were patched with yellow mud when we reached the small level spot on which the house stood.

The back door which faced up the hill was of flimsy wood with a cheap lock screwed into it from the inside. Three shoves of Nikos' shoulder tore the screws out of the wood and the door shuddered open. He stepped swiftly inside, flashing his gaze round the darkness, then signalled for us to follow him.

Inside there was welcoming dryness and warmth. We were shivering in our sodden clothes.

The house was built to the Greek peasant pattern, with one large stone-flagged room below which served as kitchen, living room, bathroom, and for some of the family, if it was large, a bedroom. In the centre of one wall was a fireplace and in one corner a brick oven with a chimney pipe that vanished through a hole in the wall. It was sparely furnished with straight-backed wooden chairs and a couple of iron-framed beds that would be used as seats during the daytime. Up the steep wooden staircase let into a trapdoor in the ceiling would be two or three smaller bedrooms. The place was uncannily, ominously, lived-in and yet deserted. There was a full ashtray on the mantelpiece and a pile of dirty dishes in the tiny sink behind the back door. Clearly, George and his wife had been arrested that day. We were safe only for as long as they remained unconnected with us.

Nikos said, 'We must not waste time. Aliki, will you go out of the house and a little way back up the slope? Keep watch for us. If you see or hear anything just run straight in here.'

Hooding the torch, we crept round collecting what we needed. The village was electrified (for purposes of propaganda, they claimed in Corfu) but it had been done austerely, as if with reluctance. In this room the supply consisted of one overhead light and a single wall plug. I clambered on a chair, pulled the light bulb out of its socket and tested the current with a sliver of silverfoil from a cigarette packet. It was on. Then I cut the socket away and added two lengths of flex, one from an electric iron, one from a table lamp, until I had an extension long enough to reach the sill of the single inward-opening window that looked out over the channel. I refitted the socket and the bulb, which was only of hundred-watt strength but would have to do.

Nikos, meanwhile, had dug about in George Milios' toolbox which he had found upstairs. He had cut a hole in the bottom of a small pewter bowl and sanded the inside to a bright sheen that would serve as a reflector. We fitted it over the socket, rested the shaky contraption on the window sill and were ready.

Nearly three miles across the channel was Corfu. Our lamp pointed as nearly as possible directly at the house on the coast where Goodwin and Terry kept alternate watches with binoculars, scanning the Albanian shoreline for our signal and with a lamp ready to acknowledge it. But now, with the drizzle falling steadily, an impenetrable curtain of rain hung between them and us. We would have to wait. It was not much after ten so we had almost seven hours of darkness left. But every minute that went by increased the possibility that Takis had cracked. I thought, as I did every few minutes, of Takis with his teeth broken, Takis screaming as an electric current was passed through his genitals. Aliki had not mentioned it for hours but I knew by the increasing strain of her manner that she lived with it every moment. Feeling guilty, I went out into the rain and relieved her of her watch-keeping duty. She said she would find some food for us in the house.

A little later Nikos came out and we surveyed together what we could see of the beach below. It was faintly visible, a strip of white sand jutting out from the foot of the hill. There were guards patrolling it at intervals of two hundred yards, stick-like figures flashing faintly in their oilskins. From beyond the headland a mile to the south came a glow from the army garrison. To the north, from a promontory past the village and the outlet of the great lagoon I had seen from Corfu, a searchlight prowled out over the water.

'All this for our benefit?' I asked softly.

'I doubt it. The searchlight and the guards have always been there. They watch continually for refugees and smugglers.'

'But they're expecting us back this way, surely?'

'Of course. But don't forget that there is a stretch of coast four or five kilometres long facing Kerkyra here. They have no way of knowing where we may choose to go from. Here we are six kilometres away from the island. They would normally expect us to set off from further north, a closer point. Unless Takis has told them.'

We took half-hour turns on watch. Half an hour seemed to be just long enough to make our clothes completely sodden again after they had spent an hour drying in the house. In a cupboard next to the oven Aliki had found cold boiled fish, gluey dark bread and a bottle of raw brandy. The bread was fresh, the presence of the Milios family seemed to haunt the house. The brandy burned pleasantly in my throat.

Every few minutes Nikos went out to inspect the weather. The drizzle kept falling and the screen between us and the island hung as heavy as ever.

114

But at one o'clock exactly the rain stopped. We waited expectantly, not daring to whisper our hopes. I went out and saw a star wink through the clouds, vanish again and emerge resolutely. But as the rain lifted a solid mist rose magically from the ground in front of us, obscuring everything more thoroughly than before. We waited in chill despair to see if it would lift in time.

We had not switched on a light or lit the fire. Most of the time we sat around in the dark thinking our own thoughts, but I did make some preparations for departing. After searching through the toolbox I found a small square of yellow oilskin that had been used to wrap up a whetstone. I took the twenty-four spools of film and folded the oilskin around them, binding it tightly with leather thongs into a small, square, waterproof package. With affection I kissed my Rollei and the long lens goodbye, took them and Corporal Billings' rucksack out on to the muddy hillside behind the house and buried them in a foot of earth. That was eight hundred pounds' worth of gear gone, making me three hundred to the bad so far. I wondered absently what I would tell the insurance company.

We waited, dozing now and then in turns on the straw-filled palliasses that covered the iron bedsteads.

Three o'clock came and there was no perceptible difference in conditions outside. The wet ground continued to give back its moisture to the air. Above us the sky had cleared to cold starlight but all around the house the clammy vapour hung.

At three-thirty, when Aliki was again on guard outside, Nikos looked significantly at his watch. I knew what he was thinking.

'Give it a bit longer,' I said.

'If Takis has talked ... ' He got up and paced back and forth. 'I don't see how he couldn't have by now. They've had him for thirty-three hours. That's one of many things I don't understand. First they wait a whole day before taking him, and then they do nothing more. They leave this house unguarded, the house of a suspect in the very place where they must expect us to go across. At first I was willing to believe it was luck. The longer I am here the less I believe it.'

'What do you suggest, then?'

'We must not signal,' he said decisively. 'If the light is seen on this side and missed by Goodwin we might as well cut our own throats.

There is still enough time for us to get up into the hills, hide there for the day and try to cross the mainland frontier tonight.'

I was desperate for something to happen. I knew I would not be able to take another day and night like this. I said, 'I'd rather try swimming, Niko. In fact I'm going to.'

He looked at me, unsettled between alarm and anger. 'Don't be a fool,' he said, 'you'd never get across the channel.'

The idea had been partly serious and partly a ploy. 'I've had enough of running,' I said. 'Safety is right across there, staring at us. I just can't face turning back for another day like yesterday. You go through the minefields if you want, I'll take my chance in the water.'

'I can swim as well as you, I think. Perhaps better. But I know that on land I have more chance of reaching safety. If you are really determined, give me the films.'

'Not a damn,' I said. 'The film is my responsibility.' Then justifying, 'if you get across the frontier you'll probably be held and interrogated for days. And the Greeks will seize the film. Don't forget who you're working for.'

For a second Nikos looked betrayed, then he narrowed his eyes shrewdly. 'What do you really want?'

'I want you to signal with that lamp,' I said. 'Because I believe this time you *are* being too cautious for your own good, uncle. This is just one more risk on top of the dozens we've taken. I think they'll see the light in Kerkyra. If there's no answering signal I'll come with you into the hills. If you refuse to signal I'm going to swim.'

He stared at me woodenly before smiling. 'Very well, you've trapped me. I'll allow you four series of flashes, which is what we decided was the most we could risk. I'm a fool to listen to you but I am not always right.'

'Get ready then.'

I went out to the back to tell Aliki what we were going to do. Then, with a new enthusiasm, Nikos and I stripped off everything but our damp trousers and boots, loosening the laces so they could be slipped off when we entered the water. I hung the oilskin package round my neck with a loop of leather and Nikos retained his pistol with a full clip of ammunition, jamming it into the waist of his trousers. He stood at the wall switch with his watch in his hand while I held the reflector just inside the window, aiming it as nearly as I could at the house on the Corfu coast.

'Ready?'

'Ready.'

He flicked the switch and counted the seconds, flash for ten, off for thirty flash for five, off for twenty, flash for one and one again a minute later, an irregular pattern which hopefully would not look like a signal to a casual observer. To Goodwin it would mean that we were in need of an emergency rescue. I tensed at the last flash, watching the beam bounce back off the wall of mist.

Across the channel not a light was visible through the vapour, not even the ones we had seen before the storm. I strained into the darkness as if by doing so I could dissolve it.

Nikos waited three minutes before making another signal. I watched for the reply that didn't come. A third time he went through the series, his gestures becoming impatient at what was plainly a waste of time.

'Once more,' I said. 'You promised me four.'

Already I knew he had been right. The mist was too thick. We were losing precious minutes of the darkness we needed to get clear of the village but I was not prepared to admit I was wrong.

He flashed the final second of light and at once moved away from the wall, ready to get dressed again. 'Come on,' he said.

I watched for a few moments and turned reluctantly from the window, slack with disappointment. Nikos was already thrusting his sinewy arms into the damp sleeves of his jacket. I remembered that I ought not to leave the lamp on the window sill and as I half-turned to pick it up I saw the reply.

A dim yellow light across the channel, barely visible, barely piercing the mist. Three short flashes and three long, three short and three long.

I started to shout something but it caught in my throat. I seized Nikos violently and whirled him to the window, forcing him to look at the light repeating and repeating the signal like a warning beacon.

'They've seen us,' he said, unbelieving. 'They've seen us.'

Across the channel Goodwin, Terry, Johnny, would be scrambling to board the big grey boat. They had taken a fix on our light and would be heading straight for it, coming as close inshore as they dared. For a moment the idea that we had triggered off all this activity was bewildering. Then we tumbled back towards the door, tripping over the lamp flex and sprawling with hasty, hysterical laughter on the floor. I picked myself up, went to the door and called Aliki in.

'They're coming for us,' I said. 'You must go, quickly.'

'Yes.' She had a little bundle of food prepared. She picked it up and in an odd, anticlimactic way she was ready. I had a wild idea.

'You could come with us. Things may be hard for you here. If they find out that you helped us ... '

'No, no.' She shook her head quickly. 'I must be with my mother.'

I'd known she would say that. We were leaving her to live with the mess we'd made of her family's lives. Guilt made me say, 'Will you be any use to your mother in a labour camp? She'd rather you were safely away.'

'She will need me most then. She and the young children. So *kalo taxathi.*'

It was better not to tax the courage she had left. I said, 'A good journey to you, too. Thank you.'

She let me kiss her but made it brief and brotherly. She hugged Nikos.

'I am sorry for all of it, niece,' he said. She nodded and left. We watched her go round the corner of the house and looked at each other.

'A good girl,' Nikos said. He knew as well as I did that he'd never see her again. He turned away and we groped about to make sure we were leaving nothing behind.

The first sound we heard was the pounding of boots outside the back door. Then came Aliki's brief terrified scream and a burst of three shots from an automatic weapon. Nikos seized my arm and we flung ourselves to the floor in one corner. He had his gun out but by then we knew that shooting would have been useless. There were too many of them. They came in through the back door, the front door and the open window and there must have been a dozen of them in the room. Shouts and torch beams chased each other through the darkness and settled on us. A big wet boot hit me in the ribs and then planted its steel studs firmly between my shoulder blades, pinning me to the floor. Hands padded down my trouser-legs, searching for weapons. Next to me something similar was happening to Nikos.

Our makeshift lamp came on, flooding the room with light. It was on the mantelpiece and from the same direction Lieutenant Jemel Kish spoke.

'You can stand up now,' he said. 'Stand up very slowly.'

15

The boot released its pressure on my back but I couldn't move. I felt like a jelly that someone had dropped on the floor. One of the troops took me under the armpits and dragged me to my feet and I stood there swaying, transfixed by the light that shone straight into my eyes. I could feel nothing else. I knew nothing but a single fact that rang through my head like the peal of a bell. It's all over, it's all over.

Most of the torches had gone off but one disc of light lingered in the doorway. Its beam still played curiously over me. Behind it I could see only the peak of a cap and a broad pair of shoulders. I became aware of another fact chiming in over the first: it's my fault, I insisted on waiting.

Nikos was standing beside me. There were soldiers all around us, smelling of damp clothing and coarse tobacco and starting to chatter excitedly now that the action was over. Somebody coughed and spat. Somebody else walked across the cleared space between us and Jemel Kish and handed over Nikos's pistol. Kish covered us with a machine carbine that peeped out between the skirts of a glistening oilskin. He reached out for the pistol, tucked it in the waistband of his trousers and said, 'Get your hands up. Higher than that.' His eyes flicked from one to the other of us and there was a hesitant smile on his lips.

My shock had settled into an aching fear as if a hole had been kicked in my stomach. But I hadn't time to think of the full meaning of what had happened. With a gun pointing at me, I couldn't think of anything except that the lunatic holding it might let it off. Now the man in the doorway stepped forward into the light.

Beneath the forage cap was a plump, smooth amber face with long oriental eyes. There were no badges on the damp cotton drill suit but I'd seen the uniform before. He was an officer of the Chinese People's Liberation Army. He stepped aside as two more soldiers came in, carrying Aliki.

Nikos tensed up beside me. 'You did not have to do that,' he said.

Kish jerked up the muzzle of his carbine. 'It is for me to decide what I have to do. She ran. I had no inclination to chase her.'

Her clothes were covered in yellow mud from the hillside where she had fallen. The front of her tunic was stained a dirty chocolate colour by the blood that had seeped through afterwards. Damp hair clung to her face, and the eyes were not quite shut so that light was reflected by glistening brown slits. The eyes told me she was dead. The soldiers stopped by one of the narrow beds and rolled her onto it.

'Now come over here and sit down,' Kish said. 'Keep your hands up.' He used the gun muzzle to indicate the bed opposite the one where Aliki's body lay.

The Chinese had started to pick his way among the soldiers, looking for something. As we moved he noticed the package of films around my neck, stepped quickly over to me and ripped it away. He undid it, looked briefly inside and shoved it into his jacket pocket. He looked at me and smiled, the way you might expect a man to smile with the security of Europe in his pocket.

'Your photographs,' Kish said, 'what you came for — and yourselves, all captured at once, like nestlings. In one day the whole episode is over.' He laughed and the Chinese smiled tentatively. It was hardly to be expected that he would understand Greek, and he didn't.

Some of the troops moved out of the way as we crossed the room and sat gingerly on the bed facing Kish. They were standing about with their rifle butts resting on the floor, and Kish seemed to realize that there were too many people in the room. He said something to the Chinese, then called out an order. The men filed out through the door; their boots squelched away across the hillside and the room seemed very empty. From a photograph above the mantelpiece George Milios and family, *circa* 1935, stared at us soulfully. The Chinese strolled to the open front window and looked out.

'Now that we have you,' Kish said, 'there remains only one small matter to clear up. Major Ma-Ling is very interested in your friends in the boat.'

The horror crawled back into me. I knew with a terrible certainty why Kish had waited till now to arrest me. He had let us draw Goodwin, Johnny and Terry into the trap.

'The shore batteries are waiting. How long will it be before they are without any doubt inside our waters? Ten minutes, do you think?'

Takis had told them everything. Everything he knew, but that hadn't been quite enough. He hadn't known the signal that would bring Johnny's boat across the channel. We had provided that — *I* had provided it — as a free bonus. Yet I found myself saying, 'Those men on the boat are innocent. They have been hired to pick us up, that's all.'

Kish tried to look amused. 'Captain Wicks is innocent, you would say? The man who has been sending his stooges in here for a year or more? And the other man, the big man from London? Major Ma-Ling is very interested in the man from London. Unfortunately it does not seem likely that he will be taken alive. He will have to be blown out of the water.'

Major Ma-Ling came back from the window and started looking without much interest through the pockets of the clothing we had left lying about. It seemed that we were going to be kept at the house until the batteries had done their work. My gaze strayed to Aliki, and she seemed to be looking back at me through her half-closed eyes. I turned away quickly. 'How long have you known?' I said. I must have been getting used to the carbine pointing at me.

Kish leaned with his free arm on the mantelpiece. 'If you mean how long have I known about Takis Varthis and his network ..: well, quite long enough. In Albania attempts from the imperialist side to spy and subvert have always been notably unsuccessful. They have no sympathy from any but a small segment of the people – the Greeks. They have had to rely on laughable, shoddy networks like that of Takis.'

I could believe that. The description suddenly seemed very apt.

'In 1950,' Kish went on, 'a stupid adventure was planned by the American CIA and your Secret Service. They tried to infiltrate the country with bands of thugs, the dregs of reactionary partisan groups from Yugoslavia and Greece. The intention was to provide a counter-revolution, but it went amiss. Almost all of them were killed or captured. At least two of them confessed that they had been helped by Takis Varthis. Should we than have arrested him? Perhaps. But instead it was decided to wait and see if he should engage in any more interesting activities. We waited eighteen years, and he did. At that time we had certain treaties, purely as a matter of expediency, with the Soviet revisionist regime' – he produced the label with a certain sarcastic relish. 'It might interest you to know that on that occasion the whole imperialist plan had been given away beforehand. By a man named Philby, in London.'

'And this time?' I said. 'Who told you we were coming?'

'Nobody,' Kish said, and stared straight at me. 'We did not need to be told. Consider the inferences to be drawn: Nikos Varthis visits his brother three times in nine months. On the last occasion, the visit coincides with the capture of a lunatic shepherd who has accidentally caught sight of a secret installation in the mountains. The next time Nikos comes in, he brings with him a man claiming to be his nephew. A man who not only bears no resemblance at all to anyone in the family, but does not even talk, or walk, or act – or think – like a Greek.' A slow smile of contempt spread across his wolfish face. 'I would have thought even the British could do better than that, Mannis. From then on it was simply a matter of diligent security work, supervised by Comrade Ma-Ling who is our adviser on internal security in this southern zone.'

Comrade Ma-Ling looked up and smiled vaguely at the mention of his name. Then he went back to the window. Surely ten minutes had gone by; where was the boat? The sea was still shrouded in mist

122

so perhaps the guns would not have such an easy task after all.

'Naturally, certain details of your intentions were not clear,' Kish said, 'until Takis was arrested. And until he made a long and detailed statement to Major Ma-Ling at three o'clock yesterday afternoon.'

So the Chinese had done the interrogating, and very efficient it had been. He didn't need Greek for his kind of work, and Takis had held out against him for less than twenty-four hours. But there was a flaw somewhere — I couldn't put my finger on it — in Kish's version of the events. Asking questions was better than sitting in silence waiting for the guns, and Kish didn't mind answering. I suspected he even enjoyed it.

'If you knew twelve hours ago where we would be heading for why didn't you wait here and grab us? Ma-Ling would have got the signals out of us and you could have called the boat over yourselves.'

Kish pushed himself away from the mantelpiece. 'Yes, I have watched Major Ma-Ling at work. But his work takes time as well, we might have had to wait until tomorrow night before sending the signal. By that time, of course, your friends would know that neither the caique nor any of its passengers had returned to Kerkyra. They would not be inclined to trust a signal from you at that stage.'

The caique and its passengers, held hostage for what we had done. The skipper, the old man with moustaches, the women in white veils. 'Why?' I demanded. 'What harm have they done? What harm have any of the Greek Albanians done to you? We are the guilty ones, the two of us.'

'The orders came from the Politburo itself,' Kish said. 'But my own reports have helped them finally to take such decisions as they have today. Network or no network, every Greek in this part of the country is a potential imperialist agent. George Milios for example' — he gestured around the room. 'If we had arrested him alone, his wife would have given you as much help as he would. This calls for thoroughness. They are under arrest. So are many others, even your mad shepherd Volni.'

Even Volni, the idiot who had started the whole idiotic business. I should have realized from that how hopeless it had been from the beginning. There was one more question I wanted to ask.

'Why did you wait so long before arresting Takis?'

Kish glanced involuntarily at the Chinese, as if to be quite sure he had not understood. 'There was a reason,' he said shortly. 'It made no difference.'

'It wasn't very sound police work,' I persisted. Had I found the flaw? 'You see, you would have caught us before we went up to the missile base. And you would have saved the life of the soldier who was killed.'

'Quite right,' said Kish, but now he was thinking of something else. He edged away to the left, keeping us covered with the carbine, until he reached the doorway. Then he glanced quickly along the hillside in either direction before coming back to the middle of the room. He seemed oddly nervous and I started thinking about the gun again. For a moment there was silence: perhaps we were all expecting it to be shattered by the sound of artillery. Twenty minutes must have gone by. I hoped on the boat they had noticed something suspicious and turned back. Nikos had said nothing for a long time; he chewed his lips and looked frequently at Aliki's body.

'Quite right,' Kish repeated. 'But waiting often brings its rewards, as we have already seen in the case of Takis. The murder of the soldier, though regrettable, has served two good purposes. It adds to the popular anger, the demand for punishment not only of the killers but of those indirectly responsible, the Greeks who sheltered them. Secondly, it establishes Nikos Varthis as a violent, desperate man. That is important to me. He did it, didn't he? You are not the man for that, Mannis. This old war horse has seen a lot of killings, and done a lot. He would do it again if it became necessary. I cannot say that Goodwin's choice of spies was altogether bad.'

From the window the Chinese major said something. He carried on staring out into the darkness.

'Major Ma-Ling thought he saw the boat,' said Kish. 'What's the matter, Mannis?'

I must have been gaping at him. I covered up quickly, saying, 'The boat?' because his earlier remark might have been a trap. It wasn't the sighting of the boat that had startled me, it was the mention of Goodwin's name. Nikos had noticed it too; next to me I felt him tensing up.

'Yes, the boat,' Kish said. 'We have only a few minutes more to wait.'

Takis hadn't known Goodwin's name. He couldn't have given it

124

away under interrogation and neither of us had mentioned it. So how did Kish know? He went on calmly talking. He was back on the subject of Nikos.

'This so-called uncle of yours, a man well versed in violence. Very much the popular picture of a spy. He carried a gun and he has already killed a man in the pursuit of those photographs. For his crimes on Albanian soil he would certainly be executed. Would one more killing make any difference to him? I think not. Would people not believe that he might make one last desperate attempt to escape? And is now, with the boat so close by and waiting to rescue him, is now not the moment when he would make it?'

He had been speaking very quietly. When he stopped the words seemed to go on whispering round the room. With a thrill I thought I knew what he was saying, but there remained a terrible ambiguity to it. He groped with his left hand for Nikos's pistol, and then it and the carbine were both pointing at us between the skirts of the oilskin. Ma-Ling was still looking out of the window. It seemed incredible that he should be unaware of the tension that had Nikos coiled up like a steel spring next to me.

'If I were to leave this house, however briefly,' Kish said, 'if the major were left to guard you with your own pistol, you would try something, wouldn't you? Between the two of you you would try to overpower him.' He laughed shortly. 'But that will not happen. Varthis is too dangerous. Too dangerous, I think, to be alive. Also dangerous enough to rid me of one of my own problems.'

The pistol came up a fraction. Kish's big mouth made an ugly, lopsided O. He made a half-turn towards the window, the pistol swivelling with him, and shot Ma-Ling twice in the back.

The shots merged into one splintering explosion that came crashing back from the walls. Ma-Ling made two jerky movements like a man in a silent film, first straightening up and turning his head as if he'd been tapped on the shoulder, then being flung by the second bullet halfway out of the window, so that he hung balanced on the sill showing us an expanse of fat behind. His left boot kicked twice at the wall, and then he was still.

Nikos and I were both on our feet but Kish had turned back to face us and the carbine was pointing at us again. More precisely, it was pointing at Nikos.

'Sit down, Varthis. Mannis, you get the film and get out.'

My head was pounding. For a moment I thought the sharp smell of cordite would make me vomit. I understood nothing except that for a few brief seconds my assumption had been right and now it was horribly wrong. The murderous glitter in Kish's eyes was wrong, and so was the way the carbine stayed levelled on Nikos's chest. Nikos sank back onto the bed.

I said, 'Are you the man Goodwin told me about?'

'There is no time to talk,' Kish said. 'Take the film.'

Shaking, I walked across to Ma-Ling, groped in his pocket and brought out the package. My hand came away with blood on it. As I turned back Nikos said to me, 'What did Goodwin tell you?'

'He said there'd be someone here to look after us if we got into trouble. Someone important. He called him a — guardian angel.'

'Is that what you call the man who shot Aliki and arrested all our network?'

'Shut your mouth,' Kish said savagely. 'Mannis, move over here.'

I went quickly across the line of fire and stood near the door. Slowly I was beginning to understand. I said, 'I go alone, is that right? And I'm meant to pretend that you won't kill Nikos as soon as I've left — kill him and blame Ma-Ling's death on him.'

'Can't you see?' Nikos said. 'He's not taking the risk of giving himself away. This will have to look good. He had to leave the house briefly and while he was out we killed Ma-Ling and escaped. Kish got me — the gun will be found in my hand — but you had gone ahead with the films. Unfortunate. Someone must pay to keep your cover intact, Kish, isn't that so? Is this the kind of friend the British are making these days?'

'You brought this on yourself,' Kish said. 'I am here only to see that the film reaches the right people. I did my best for you, I delayed going to Takis's house till the last possible minute, until Ma-Ling was becoming suspicious. I tried to concentrate our search upon the mountains while you reached the coast. And then you killed the soldier. What happened after that was out of my hands.'

'I don't believe you,' Nikos said quietly. 'You smashed up our network too thoroughly not to have wanted to do it.'

Kish turned to me. His long face seemed hideously cruel. 'Are you going? I can still kill you both and take the films to Goodwin

126

myself.'

'You must do as he tells you, Michael,' said Nikos. I couldn't speak; my insides were twisted up with horror. How could Nikos be so calm? He said to Kish, 'What about the guards?'

'They are all out looking for the boat. I sent them far enough away not to hear the shots. Mannis, walk down the hill directly in front of the house. Don't run. Wait among the rocks above the beach until the guard on that section is walking away from you to the south. He knows you are coming, he does not want to have to see you and raise the alarm. Then swim.'

I still hesitated. 'One other thing,' he said. 'The carbine is louder than the pistol. It may draw the guards' attention up here. Afterwards they may fire on you but you should be out of sight by then. Now go.'

I tried to make Nikos look at me, give me some clue about what he was going to do. He couldn't just sit there waiting for Kish to shoot him in cold blood, I knew he couldn't. And I couldn't walk away knowing he was going to. Kish and Nikos — they seemed so alike, suddenly, in the way they made the films matter more than anything else. They assumed they mattered to me as well, they could never understand that the precious film that I clutched in my right hand meant nothing any longer. I would have thrown them into the sea if I thought it would help Nikos.

He sat there staring at Aliki's body on the other bed. 'Go, Michael,' he said.

So it was up to me, entirely up to me.

I turned and took two paces towards the door. I half-turned back as if to look once more at Nikos, and flung the package of film at Kish's head.

It is impossible to say in what order things happened then. They blurred together and I recorded only a series of swift impressions. One was that the oilskin package wasn't wrapped up as tightly as it should have been. Ma-Ling had undone it, and it unwrapped itself as it was thrown. What hit Kish was not a hefty little missile but a shower of red and mauve and yellow 2¼-inch film spools that went bouncing and clattering all over him and the wall and the floor. There was Kish raising his free hand instinctively before he realized how harmless the throw had been, and knocking the makeshift lamp to the floor. There was Nikos bounding off the bed towards him, and there were the shots — a burst of five or six that rent the darkness as I dived, banging my elbows bruisingly on the floor. Bits of plaster and shreds of hot nickel spat and sang around me. And then, in the sudden quiet, there were the terrible animal grunts that went on in the centre of the room for two or three seconds before I heard the same snapping noise I'd heard the night before on the mountain.

I saw Nikos, in silhouette, get to his feet. He breathed in long agonized gasps and he was bent over double.

I scrambled up. 'You're hurt.'

'My hand, that's all. Get Kish's torch, find the films. Quick!'

The torch was clipped to the Albanian's belt. He was lying with his head and shoulders jammed into the fireplace and as I passed the beam quickly over him I saw that his head lolled at the same grotesque angle as the soldier's had the night before. The carbine lay a few feet away. I shone the torch on Nikos.

He stood with his right hand clasped between his knees, grimacing with pain. The fingers were a mass of bone and blood. He'd used the hand to knock the carbine out of the way and taken the first two shots between his fingers. 'Get the film, for God's sake,' he said as I stared at him. 'The guards have probably heard the shooting.'

I picked up the oilskin and groped around for the spools. Soon I had about eighteen or twenty of them: the rest had rolled into corners and under the furniture and there wasn't time to look for them. Nikos had picked up the carbine and stood guard at the back door. The shattered right hand hung by his side.

'You took your time,' he said. '*Ela*, let's go.'

For fifty yards we trotted northwards along the hillside at the same level as the house. Then we saw the first guards coming diagonally up the slope from the other direction. The steepness of the hill had cut down their speed, but now within a couple of minutes the alarm would go right up and down the coast. We waited until they went into the building then ran, stumbled and rolled down the hill, cutting and bruising ourselves on the stones. We stopped among the boulders fifty yards above the beach to reconnoitre: the only guard that was visible was coming towards us from the left. That would be the one Kish had said would let me through, but we had to wait for him to turn.

He took an agonizing time to reach the end of his beat. The exertion had got Nikos's wound bleeding badly and he stared at it with a fixed scowl, letting the blood drip onto the ground. There were still no sounds of alarm from the hill behind us.

'Are you going to make it?' I asked.

'Yes.' The mist was still over the channel. Johnny's boat had obviously not been sighted, in spite of what Ma-Ling had thought. That was, if it was still out there. Nikos was looking at me.

'What did you make of Kish?' he said.

'A ruthless bastard, that's all. And a clever one. Goodwin will be sorry he's dead.'

'Goodwin has a lot to answer for,' Nikos said slowly. 'Kish wiped out the network ....' He let the sentence die out, then said decisively, 'I'm coming with you on the boat. All the way, I mean — to Malta.'

I stared at him. 'You're mad. You need a doctor.'

'There are penicillin and other things in Johnny's medicine chest. I can last for a day or two. I want to ask Goodwin some things.'

'What sort of things?'

'Quiet,' he said, and gripped my arm. The guard was coming past on his way back.

We let him get a hundred yards to the south, stood up and ran side by side for the dark line of the sea.

The rocks gave onto difficult beach sand. The package of films that I'd knotted round my neck bounced against my chest and Nikos carried the carbine clumsily. We crossed the firm sand close to the waterline and were racing into the sea with high-kicking steps, flinging off our boots, when the first shout came from somewhere far to the right. It was echoed by another from the hill behind us.

We lunged forward into the black water and swam. I swam as I'd never swum before, feeling my heart trying to burst and my lungs screaming for more air. I was about sixty yards out when the first bullet pocked the water a yard from my head. Time to dive; I went down, swan a dozen suffocating strokes in a new direction, came up and went down again. When I surfaced the sky and the flat sea were lit greenly by a flare. I dived as the water around me was slapped by another three shots. How long would it be before I blacked out from oxygen starvation?

Coming up again I realized that the mist was beginning to protect me. Nikos was off to the right somewhere but for the moment I had lost sight of him. The shore was a dim line with tiny moving lights on it. I took two breaths instead of one before diving again.

Another flare went up; its light was thrown back by the curtain of mist. There was no more shooting but now they began firing random mortar shells. The nearest landed a hundred yards ahead of me and I must have been a good three hundred yards from the shore. I swam on more slowly, feeling the dead weight of my limbs and noticing for the first time the slight chill of the water.

Where was the boat? I swam another three hundred yards in what I hoped was a straight line. They could have a gunboat out looking for us at any minute, and still Nikos was nowhere to be seen. Suspended in inaction, I turned on my back and it was all I could do to stay afloat; exhaustion was starting to overwhelm me.

I couldn't tell how long went by before the muffled thud of a diesel engine and the gurgle of a slowly turning propellor came from my left. The grey flat shape of the boat was suddenly sharp against the haze, lightless and sinister. I splashed a hand feebly on the surface and heard Johnny Roth's voice, as if right next to me, say 'Here's one of them. In a bit to starboard.'

Hands drew me under the rail, dropped me like a wet fish on the deck where I lay in a spreading pool of water, propped me up, wrapped something around me. I couldn't bring myself to the effort of opening my eyes. Johnny said, 'Done in, but no wounds.' Gently the loop around my neck was severed and Goodwin said, 'The films?'

'Pick up Nikos,' I said.

'Of course,' The neck of a bottle was forced into my mouth. With the liquid fire spreading through my chest I dissolved into unconsciousness.

130

16

Once I woke up — it must have been only an hour or two after I had been pulled aboard — and saw the yellow early morning sun pouring through a scuttle somewhere to the left of my feet. There was a soft texture of warmth around me but my head ached and my mouth tasted foul. The boat rolled gently and far off was the steady hammering throb of engines. It was only a brief moment of restlessness and a minute later I was sinking back into a vast and bottomless sea of sleep.

When I rose to the surface finally the light had changed, it was soft and pink and angled in low from the right. Freeing my left arm from the folds of the sleeping bag I looked at my watch. Not surprisingly it had stopped. But it was almost sunset, surely; I must have slept for more than twelve hours.

I lay naked in a bunk on the starboard side of what must have been a saloon in the forward part of Johnny's boat. It was not a saloon in the yachtsman's sense, merely a part of the boat sparely equipped for eating and sleeping. There was a low bunk on either side with a bare foam-rubber mattress on it, a table secured to the deck between them with a top that folded down to the sides, two small lockers against the forward bulkhead, on either side of a doorway leading further forward, and that was all. No carpet, ornaments, books or anything to soften its utility. Through the doorway I could see a tiny galley crammed in on the port side, a toilet facing it across the gangway and yet another door, closed, that must have led into some tiny compartment right in the bows, perhaps a cable-tier for the anchor chain. Below decks the boat was painted the same dull grey as above; with its spartan fittings it looked exactly what it was, a workman's tool, not a pleasure cruiser.

Behind me to the left wooden steps led up through a hatch to the wheelhouse where someone would be at the helm. Any sound that might have reached me from there would be swallowed by the thundering of the powerful engines that sent a continual low vibration through the whole craft.

I pulled myself gingerly out of the old army sleeping bag and swung my feet down to the deck. Then I stood up, testing myself for damage. Apart from general aches that reached into every corner of my body there didn't seem to be any. In my mouth lingered the faintest etherous taste of the drink I had been given when I came on board.

Now that I was fully awake a name presented itself urgently to my mind: Nikos. Had they found him? I hadn't seen him since the bullets began to spit at us in the water.

There was nothing in the saloon for me to wear. But I found a grubby pink towel on the opposite bunk and was wrapping it round my middle when the companionway from the wheelhouse creaked. Goodwin appeared in sections, feet first in sturdy leather sandals, then pale blue lightweight trousers, a faded orange shirt and finally his dark Levantine face and grey mop. He stood with his head bent slightly under the low beams of the saloon, looking at me with a kind of proprietary pleasure.

'So you're vertical at last,' he said. It was odd to hear English spoken again.

'Nikos,' I said. 'Did you pick him up?'

'Nikos is safely back in Corfu. We dropped him on the first beach we saw and pulled straight out.'

The memories of the night before were returning to me very slowly. 'He was muttering about coming to Malta with us. Did you talk him out of it?'

'Terry must have done that. Frankly' – Goodwin looked apologetic – 'I hardly said two words to him. I had to leave him to Terry. You know the Albanians were lobbing mortars at us. Just as we reached Nikos they started firing a few big shells at random too, and the mist was lifting. Between dodging the rounds and hoping there weren't any curious Greek policemen waiting to meet us ... and then I was busy checking your films as well.'

'Of course,' I said coldly. 'The films come first. Did you bother to notice that Nikos had a couple of holes shot in his hand?'

'Yes, I did. As a matter of fact I decided to put Terry ashore to look after him. It makes running the boat more difficult but I didn't want Nikos passing out and bleeding to death on the beach.' He looked at me self-righteously. 'Satisfied?'

'Yes, all right.' Suddenly it seemed no longer important to be bitter. 'You know Kish is dead?'

Goodwin nodded. 'It's a loss to us. Personally speaking, though ... I've never met him, but from what I hear of the circumstances I can't say I'm sorry.'

'He was going to kill Nikos. He got a lot of other people out of the way as well, broke up Takis' network. Presumably it was his zealous way of covering himself. When did 3 Committee start employing genocidal maniacs?'

'I wasn't to know all *that* would happen,' Goodwin said sharply. 'You don't understand these things. A man like that works entirely to his own rules. If I had known ... ' He shrugged and then smiled cautiously. 'What's the use of speculating? We can talk about it later. You've done a good job, Michael, A-one. London is pleased.'

'Thanks for nothing,' I said.

'Your suitcase is back aft if you want to clean up and change. I'll bring you some hot water for a shave. You haven't seen yourself in a mirror lately, I suppose?'

'No, but I can guess.'

I went stiffly up the companionway and found Johnny at the wheel, standing in a relaxed wide-legged stance in his uniform of white shorts and T-shirt. He gave me a slit of a grin.

'Hello, how you going?' He flattened his 'o' slightly in the Australian way.

'All right, Johnny. The sleep's done me some good. How far to go?'

He made a clucking sound of annoyance. 'Three hundred miles, three quarters of the way. Had some generator trouble this morning and had to cut right back — or did Joe tell you?'

'No, he didn't. Is it bad?'

'He's fixed so he'll hold but it delayed us by six or seven hours.'

'So we won't reach Malta before — when? Tomorrow morning?' I laughed. 'Terry always said this hulk wouldn't get us there. Maybe he was right.'

Johnny gave me a quick flat look. So I'd forgotten that he and Terry didn't like each other but there was no need to be humourless about it. He turned back to the binnacle and said, 'It's sum'ming you can't foresee.' Which for him seemed to settle the matter.

I went up the single step from the duckboard flooring to the narrow deck space running down the port side. The boat dipped and rose against the long easy swell, lifting a white bow wave in an unvarying arc. The sea burned with a red peardrop sun hanging just above the horizon, fine off the starboard bow. I took a few deep breaths of the clean air and made my way aft, past the clamorous engine room to a low doorway looking out over the stern, which led down a couple of steps to what was normally a cargo room for Johnny's merchandise. A couple of steel-framed bunks hung along the starboard side and there were a water tank and washbasin against the forward bulkhead. A steel mirror swung with the boat's motion from a hook on one of the bunks, and I approached it warily.

Beneath the five days' growth of gingery beard the skin was pallid and streaked with dirt. The eyes were puffed up and there was a long scratch across my forehead from a thorn bush I had blundered into while running from the System V base. My mother would have turned in her grave.

I went to the suitcases that were lined up on the deck and took some clothes out of mine. I put it back and then stood looking rather dumbly at them, all four of them, until Goodwin arrived with a bowl of steaming water. From then on I concentrated on shaving and cleaning up, washing away from head to toe the accumulated grime of four days. Installing a shower simply wouldn't have occurred to Johnny Roth. I dressed in slacks, plimsolls and a cool shirt and felt fresh and alert when I got back to the wheelhouse.

Darkness was settling over the water. Johnny was still at the wheel with his easy sailor's stance and Goodwin was wedged in behind him, fiddling with the transceiver with one hand and holding the earphones with the other. He stopped and looked up when I came in. I remembered his touchiness about making his calls in private but this time I didn't give a damn. The sliding door into the engine room was open and by the dim light above them I saw the long shapes of the three diesel engines, strangely inert for all the noise they made. The air round them was hazy with fumes. Remembering the antagonism between Terry on one hand and Goodwin and Johnny on the other, I realized how very convenient it must have been to put Terry ashore.

Goodwin put down the earphones. 'You're looking better every minute,' he said. 'We'll have some grub ready soon.'

'Terry must have left here in a hell of a hurry,' I said casually.

'Why?'

'He left his suitcase behind.'

I didn't know why I had waited until they were together before mentioning it. Goodwin stared at me for a second and then burst out laughing. 'Oh, the bloody idiot! Well, he got into a flap about getting ashore, didn't he? We had too much on our minds to make sure he took his woollies with him.'

Johnny sniggered. 'Sure. He didn't like the sound of the shells falling so close. Some people do funny things the first time they're under fire.'

'Anyway,' Goodwin said, 'there can't be anything vital in the case. If his passport's in there we'll send it on to him.'

'Daft thing to do,' I said, laughing it off. I turned away to look through the weather screen at the black horizon ahead, stark against the last silver line of daylight. Were they, an unkind voice in the back of my mind asked, protesting too much? And then I caught it, reflected from the weather screen by the dim light thrown up from the binnacle, the exchange of a glance between them. Just a ghost of a glance, the casual shifting of Johnny's head to look unnecessarily at the coloured throttle levers on his right, the movement of Goodwin's gaze to a point in the darkness beyond me, a swift coincidence of their eyes, blankly significant.

As I watched the line of silver narrowed and dimmed, and then vanished suddenly as the black curtains of sea and sky were drawn together.

17

Dinner that night was good. It was my first hot meal in four days and we made something of an occasion out of it. Goodwin worked on the spaghetti and meatballs to make it less obvious that they'd come out of cans. With them we drank a couple of litres of light red Greek wine. Johnny had his at the wheel and I sat with Goodwin at the table in the saloon.

Goodwin didn't eat much. He sat watching me in an amused, paternal way that gradually became irritating, and topped up my glass whenever it got down to the halfway mark. Finally I had finished and he produced two cigars.

'To celebrate your safe return,' he said. 'Now tell me about Albania.'

'The firm is never far from your mind, is it?'

'I should have given you an informal debriefing hours ago,' he said. 'I'm supposed to send them a coded summary in Malta. The real thing will have to wait until you reach London.'

So I told him, starting at the beginning. There were parts he invited me to skip, parts he already knew about from Kish. It became clear that Kish had been a very valuable informer and I wasn't surprised that Takis' network had known nothing about him. Being a junior officer in the SSSh he'd had no access to high-level state secrets; but with his job and by keeping his eyes and ears open he had learnt most of what there was to know about troop dispositions and security arrangements. He hadn't known that System V existed until Takis' information was passed back to him; even if he had, he would not have taken the risk of procuring photographs himself. He'd simply agreed to help us if our plan came unstuck — and without, of course, specifying what kind of help he would give. If a few incidental murders were involved, that was on his own conscience. The thought of Kish made me sick.

It seemed that he had various channels for getting his information out, none of them as crude as Takis' methods. One was a transmitter that he used to signal to a listening post somewhere in southern Yugoslavia. From there by some means or other the messages were passed to a small number of officers with a high security clearance. In this case Goodwin alone had received them. Goodwin had been kept informed of our movements from the time we entered Albania until we were holed up in George Milios' house on the coast. I smiled sarcastically.

'Well, that's the man you should thank. He got the films out for

136

you – at a price.'

'Yes.' Goodwin looked thoughtful.

'How did we get him on our side in the first place? He's not what I'd call good public relations material.'

Goodwin smiled and waved a finger at me. 'Question disallowed. You already know more than is good for you.'

I went on talking. I wanted my responsibility shared, the debt of guilt that I owed to a dead girl, a dead soldier and a thousand Greek Albanians.

I had forgotten the important thing Nikos had told me to remember, the position of the System V base. But on an ordnance map that Goodwin produced I was able to pinpoint it and trace the various routes we had taken to and from the coast and the site. I described the rockets and their launching ramps, the garrison, the road from the base to Koritsa. And I mentioned that the base was supplying its own electricity and there seemed to be no launching control gear there. I did not have the notes I had taken at the time, of course, but I remembered most of the details.

Goodwin listened intently, nodding once in a while. When I finished I noted with satisfaction that he was tense and drawn. The weight of it had settled on him too.

'What about the rockets?' I said. 'Do they sound as you expected?'

'Just about.'

'And is the base still non-operational?'

'My opinion's not a qualified one,' Goodwin said, 'but from what I know of it, yes. We've caught them in time. You realize that you and Nikos are the first outsiders to have seen one of those missiles?'

'I'm privileged. Look, Joe, can something be done about the people who were sent to labour camps? Through diplomatic channels, I mean.'

'I'm afraid the damage has been done. The Chinese can't replace what they've lost, secrecy, not even if we give them your head on a platter. Apart from the fact that we have no diplomatic relations with Albania we're the last ones to start pleading the cause. We sent you in there. But if it makes you feel any better the Yanks would probably have tried something similar.'

'The Yanks know about System V?'

'They picked it up on a routine U-2 recce flight on Monday, I gather. But with the camouflage you mentioned they can't make head or tail of their photographs. Your ground-level shots are the definitive article, the only ones we'll get now.'

'So,' I said, 'you're co-operating with the Americans by now?'

'No.' Goodwin shook his head quickly. 'The UK liaison office of the CIA gave us their report and we looked politely surprised. It's all been fed back to me.'

'Why? It doesn't make sense.'

'Because the mangy old lion wants to show that his claws are still sharp, that's why.' His voice was suddenly bitter. His cigar had gone out and he started to re-light it, then changed his mind and flung the butt into a corner of the saloon. 'Prestige ... it's become as important to them in Whitehall as the films themselves. And much more important than the fact that you and I risk getting our balls blown off to produce them. They won't let anyone have a look in until they can lay the stuff on the table and announce that it's a British product. Made one hundred per cent by British labour. They'll be slapping each other on the back tonight and telling themselves the old firm is as good as ever. Put one over the almighty Yanks and the KGB. Those films are a very hot property, the hottest since Cuba: that'll put the Americans in their place, teach them not to trust us as they used to. And we can get back to pretending that Philby, Burgess, Maclean, were just mishaps of no consequence at all. We'll be restored to our rightful place at the head of the table and we don't belong there, I can tell you we don't. Look at the mess in Albania. More important, the personal messes that no-one at the top ever finds out about ... '

'Joe!' Johnny was calling from the wheelhouse, over the sound of the engines.

'They'll bloody well learn,' Goodwin said, standing up and looking at me darkly. Then he glanced at his watch. 'I'm ten minutes overdue to relieve Johnny. I'll have a mutiny on my hands.'

He got up, went to the hatch and vanished in sections up the steps. I had warmed to him slightly but realized I still didn't know him. He seemed to change his personality like his clothes, wearing whatever suited the occasion. Tonight he was playing candid and cynical, at other times he'd been quite the opposite. And I could think of no reason at all for his persecution of Terry, deliberate and unjustified with a hint of caste to it, leading Goodwin to find the first excuse he could to get Terry off the boat. At the other extreme, and equally strange, his friendship with Johnny Roth. Why the silent communication between them, the tacit agreement to keep something from me?

Perhaps because I'd drunk a lot of wine, I decided I was making too much of it. The simple explanations for things were almost always the right ones. I knew Terry even less than I knew Goodwin; perhaps he was really an unpleasant little man. Goodwin and Johnny had worked together before, it was natural for them to have confidences that they wouldn't share with a newcomer. Forget it, I told myself.

Johnny came heavily down the steps into the saloon, sandals, tree-trunk legs, heavy torso and simian face, walnut-coloured in the dim light. He eased himself onto the bunk opposite.

'My neck,' he said, arching his head back and massaging the upper vertebrae. 'He gives me hell on these four-hour watches.'

'Maybe I could help out by joining your roster,' I said, feeling guilty. 'I've steered courses before.'

'Naa, I wouldn't worry. We can manage. The old neck gets a bit stiff in the last half-hour or so, that's all. I got kicked by a wog policeman in the Congo.'

'I know the feeling,' I said, remembering the Albanian boot in my ribs. Johnny smiled blankly, uncertain whether he was meant to laugh. 'I need a drop of the hard stuff,' he said and went to one of the lockers. He came back with a full bottle of Daiquiri. 'Have some?'

Johnny never addressed me by my name. Sometimes I wondered if he knew it. 'I'm an ever-open door,' I said.

I sipped at the four-finger tot, a Tom Blakeney tot, and said, 'Any idea when we'll reach Malta, Johnny?'

'Malta.' He repeated the name, his slow brain with difficulty evicting whatever thought had just occupied it. 'Oh, about eight or nine in the morning, I reckon.'

I told Johnny some newspapermen's jokes and he told me some stories about the Foreign Legion. After half an hour he stretched himself out on the bunk where he and Goodwin slept alternately, leaving the Daiquiri to keep me company. I sat mellowing for another hour, thinking the past week into perspective. The further we moved from Albania the less real its existence seemed, a country from a nightmare. Eventually I might be able to think about the whole episode with detachment.

The next morning I found out why Malta hadn't been in Johnny's mind.

18

At first the sound of the engines was different. The pitch seemed higher and the roar fuller-throated and I realized it was this that had woken me. Gathering my faculties slowly I heard that the rush of water against the hull was more frantic; the prow of the GSP had lifted so that I tended to slide head-first down the bunk. We had picked up speed, perhaps because we could afford to burn more fuel now that we were close to our destination.

It was six-thirty by my watch (my own one now, set two hours in advance of GMT). I debated the chances of going back to sleep and decided they were minimal. Across the way Johnny was hunched under a grubby blue blanket, asleep. Goodwin must be taking the last watch; the least the passenger could do was get up and make him a cup of tea. Then laziness overcame me and I lay there for another twenty minutes.

When I finally got up, padding forward on bare feet to the galley, the sunshine was strong on the water that raced past the twin scuttles at either side of the saloon. I found the kettle full, put it on the gas ring, got it going and walked back to my bunk to get dressed. And as I passed the porthole again I realized there was something wrong with the sunshine. It was coming from the wrong side.

Well, 'wrong' wasn't the word to use. The sun was where it should have been at that time of the morning and that time of year, just south of east. And that was directly behind us, or rather off to starboard by just enough to throw a thin crescent of sunshine against the bulkhead through the starboard porthole. The morning before, when I had woken up briefly, it had been shining at about the same angle from the port side. The evening before, the sunset had been to starboard.

Sometime in the last twelve hours we had changed course by about ninety degrees.

That in itself wasn't very startling. I hadn't given a thought to the course we were steering and for all I knew it might involve several changes of direction. Even so ninety degrees, a full quarter of the compass, seemed a bit drastic. Maybe I had it all wrong; if I had to be curious at that time of the morning why didn't I go up to Goodwin at the wheel and ask him?

The kettle boiled over and hissed on the flame. I went back to the galley, found two enamel mugs, tinned milk and a teapot and made the tea. While I waited for it to draw I pulled on slacks, shirt and plimsolls. Then I cast around vaguely for a map of some kind. I hadn't seen one on board. Come to think of it, I hadn't even seen the charts we must be using. There was a cupboard in the wheelhouse that might have been a chart locker but at least one chart is normally left out and pinned to a board for easy reference. It was almost as if they'd been deliberately kept out of my way. No — what was I thinking! The mundane, common-sense side of me, the side that favoured simple explanations and wouldn't believe that the noise downstairs was really made by a burglar, told me not to be a fool. But something more imperative urged me to work this out for myself. Then and there.

From memory I tried to fix a map of the Med in my mind. As I hopped from one land mass or island to another the ones I had put in place swam out of the picture, but finally I got most of them pinned down. Greece was on the eastern side, with the Albanian border and Corfu up in the right-hand corner. To the left was Italy, with the toe of its boot a good way further south. South again to Sicily and then again, for something less than a hundred miles, to Malta. As far as I could see the course from Corfu to Malta should be about directly south-west — give or take a few degrees — with no

141

need for alterations.

Retaining the picture, and trying to pour tea at the same time, I started to work out our present direction in relation to the sun. By now, getting on for September, it had moved a fair way to the south. How much? I hadn't the foggiest, but for argument's sake say it rose to the east by south-east — old-fashioned direction-plotting, leaving out degrees on the compass for now.

With a start I dropped the mug I was holding, and scalding tea ran over my left hand. Johnny Roth stirred as I cursed, sucking my wrist. Calmly enough I picked up the mug, finished pouring and leaned back against the bulkhead.

Our direction was somewhere between north-west and west-north-west. It was impossible to reach Malta on such a course. Unless — a gleam of hope — unless Johnny's navigation had led us so badly astray that we were having to correct by ninety degrees. I glanced at his sleeping bulk and decided, reluctantly, not. Johnny handled his boat too well to be a dud at the most basic element of seamanship. Perhaps a momentary lapse in Goodwin's steering? No — the crescent of sunshine was still there, moving half an inch left and right with the roll of the boat, just a little lower and thinner now that the sun was higher. I'd been awake forty minutes; we were travelling, I guessed, at twenty-five knots. At the very least we'd moved twelve or fifteen nautical miles on this course.

I stood, reluctant to move, and watched the tea cooling off. There were still a thousand simple explanations that I wanted to believe, but more and more the balance tipped against the common-sense scheme of things. I wanted to confirm what I suspected and do so without Goodwin or Johnny knowing. The explanations, simple or not, could come later; in the meantime everything must be normal.

I found that a cold film of sweat covered me. A rank rotten smell came to me for a moment and I wondered if it had something to do with my own nameless fear. But it came from somewhere in the constricting space of the boat whose bulkheads seemed to be closing in on me. I must move. There wasn't much time. Johnny had said we would be in Malta early this morning. If Malta didn't appear on the horizon I could only be expected to wait so long before asking why. All right, start by giving them the chance to volunteer an explanation. If they didn't take the chance I would do some ferreting of my own.

The tea was tepid but I wasn't going to waste time making more. I added the milk, stirred in some sugar, tried to make myself look cheerful and went to the wheelhouse.

Goodwin smiled through the dark shadows round his eyes. Lines of strain were etched in at their corners, drawing the skin tight over his cheekbones. Time you had your share of it, I thought.

'Thank you, Michael.' He cleared his throat after the hours of silent watchkeeping. 'This is very good of you.'

'It's a pleasure.' I returned the smile but I'd never been much of an actor. He gave me a quick, curious glance, perhaps noticing some stiffness in my manner. I decided this wasn't the time to sneak a look at the compass but I was determined to linger all the same.

'Did you sleep well?' he asked.

'Very, on Johnny's grog.' Perhaps pleading a hangover would explain my nervous tension. 'Left me a bit fragile though.'

There was the same gentle swell on the sea though it was rippled now by a breeze. The rearing boat at its higher speed seemed to skim over the water, barely touching it. No land was in sight. For a while we sipped tea in silence as I groped for innocuous conversation and found none. Normal questions of interest — how fast were we moving, how soon would we be there? — had assumed hidden motives. But I was giving him his chance to explain and he wasn't taking it. Finally I said, with unintended abruptness, 'I'm going aft to clean up,' and stepped out of the wheelhouse.

At the stern I crouched quickly out of sight between the open double doors of the cargo room and took off my watch. If there was one thing I thought I could remember from my infantry training it was direction finding by the sun. I wound it back two hours to GMT, twenty to six, and pointed the hour hand at the sun. Slicing the distance between that and the hour hand in two I found true south, something more than 120° to port. It was all I needed to tell me my guess had been right. I stood up slowly, winding on the watch again, looking out over the churning wake to the faint haze of the horizon.

I grasped again at the shards of my map, trying to superimpose our course. We had been on the right course the day before, I was sure of that. Now, if before we had reached Malta we had turned to the north-west we would bump into Italy or Sicily very soon. Unless we were going through the Straits of Messina, or through the Malta Channel, south of Sicily. Or had we already passed Malta and turned back in a V around it? No, after the generator breakdown we couldn't have come that far.

But had there been a breakdown? I knew now that I could accept no statement from Goodwin or Johnny at face value. Remembering one thing they had said I glanced into the cargo room. Terry's suitcase had gone.

Helplessness or terror – I don't know what to call the empty feeling that grew inside me as I stood gripping the rail and staring back along the wake. For about a minute I was motionless, letting a series of memories fall into place, letting them form the beginnings of a picture that I had never seen before. Had I been blind or stupid or both?

' "What is this life," ' said Goodwin at my elbow, ' "if, full of care, we have no time to stand and stare?" Is that how it goes, Michael? You really are lost in thought. It's time we had a brief chat.'

I didn't really want to look at him. I turned round because something made me wonder whether his eyes were different, whether they would show me the complete man I had never seen. They didn't, though the expression was something new, a nervous, tentative one. He had a gun in his hand, and somehow I had expected him to. It was a service .38.

'What's happening?' I said. 'Or do you want me to guess? I've worked out some of it already.' Now that things seemed to be getting into the right order at last I was calm; the fear had become a finite, controllable thing settled tightly in the pit of my stomach.

Goodwin smiled faintly. 'Let's hear your theory.'

'You're not going to Malta, I know that much. That means the films aren't going to 3 Committee. Who's getting them?'

'You're warm,' he said. 'Have another guess.'

'Only one side can want them as badly as we do. The Russians.'

'Close enough. The East Germans are actually doing the staff work.'

'And you're crossing over to them,' I said. My own voice sounded

144

strange; it seemed to be coming from someone else.

'I had to cross over anyway. One doesn't like to arrive empty-handed.'

'Tell me one thing,' I said. 'You're not doing it for love. How much are they paying you?'

His eyes blazed angrily for a moment. 'You're over-simplifying,' he snapped. 'You do it all the time. Everything has to be black or white and it limits your judgment. That's why you haven't caught on till now.'

I nodded. He was right. But I couldn't summon up anger at myself or even at him, and I was left in a strangely neutral state. The boat went rushing on; Johnny must have come to the wheel.

'I'll tell you a story,' Goodwin said. 'You'll remember a brief part of it because you were there yourself. Jerusalem. Last summer.'

Jerusalem in the wake of the June war. Goodwin staying at the same hotel as Tom and I.

'It's not a story I'm proud of but I'll tell it to you anyway. It may teach you something. It was my first bad mistake in twenty years.'

'Last night,' I said dully, 'you were going to tell me about personal messes. Is this one of them?'

'It is. I used you to take those photographs in the Sinai but that was purely incidental. I'd come to collect some documents from an Israeli cabinet minister. They gave a complete breakdown of their losses in the war − the real losses, not the ones they gave out. The fellow was a worrier. He was anxious about us and the Americans freezing their arms supplies the way the French had done. He thought he could do some good by leaking the figures to us, showing us how bad it really was. Quite a good idea, as long as it didn't rebound.'

'But it did?'

'It was quite well planned. It was a mistake to send me there in the first place; I've told you before, I'm too well known. After I'd met him I was walking down King David Street on my way back to the hotel. There was an air-raid warning, a false alarm as it turned out. I got caught up in a crowd running for a shelter and the briefcase with the papers in it was snatched from me. I saw the man who did it but he got away on a scooter before I could catch him. I knew him, too: a dirty little yid called Schloss who'd done a bit of leg-work for the Americans. One of the fly-by-nights we get around the edges of this business, who'll work for anybody at the right price. What I didn't realize was that I'd been *meant* to see him and recognize him.

'I should have got on to London right then and told them the whole thing was blown, put myself on the carpet. But I didn't — that was my first mistake. You see, I knew Schloss would be offering to sell me the documents back. The source was easily identifiable; he would figure out that we'd be willing to pay more than anybody else, just to protect our source. I sweated it out for a few hours and sure enough, he phoned me. By that time I had my own plan worked out.'

Goodwin wasn't pointing his revolver at me. It was just a formal symbol of his authority, of the fact that he was calling the tune. Sensing that I recognised this he put it back in his pocket. He said, 'My second mistake was killing Schloss.'

Perhaps he expected me to react. When I didn't, he carried on. 'It wasn't I who did it — physically, that is. There had to be two of us, one to meet him and one to follow him afterwards. Someone he didn't know. He was careless because he thought he had support from the rear by the people who'd arranged the whole thing. The details don't matter much: I pretended not to know who'd taken the briefcase and demanded proof that he had the documents. Schloss agreed to give me a photostatic copy of one page. He convinced me that he was greedy for the money, so greedy that he'd hand the photostat over to me rather than put it in the post. After that it was easy. We met. Johnny Roth followed him home.'

Goodwin glanced towards the wheelhouse and back at me. 'He did it for a reasonable fee. Afterwards we became friends.' He laughed harshly. 'It had to be done, even an outsider can appreciate that. I had to protect my source. We found the papers there, just stuck away in a cupboard in Schloss's dirty room in Talbieh. It was far too easy. We drove out to the Kidron valley and dumped the body down a well. That's where the Jews expect the Resurrection to take place, did you know that? This one came back all right. It was the day you went out to the Sinai. When I got back to the hotel a man called Wolf-Dieter Kranz was waiting for me. Do you remember him?'

146

I remembered him. The small, dark self-assured man Goodwin had been talking to that night. Then I remembered that I'd seen him since. He was the man Goodwin had met — or not met, rather — at the Horse and Hounds in St Johns Wood.

'He's an East German who travels on a Federal passport — when it suits him. He'd put Schloss up to it and double-crossed him by letting us kill him. And needless to say he had his own photostats of the documents put away in a safe place. He offered me a choice: I started working for him, or copies of the papers would be sent to the right people, 3 Committee and the Israeli police. Plus details of the murder, which added just enough dirt to make 3 Committee wash their hands of me and was, conveniently, an extraditable offence. What do you think you would have done?'

'I'd have wept on 3 Committee's shoulder,' I said. 'I'd have told them the whole story. Don't tell me you couldn't see the consequences of doing otherwise.'

'Don't be naïve,' Goodwin said. 'Nobody weeps on their shoulders. Do you think I matter to them? Do you think my life is worth a tuppenny damn against their precious reputations and the respectability of the Foreign Office? The rule is not Don't hit below the belt, but Don't be caught doing it. I'd been caught. In their eyes the moral outrage wouldn't be killing Schloss but making a mess of it. Furthermore, I'd done it without consulting them so they could throw up their hands in a suitable show of horror. They'd throw me to the wolves to keep them away from their own door, don't worry. This way my skin is still whole. Besides, Kranz has been quite generous.'

He gave me a tentative smile. I said nothing. The numbness of shock had spread all through me. 'Now just behave yourself and you'll be all right.'

'What sort of guarantee is that?'

'No guarantee at all. I'm making the rules. I postponed letting on to you for as long as I could because the less time you've got to brood about it the better. Now you know as much as you're going to find out, I'm not explaining any more. Do what you're told and you'll come to no harm. Otherwise I might have to turn Johnny loose on you; he's not such a nice fellow when he's cross. I don't want you hurt. Besides, I owe you a favour.'

'Oh yes?'

'It's you, in a small way, who made this unscheduled part of the voyage possible. You gave me my first positive lead to the Americans.'

I didn't want to talk to him but he provoked the question. 'Americans?'

'The clumsy buggers who were following me about London. They could only have been Americans. They've been sniffing about for a few months now but I never realized they were that close to blowing me. Not until you gave me that car number.'

'Christ,' I muttered. I felt sick at my own stupid gullibility. I'd taken in all Goodwin's lies and ambiguities, every one.

'Fortunately,' he said, 'partly because of what I explained to you last night, there's a certain lack of communication between them and 3 Committee. Especially in view of the work I've done on System V. The Americans suspect me but they have no proof. They have no idea where I am. Our own people are still cheerfully waiting for us to arrive in Malta. Now, so that there won't be any misunderstandings, suppose we go and talk to Johnny.'

The sun was hot now and Goodwin's face ran with sweat. He motioned for me to go up the deck on the port side, and he followed.

Johnny was at the wheel. Now that I knew he'd been a paid executioner it wasn't difficult to see him in the role. He stood with his forearms resting between the spokes and huge hands hanging in front of the wheel, an oddly gorilla-like stance. He knew what was happening and he looked at me with quick menace before turning back to the binnacle. Goodwin came into the wheelhouse after me and stood on my left.

'I've been bringing Michael up to date,' he said. 'He knows we've got no time for melodrama and no use for quarrelsome passengers.' He looked at me. 'Johnny thought even one passenger was too many. Bear that in mind, Michael — perhaps he still thinks so.'

He spoke in a quietly intimidating way but the words had the wrong effect on me. They brought back a memory, and with it a rush of fury.

'Nikos!' I shouted. Goodwin backed off a pace and his hand went to his trouser pocket. 'You bastard, you didn't take Nikos on board!

What did you do to him?'

He said nothing, keeping his dark eyes dangerously on me. A tic had appeared on his left eyebrow. 'Come on, tell me what you did with Nikos.' I said. The anger that had been building up inside me burst out all at once. 'Did you shoot him in the water or just leave him to drown? Or did you let your tame gorilla here get at him? No – you wouldn't have, Nikos was too dangerous even for him. A dangerous liability, and once I was on board with the films you had everything you wanted, didn't you? And, oh, Christ!' – the memory of my own blindness made me angrier. 'You gave me a mickey finn the minute I came on board so that I wouldn't know anything about it – of course, I could still taste it last night when I came round. I should have realized the minute I saw you that you didn't know anything about Nikos wanting to come to Malta with us. I've been bloody stupid and ... Goodwin, you bastard!'

The words seemed as tame and helpless as I was, but I went on. 'What about Aliki who was killed, and all Takis' people who've been sent to labour camps? They don't matter to you either, do they? I suppose it's easy for you two, it must get easier as it goes along. Start by killing some little Jew and it doesn't matter where you stop.'

Johnny made a move towards me but Goodwin held up his hand. 'Nikos wasn't killed,' he said quietly. 'we didn't find him, that's all.'

'You mean you didn't look.'

'For all we knew he was dead already. If not we left him with the chance of swimming to Corfu. A slender chance. It got him out of the way, that was the important thing. He knew too much about Kish.'

'There was nothing left to know about Kish. He was dead too.'

'Your simplicity is almost touching, Michael. You never cottoned on, did you? But Nikos would have, sooner or later – I knew that as soon as Kish had to show his hand. Kish was a Soviet agent, not a British one.'

Goodwin stared through the weather screen as if there was something of interest in the sea ahead. I had the sudden hideous feeling that he controlled and accounted for everything I did, even before I did it. Kish made sense at last – his destruction of the rival British network and his need to kill Nikos. Goodwin had completed what Kish began.

'You wouldn't have lasted five minutes in Albania without Kish,' Goodwin said. 'Relying on Takis' network would have been suicidal. We've had no-one worthy of being called an agent there for years, and picking up System V was a ridiculous fluke. The Russians are a different matter: they consider the country to be in their sphere of influence. Before the split, bright young Party men used to go to Moscow for training. Kish was one of those who came back believing the salvation of socialism lay that way, and not in Peking. So why not use his resources? For the Russians and Kranz it was as good as sending their own men in with no risk of embarrassment. Kish got what he wanted too: an excuse to eliminate his rivals as well as seeing that the films went to the right place. So you've got Kish to thank for getting you out. It meant blowing me, but that had to happen anyway. And what gift could I bring more welcome than those films? Once the GDR people have passed them on to the Russians they'll be able to take the initiative in putting the pressure on Albania. When the photographs have been analysed *they* will have the margin of certainty no-one else has. They might even invade, and this time with a far better excuse than they had in Czechoslovakia. European security at stake – very philanthropic. The fact that the Chinese will be chased out and Albania taken back into the fold will be merely incidental. The Russians have the strength of will to do it, you see, something we've been lacking in the West for a long time.'

'I think you actually believe in them,' I said. 'I'm inclined to think you made up the story about killing Schloss and being blackmailed.'

'It happened, all right,' Goodwin said. 'You might say I believe in accepting the inevitable. We're making the best of the situation, Johnny and I.'

He looked at me and the tic raced across his eyebrow. 'I'm talking too much. It's time we put you away somewhere safe.'

'Where are we going?' I asked. 'You can't sail this crate all the way to East Germany.'

'We're going nowhere that needs to concern you. You'll be looked after ... kept in protective custody as they say, till Johnny and I are safely out of reach. In the meantime remember that I'm not afraid of drawing blood. You won't get a second chance to do anything silly.'

'I'm surprised I got a first chance,' I said, and Johnny muttered something behind me. Goodwin said sharply, 'I wouldn't kill you without a reason. Don't give me a reason, that's all.'

'You've been clever, Goodwin,' I said, and I meant it. 'Pretty bloody clever. I'm only beginning to realize how well you've attended to the details. There was no breakdown yesterday, was there? But you reported a breakdown to the people in Malta to explain your delay, to give you time to get well clear of the area where they'd eventually start searching. I'm surprised you didn't ask your Russian friends for a destroyer escort. I've just got an idea, you know' – I felt the anger welling up again – 'I've an idea your own cleverness may betray you. It's what happened to Kish. He was clever but he had a flaw, he judged people by his own standards. He thought everybody attached as little value to life – other people's lives – as he did. He thought I would run out and let him kill Nikos because the films must be more important to me than Nikos was. Maybe you don't care about Nikos or Aliki or a thousand people who've been betrayed, but I'm one of those odd people who do care. Maybe you can't believe that when I get out of this I'm going to make a career out of finding some way of making you answer for it. Somewhere. Sometime.'

For a moment Goodwin seemed to lose control of his facial muscles. His mouth worked sideways and the tic danced across his brow. I thought he would do something to me but it was Johnny who seized my arm and whirled me round to face him. I stopped in time to see the big brown fist coming at me, felt the impact and had an instant of blackness. I came out of it as my head struck the duckboards at Goodwin's feet. The area round my mouth was numb. I wiped it with my wrist and a streak of blood came away.

'I've listened to enough bullshit,' Johnny said. He bent down, seized me single-handed by my shirt front and jerked me to my feet. He drew my face close to his. The blank blue eyes were cold with fury and his nostrils flared. 'I didn't hear what you said, Greek hero. Are you going to say it again?'

I said nothing and he shook me. 'It's all right, Johnny,' said Goodwin, who'd recovered his composure.

'No, it bloody well isn't all right,' Johnny said and flashed him a

151

look. He was not in a mood to be contradicted. 'I told you we shouldn't have brought him in the first place. Now he's here he'll shut up and do as he's told. Not scared, Greek hero? All right, I'll show you sum'ming that'll scare you.' He let go of my shirt and seized my right arm, twisting it painfully behind my back. He manoeuvred me past the wheel to the door.

'No,' Goodwin said with some anxiety. 'There's no need, Johnny.' But Johnny's thought process was like the charge of a buffalo: he didn't stop till he got there. 'Take over the wheel,' he said to Goodwin and pushed me up the step onto the deck.

There was a brisk wind that was cool on my skin. Johnny marched me right up to the prow. In the deck here was a circular hatch cover, padlocked, which I guessed led down into the tiny compartment whose door from the saloon was always kept locked.

Holding me in his right hand Johnny groped in his left pocket for a bunch of keys, undid the padlock and flung open the cover.

Below it was dark, except where slanting sunlight showed the end of the hawse-pipe and the two top rungs of an iron ladder. From it came, overpoweringly, the same stench I had noticed earlier when I was in the galley, right next to that locked door.

Johnny pushed me up to the hatch until my feet jammed against the coaming. I turned to look at him coldly, yet afraid of what he wanted me to do.

'Go down,' he said woodenly.

He let go of my arm and I stepped onto the top rung of the ladder. I went down step after groping step, at each knowing more certainly what I would find at the bottom.

The smell was nauseating. My feet crunched on a pile of anchor chain and I stood gripping the uprights of the ladder, blinking away from the circle of light above me to accustom my eyes to the dark before I turned around. Then I turned.

Terry Wicks sat in an ungainly slouch in one corner, staring at me with wide, incredulous eyes. There was just enough light for me to see the mass of livid bruises on his throat. He'd been throttled by a pair of large, very strong hands.

Suddenly, in terror, I thought Johnny was going to close the hatch on me and I scrambled up the ladder into sunlight. The big, strong hands seized me again and I was frog-marched aft down the

152

deck to the double doors that led into the cargo room. Johnny let me get onto the top step, then released my arm and gave me a brisk shove down the other two. I landed on my side and heard the doors slam and a key turn in the lock.

I lay there for quite a while, unable to make the effort of standing up.

19

Things had got themselves into perspective, at any rate. Everyone's role was clear and there was no more need for double-talk. The haze that surrounded so many events of the past week had lifted. If I could do nothing else I could at least think about them clearly.

Exploring under the iron frames of the bunks I found a canvas awning. Johnny had rigged it on the foredeck while we were in Corfu to make his boat look less like the warship that it was. I spread it over the sprung mesh of one bunk and lay full-length on it, making myself as comfortable as I could. The diesel fumes, drifting from the engine room just forward of my cell, were suffocating. I lit a cigarette, holding it delicately between my swollen lips, took the first deep, dizzying draw on it and started to think.

Goodwin had done it well. I had to admit that, in spite of my short-lived show of bravado in the wheelhouse. From the start he'd planned with his East German mentor, Kranz, to give the results of this mission to the other side. In some way the Americans had been onto him and he'd walked out from under their noses. By pretending to take me into his confidence he'd insulated me, even to the extent of casting suspicion on Tom Blakeney who'd been too curious for Goodwin's liking.

Did curiosity explain why Tom had stolen my spool of film from the Newsflash office that night? No — there was still no explanation for that incident. It probably hadn't been Tom after all, it had been the man from the green Cooper, one of the Americans who were watching Goodwin and had seen me taking the pictures.

It was too late now to matter. London seemed a long way off and Goodwin had covered his tracks. The two men who might have stood in his way had met a swift end, Nikos and Terry. I thought of the body still riding with us and shuddered. A point had been reached where Terry must have started to realize what was happening, and at that point the executioner stepped in – Johnny Roth. Johnny would have liked to do the same to me, and although he might not realize it the feeling was completely mutual. I'd changed, that was for sure. For the first time in my life I was willing to kill someone.

Where were we going? That was the important unanswered question. Our course was a puzzle: as it stood it would take us to some point on the arc of the Mediterranean coasts of France or Spain, or possibly to Sardinia or Corsica. Then what? Kranz would have arranged some way to get Goodwin and Johnny quickly to eastern Europe – quickly enough to slip through the net of British Intelligence that must already have started spreading around them.

Without much hope of learning anything I inspected my surroundings, starting with the contents of Goodwin's and Johnny's suitcases. There was nothing in them but a few clothes – not even their passports and certainly not the films. From my own suitcase, my passport had gone. I looked around the cargo room.

It was about fifteen feet long with a roof raised down the centre to a foot or two above the level of the outer deck. On either side of the raised central canopy two portholes were set, looking out over the narrow deck, under the rail and across the water. These at least would allow me an idea of the sun's position and of any change in course. But even as I thought of it the sunshine was blotted out by a cloud. The ripples on the water had expanded into choppy whitecaps. It looked as if a storm was approaching.

For the rest, the place seemed to have been specially prepared for my occupation. Goodwin hadn't missed much. The few loose items of equipment that lay around were entirely harmless, the washbasin, a couple of oars, half a dozen basketwork fenders, three old-fashioned life-jackets with cork fillings. It would not have been

154

difficult to break out, to kick through the flimsy wooden bulkhead to the engine room or use an oar as a battering ram against the doors, but where would it get me? Goodwin knew I had no chance of escaping, he had put me in here to keep me out of the way. He knew that the lesson had got home: I wouldn't get a second chance.

Soon there was nothing more to do and nothing to think about. I lay on my bunk smoking and letting a fit of depression settle over me. It was aggravated by a headache from the diesel fumes, and outside the weather worsened in sympathy. Black clouds rolled over us from the west and the wind drove the waves higher, throwing foamy barrelfuls across the deck at my portholes. The boat began to plough heavily into the seas, pitching forward with long regular sighs and a creaking of timbers. It wasn't built for this kind of weather. At every pitch, as the screws rose from the water to flail at the air the drive shafts under the deck below me screamed in alarm. Water began to drip, then trickle, then stream through the crumbled caulking of the old timbers above me. The enamel washbasin skated back and forth across the rolling slippery deck. We'd ridden into one of the Mediterranean's sudden and furious summer storms.

Feeling a faint clutching of seasickness I lay still on the bunk, doubling the canvas awning over me to keep dry. I had found in the past that as long as I stayed horizontal it could be endured and I was likely soon to drift off to sleep. The last thing I heard, with malicious satisfaction, was Johnny Roth cursing as he was flung against the engine room bulkhead.

Those summer storms can be frightening but they don't last long. Johnny knew this and he was taking the chance of driving the GSP straight through it. It would be his last voyage on the boat anyway, and as long as it got us wherever we were going without actually sinking, it didn't matter what sort of hammering it took.

When I awoke the wind had gone down but the seas were still running high. Clouds raced low across the sky though a pale patch behind them showed where the sun would soon emerge. It was two o'clock: I'd slept a lot on the boat: perhaps I hadn't realized how deeply exhausted I was. Now I felt at my optimum strength and alert, even cheerful enough to talk to my captors.

Someone was moving about the engine room again. I heard the clink of light metal on heavy. I got up, knocked on the bulkhead and

155

called, 'Johnny?'

There was a suspicious pause before he said, 'What?'

'I haven't eaten since last night,' I said. 'Is there any chance of getting some food out of you?'

'You can wait,' he said shortly. 'It won't kill you.'

So he was still in a bad temper. The storm, and apparently some fault in the engine room – a real one this time – had disrupted their working routine and neither of them was getting enough rest. They were losing strength while I gained it and that was one small improvement in my situation.

It was nearly two hours before they fed me. Goodwin's sandalled feet came past my scuttles on the port side and he unlocked the doors. 'Here,' he said, and thrust two rough-hewn sandwiches into my hand. He was about to close the doors again when he saw the deferential question in my eyes and hesitated.

'Can you find me a blanket somewhere for tonight?' I asked.

'You won't need one,' he said.

'What do I do when I want a piss, and that sort of thing?'

'Use the bilge. There'll be an opening in the deck somewhere.' He thought for a moment and said, 'If you've got any more requests you'd better save them till I'm back on watch. Johnny won't appreciate being bothered.'

'Are you tired?' I said.

Anyone else might have succumbed to a very slight need for sympathy. But Goodwin smiled and said, 'Not tired enough to forget what I told you earlier. Behave yourself. Johnny's lost some sleep fixing a leak on the fuel line. He only needs one excuse to get hold of you when I'm not around to stop him.'

He locked the doors and walked off.

So I wouldn't need a blanket. That was one thing I'd learnt, wherever we were going we'd be arriving that night. And the fault in the engine room had been fixed, which from my point of view was a good thing. Goodwin's escape plan was precisely balanced: if anything went wrong with it the first ballast to go overboard would be me.

The sandwiches were corned beef slammed between thick slices of unbuttered brown bread, none of Goodwin's usual finesse about them. Captives must, of course, be shown that things are done for them unwillingly. I ate them anyway, and drank some water, then found the trapdoor at the forward end of the cargo room that opened into the bilge. It was a small removable square of deck planking that I hadn't noticed before, and it lifted off the struts to show filthy brown water slapping about in the bilge. The three long propeller shafts ran under the deck here as well, humming along at a couple of hundred revolutions a minute and spraying bilge water over my feet as I stood and urinated into it. I replaced the cover and lay down on the bunk again.

With desperate speed the rest of the afternoon slipped away, the boat leaving mile after mile in its churning wake. Behind us, perhaps two hundred miles away, the planes of the RAF would be out searching for us. Even if they were nearer than that, even if 3 Committee by some chance already suspected what was going on and had thrown all their resources into the hunt for Goodwin, there was still a lot of sea to search for one small boat. And soon it would be dark. There was radar of course, but I knew that radar couldn't distinguish one boat from the thousands of pleasure craft that were pottering about the Med at this time of the year, especially since they didn't know what course we were on. If there was any hope of saving the films it didn't lie in that direction.

I smoked all but one of my packet of cigarettes and then fidgeted about the place, trying to resist taking out the last one. It was soon after six, with the light already fading, when I glanced through a porthole and saw the coastline. I might not have seen it at all, with my line of vision practically at sea level, but for the high dark cliffs that rose just above the crests of the shifting, heaving swell on the port side of the boat. I felt the anxiety tauten inside me: was this our destination?

But soon it was obvious that we weren't going towards them. They drew abeam of the boat and in thirty minutes they were fading away to the port quarter, big ragged shapes settling down in the dusk. How far away had they been? I tried to remember what I'd once known about sight distances at sea level but couldn't settle on any guess between three miles and ten. Assembling my imaginary map again I ran through the possible landfalls we might make. France or Spain? No. I couldn't be sure of our speed or of the actual distance involved, but it seemed impossible that we could have come

157

practically from one side of the Med to the other in thirty-six hours. Sardinia was the only island of any size that we might have reached, but I didn't really believe our course had been northerly enough to take us there. So the cliffs could only have been part of a small island and I was damned if I could imagine which one. There are many more in that part of the world than a casual glance at a map would suggest.

I'd settled on that idea but I was still straining my eyes to stare out into the gathering darkness. And in the last few minutes of daylight I saw more cliffs — lower cliffs this time, but part of a much more substantial coastline that reached away to the vanishing haze of light in the west.

I sat down heavily on the bunk and remembered an area I hadn't even included in my map. A whole continent. Africa.

The Barbary coast of North Africa stretched, as I remembered, in a long fairly unbroken line from the western edge of the Gulf of Libya all the way to the Straits of Gibraltar. The southern tip of Sicily seemed to be on about the same latitude as that coastline, so through the Sicilian Channel from the area of Malta, further south, the course would be — incredibly enough, west by north-west.

The first land I had seen had been the cliffs of Cap Bon on the north-western tip of the gulf. Then the coastline dipped again into the Gulf of Tunis and the land we were approaching now was the start of the Barbary Coast proper. It all fitted together. We would travel parallel to that coastline and somewhere along it Goodwin would have his rendezvous with the East Germans.

Suddenly I wondered what I was getting excited about. The proximity of land didn't alter my predicament one bit, it was just ... tantalizing. Tempting. Somehow I felt that Goodwin and Johnny hadn't intended to come this close to land so soon; they'd probably lost way against the storm. But now they were here and within a few hours at the most from their rendezvous, would they waste time putting out to sea again? I doubted it. They'd stay a couple of miles offshore until they drew parallel with the jumping-off point, then slip in and beach the boat. That gave me just one possible advantage. Earlier on I had thought — and dismissed the thought as suicidal — that if I could somehow subdue the two of them and find where the films were hidden, I would head the boat to wherever I guessed the nearest land was. Now I knew where it was, no more than twenty or thirty minutes away, and if I could get control of the boat for just that long .... It *was* a tempting thought, and the least I could do was chase the thought through to its conclusion. I drew out my last squashed cigarette and smoked it very carefully down to within a quarter-inch of the end. I hadn't a lot more time but I couldn't afford to skip over anything. If I did, I was as good as dead already.

First I had to get out of the cargo room, but breaking out was too risky. I'd have to wait till Goodwin or Johnny came to open the doors, but again, that might not happen till the end of the voyage. The answer was to trick them into opening the doors for me, trick them carefully enough to retain an element of surprise. Then I had to tackle the two of them, one by one, obviously – I'd be an idiot to take them both on at once. Goodwin was asleep, but I knew they were working four-hour shifts so he'd be taking over at eight o'clock. Barely an hour away. Which did I go for first – Goodwin with his revolver or Johnny with the strength of two men? I decided it would have to be Johnny: if they were really close to their destination he might not bother to go off to sleep when Goodwin relieved him at the wheel, and that would leave two of them awake.

So Johnny it was. Sometime in the next hour, before Goodwin was roused, I had to lure Johnny back aft and into the cargo room. If I could kill or disable him right there so much the better.

For a minute my determination faltered. In a fair fight Johnny would tear me limb from limb and enjoy doing it. But then it needn't be a fair fight: I'd learnt some painful lessons growing up on the tougher streets of Camden Town. I stood up and ground out the butt of my cigarette. It was quite dark now, but there were lights in the roof of the cargo room and I found the switches and turned them on. There was only one choice for a weapon: I picked up one of the oars, leaned it at a slant against a bunk and jumped on it. A two-foot length of wood came off the end. It was a messy break with long splinters but it made a handy club. Waiting to make sure the sound had not been heard I hid both broken pieces under the awning on my bunk, but I needn't have worried. The engines made a barrier of noise between me and the forward part of the boat.

Glancing out of the port scuttle I saw we were still close to land. There were one or two faint lights shimmering against the horizon,

159

and beyond them a greenish glow reaching up into the sky that suggested a city or town quite close by. It seemed incredible that the ordinary sane citizens should be unaware of what was going on off their shores. I turned my attention to the trickiest problem: how to draw Johnny away from the wheel and back to the cargo room.

Something would have to attract his attention back aft without attracting it to me; something important that would make him leave the wheel but not important enough to make him wake Goodwin. Something Johnny thought he could attend to himself fairly quickly. What? Minor engine trouble would be ideal, but there was no way I could cause it. Something affecting the steering, perhaps: the rudder cables would probably run under the deck of the cargo room, and if I could find a way of jamming the rudders Johnny would be quick to investigate. I lifted the bilge cover and peered round in the darkness below. There seemed to be nothing but dirty water and the humming propeller shafts. I crawled all round the room under the bunks, probing with my fingers into the gaps between struts and planking, but there was still no sign of a cable. It must have been accessible from somewhere but clearly not from there.

At seven-thirty I was still stuck for an idea and I was getting nervous. I wished I had kept my last cigarette to help me think. The propeller shafts were spraying bilge water up through the opening, and I started to replace the cover. Then I had an idea.

It wasn't a brilliant idea; it wasn't even good enough to excite me and it probably wouldn't work. I remembered taking pictures at the finish of an offshore power boat race in Cornwall, when one of the boats had limped in with its propeller fouled by a tangle of rope. The rope had not only wrapped itself around the screw but had worked its way up the shaft through the journal box at the stern. What if I could do the same in reverse, foul one of the propellers from inside the boat? Or if that was too ambitious, couldn't I just gum up the works enough to bring Johnny looking for the trouble? It shouldn't be too serious, I must remember that—just enough fouling to slow down one propeller and heat up the engine. He'd notice it very soon.

I assembled my meagre resources. There are bits of cordage everywhere on a boat if you look for them — on the old fenders, on the awning, a coil of thicker stuff tucked under a bunk, and even the cords of the lifejackets. A lot of them were frayed and perished. I ripped them loose and knotted them roughly together, starting with the thin line at one end. It would work its way into the housing more easily. For good measure I got a T-shirt out of Johnny's suitcase, tore it up and knotted shreds of the thin cotton fabric in at intervals. Then I was ready. I hesitated for a moment – inevitably there is a pause on the brink of doing something desperate, and this time I knew I would get no second chance. Then I flicked the line into the opening and watched it coil rapidly round the starboard propeller shaft.

The line had to grip the shaft but still be loose enough to work its way down the slope to the stern. The coils vanished into the darkness and the murky bilge water – thin cord, then thick rope and strips of material, and finally it was all gone, forty feet of it. The shaft didn't slow down. I opened Johnny's and Goodwin's suitcases and methodically tore their shirts, underpants and socks into strips and fed them into the bilge. Sooner or later the works were bound to clog up, but it was already ten to eight. In a sudden hysterical frenzy I tore my own shirt off and wrapped it round the shaft, then forced the lifejackets in after it. I started to drag the big awning to the opening.

I hadn't, of course, considered the possibility that I might succeed too well. Something among the rubbish I had thrown into the bilge had all at once forced itself very securely into the journal. Instead of slowing down, the shaft stopped completely and broke the universal joint at the other end with a wrenching crack that made the boat shudder. The shaft subsided into the bilge water and the starboard engine screamed for a few moments before Johnny throttled back. Then his feet came pounding down the deck.

I'd expected him to be slower. Not knowing where the trouble was, he would first have looked over the stern at the propeller, then come into the cargo room and lifted the bilge cover. That was when I'd been going to hit him. Now I squatted among the evidence of what I had done – the cover off, the suitcases empty, a yellow sock floating on the bilge water. He flung the double doors open and took it all in at a glance.

I stood up and edged towards the bunk where my length of

broken oar still lay. Johnny came in one bound down the steps. His eyes were flat and glazed and he stood with his shoulders loose and arms hanging in front of him. He said, 'I've been waiting for you to do sum'ming like that, buster.' He came towards me.

20

The boat was rolling badly — a fact I had hardly had time to notice. Johnny had abandoned the wheel and with her rudders swinging loose the GSP took the line of least resistance, moving broadside-on to the swell. Now she lurched and threw Johnny very slightly off balance as he charged at me. It gave me the half-second's grace that I needed to seize the club and aim a swinging left-handed blow at his head. He got his arm up in time to take most of the force, but the round end of the oar caught him across the cheek and he fell back a foot or two. I lifted the club and brought it down with all the strength I had on the top of his balding head.

If only it happened the way it does in films; if only one clean blow would put a man conveniently down and out. Johnny's scalp split into a grin of gleaming white tissue, but he lunged at me again with his hands bunched into claws and his eyes burning with fury and pain. He was too close for another swinging blow. Just as his hands began to close around my throat I drove the round end of the club into his belly. It hardly gave at all. The club rebounded from gristly muscles but air was driven out of him with a quick hiss and it took him a moment to recover.

I panicked. I admit that facing this indestructible animal of a man, I lost my nerve. Instead of following up my slight advantage I bolted for the double doors with some wild idea of locking him into the cargo room, but he flung himself after me in a full-length dive. I had reached the second step when I felt his hand close around my

162

right ankle, and I went on scrambling insanely out onto the deck and dragging him after me. I hopped for three paces along the port rail before I fell. And Johnny fell on top of me.

There were only two feet of deck space between the rail and the cargo-room bulkhead, with no room for movement. Johnny pinned me down like a fly to the wall on the rolling deck, my hips caught in a scissor grip between his thighs. The big hard fingers clutched at my throat as I bucked and jerked, trying to get him off my middle. But the pressure became stronger, I felt his thumbs probing for my windpipe and sinking slowly between the straining tendons of my neck.

I needed my hands to break his grip. The right one was trapped beneath me and the left one, curiously, still held the broken piece of oar. I struck convulsively upwards with it, felt the splintered end stick into something and heard Johnny's gasp of pain. I jabbed it into him two or three times more before he freed a hand momentarily from my throat, took the club and flung it overboard. Then both his thumbs were pressing into my larynx again, harder than ever, and my head swam. My free hand, soaked in sweat, clawed feebly at Johnny's wrists. My consciousness narrowed and dimmed. I felt the hands at my throat, saw the wide dark face looking into mine, heard both our hard breathing — nothing else. In the sick dizziness of strangulation I knew that Terry Wicks and the Jew called Schloss had felt and heard and seen the same things, though not the warm rivulets of blood that ran down Johnny's arms and made his hands slip on my throat. Gallons of blood, it seemed, more than anyone had a right to.

I was only a few seconds away from unconsciousness. Johnny arched his back. The pressure of the hands weakened and then tightened up in a sudden convulsion as he fell, senseless, on top of me. Incredulously I heaved him aside and broke his grip. There was blood everywhere, with a sharp sickly smell I knew but couldn't place. I stood up, feeling a spasm of giddiness, and by the starlight I saw the jagged splinter of wood that had pierced the carotid artery in his neck. It was still sticking out at a funny angle, with little volcanic bubbles of blood welling around it.

The boat rolled violently and flung him against a steel stanchion, and I remembered what I still had to do. I made my way up the two steps to the foredeck. In the wheelhouse, the grey panelling reflected the dull gleam of the dashboard and binnacle lights, and the wheel spun wildly. Incredibly, Goodwin was still asleep. Johnny had planned to take care of me without Goodwin interfering.

I had another moment of dizziness and leaned in the doorway. My throat felt as if it had been through a mangle. Through the saloon hatchway I could see the lower half of Goodwin under a blanket on his bunk. He was worn out, too tired even for the sound of my sabotage or the crazy rolling of the boat to have woken him. And with him, somewhere down there, were my films. I could tackle him right away – but no, I'd be pushing my luck too far. I was shaking; I simply wasn't up to another fight. And then he had a revolver and was twice as cunning as Johnny. I decided I would have to keep Goodwin safely out of the way for as long as it took me to reach land. The films would have to wait. I'd noticed that the wooden saloon hatch could be locked from the outside: there were a staple and hasp but no padlock. The only other exit was through the hatch in the bows where Terry's body was, and that was padlocked from the outside. I slipped into the engine room, to the workbench on the starboard side, and found a short file that would do as a pin to secure the hatch. I closed the hatch gently, thrust the file through the staple and turned my attention to the wheel.

During Johnny's absence the boat had turned with the seas and the compass was wandering between north and east. With two engines still running we'd probably covered several miles in exactly the direction I didn't want. I brought the boat bucking across the swell to face due south and punched the port and centre throttles down to full speed.

We were still within sight of land. Far ahead of me there were a few lights, and a long way to the west a winking glow appeared at intervals – a lighthouse. Driving the boat through the black, heaving sea I felt a strange elation: I was at the controls, for the first time since I had left London I was acting on my own initiative. With the odds stacked against me I was winning.

The feeling didn't last long. It was ten past eight when I came into the wheelhouse, and at twenty-five past I heard a movement from the saloon. Goodwin was awake. As I expected, he noticed at once that the hatch was closed and called out, 'Johnny?'

I bit my tongue to prevent myself replying. Let him work it out for himself. The shoreline was visibly closer now and I was getting about eighteen knots out of the boat. Goodwin banged on the hatch. 'Johnny, are you there?' he shouted.

He knew someone was at the wheel and if it wasn't Johnny it could only be one other person. I was suddenly aware how flimsy the wooden partitions were between the wheelhouse and the saloon.

His voice came coldly from right beneath the hatch. 'It's you, is it, Michael? You're not going to get away with this, you know, you'd better think again. Open this hatch while you've got the chance, and perhaps we can pretend nothing's happened.'

I still said nothing. I wasn't falling for that kind of bluff. He waited a couple of seconds, and then his gun gave a muffled roar and the wood around the hasp splintered. It didn't give; the bullet flattened itself around the file but a screw was torn loose from the hasp. Two or three more shots and he'd have weakened it enough to break through.

I let go of the wheel and looked around me desperately. Another shot went off and the bullet tore through the roof of the wheelhouse. 'Too late to change your mind now, Michael,' Goodwin called.

The chart locker aft of the wheel was made of heavy teak. It was screwed down to the deck, but everything on that boat was rotten. With a couple of heaves I upended it and pulled the screws out. The doors fell open and pencils, rolled charts and protractors came spilling off the shelves. I dragged the locker across the duckboards and slid it over the hatch just as another shot broke the hasp and sent it spinning away. Goodwin shoved against the hatch. Standing on the companionway and pushing upwards he didn't have a good enough purchase to move the locker. That would give him something to think about. I went to the wheel and swung the boat back to face south. Ahead of me the coast bulked in a black uneven line and below it was a faint strip of white. A beach — I was close enough to see it, no more than five minutes away. Five minutes, plus a few more minutes to get away before Goodwin could free himself, that was all I needed.

The next shot came through a temperature gauge on the dashboard. It missed my head by six inches and the shattered gauge sprang from its socket and swung on a length of red cable like an umbilical cord. I dived to the duckboards He was firing straight through the thin partition at where he guessed I'd be standing. Another bullet lodged in the wheel; the third spun off the binnacle and the starboard light above the door frame disintegrated in a shower of splinters and green glass.

The boat veered wildly to port. Still lying down, I seized the lower spokes of the wheel and spun them to starboard, but the rudders over-corrected and pitched us straight into the swell. I'd lost all sense of direction and I couldn't stand up to see where the shore was. The GSP reared and fought like a mishandled horse.

The shooting had stopped. Too late, I realized Goodwin had had six shots and must be reloading. I'd missed the chance to stand up and get my bearings. The next series of shots came through the dashboard in a methodical zigzag pattern. I pressed myself down to the duckboards as bullets thumped into the panelling behind me, waiting for the one that sooner or later was going to be low enough to get me in the ribs or the head. Goodwin must have fired five times before we hit the rocks.

We would have hit them anyway. Even if I'd been standing at the wheel I wouldn't have seen them, a flat water-smoothed line of rocks standing in shallow water a hundred yards offshore. In calm weather they would hardly have broken the surface. In this weather the seas rolled smoothly over them.

We were moving at eighteen knots. There was a terrible jarring bump and the boat reared and slithered like some huge animal crawling onto land. The copper sheathing on the bottom tore away with a shriek. The lights went out; the deck tilted fifty degrees to starboard and things were falling and breaking all around us. The boat went on clambering over the rocks. I was flung, still clutching a square of duckboard, out of the wheelhouse and against the starboard rail. The prow dipped suddenly and I rolled forward. Then nothing was happening except hissing and crackling and a smell of diesel fuel as the engine room began to flood. I scrambled to my feet and found I was trembling. The boat had come right over the rocks and dived nose-first into the water on the other side. The stern reared up with broken propellers silhouetted against the sky and a length of rudder cable trailing out behind it.

There was a noise from the saloon and I remembered Goodwin. Glancing into the wheelhouse I saw that the chart locker had slid to the other side and the hatch was open. I could only do what I'd intended to — get away, though without the few minutes' start I had hoped for. I lowered myself quietly over the rail and waded for the shore. The water was cold, waist-deep and calm in the lee of the rocks. I had almost reached the beach when I turned and saw Goodwin stepping out of the wheelhouse door. He saw me too. He raised his revolver to shoulder height, aimed in the regulation fashion and fired the last round in the breech at me. I flinched instinctively, but I was eighty yards away from him and I knew as well as he did that it was only a token shot. It fell twenty yards short. I ploughed my way up to the sandy beach and turned again. Goodwin wasn't following me. For the moment I didn't wonder why.

21

There were two possibilities open to me. I could wait and see what Goodwin did next, or I could go looking for help of some kind. My original idea had been to get hold of the films before beaching the boat, and with them head for the nearest British consulate. That had misfired: Goodwin still had the films as well as a gun, even if I had upset his plans for a rendezvous with Kranz.

I remembered the radio, and cursed my stupidity. Christ, I should have wrecked the radio. Bolted down on its steel table in the wheelhouse, it was probably intact after the crash, and Goodwin could use it, as he'd used it all along, to communicate with Kranz. Without it he'd have been as helpless as I was, stranded on the shores of some foreign country whose name I didn't even know. Peering at the wreck of the boat, I thought I could see him moving about in the wheelhouse. No wonder he hadn't chased me ashore: it was more important now to let Kranz know where he was and arrange to be picked up. It might not take very long, depending on how far away the original rendezvous point was. And Kranz wouldn't be alone.

That settled it. I was reluctant to let Goodwin and the films out of my sight but there was no point in waiting here to see him spirited off to safety. I'd have to get some help. But where did I start looking?

The beach stretched as far as I could see in both directions. It was a narrow beach that ran up against a dark line of vegetation about twenty yards away, and there wasn't a sign of life anywhere. From the boat scattered lights had been visible when we were a mile or two out at sea, but now there was nothing. I might have been imagining it, but I thought there'd been a rather more concentrated grouping of lights a little way to the east. It seemed as good a way to go as any. I squelched up the beach in my soaking plimsolls and picked a way into the vegetation. It was a thicket of low bushes with thorns that snatched at my naked chest and arms. The starlight was bright but it still took an interminable time to find my way round the toughest barricades of thorns. Finally they thinned out and there was a sandy track in front of me running parallel to the beach and vanishing up the side of a hillock to the left. That was the way I wanted. I followed the meandering of the track, which became stonier and more precarious as it traversed a cleft between two low hills and – ah, people did actually live here. On the gentler slope of the hill to the right there was some cultivation, vegetable patches and what might have been a small vineyard. Higher up were the low grey shapes of a couple of cottages: peasant homes, no doubt, shuttered and unlighted, but they weren't what I really wanted.

What I wanted were a telephone and the number of the nearest British consul – no, the Embassy would be better if there was one. A consul would be out of his depth. Embassies had people like military attachés with some sort of direct access to 3 Committee in London. If they could get things moving fast enough there might still be time to stop Goodwin. If not – well, I preferred not to think about that. I'd have done everything I could. In the meantime whatever country this was I had entered it illegally, without a passport, and I had to stay clear of the local police. Sooner or later Johnny's boat was going to be found, and that would lead to some awkward, not to say unpleasant, questions. I had left a man bleeding to death on board. Goodwin wouldn't help him if it meant putting himself and the films at risk. When Goodwin vanished I would be left to do the explaining. With something like panic quickening my pace I hurried along the track.

A few more vineyards and fields of crops clung to the hillside, and elsewhere there seemed to be just the usual Mediterranean scrub. I walked for half an hour before coming abruptly into the village.

By virtue of widening slightly and turning sharp left around an outcrop of rocks, the track I had been following became the main street. It was an unmade, rutted and water-runnelled street that descended sharply between two rows of low, whitewashed houses to the sea. There were lamp standards at intervals holding bare bulbs that made harsh points of light but illuminated very little. The village was built round the steep shores of a small bay. The main street ran straight onto a jetty with stacks of corkwood standing on it, and fishing boats lay at anchor in the silvered water. I realized that the track had taken me round the back of a headland and brought me out on the coast again. And this was the cluster of lights I had seen from the boat.

The hub of the village was down near the jetty and I started to walk towards it. From radios in the houses around me came the high wailing tones of Arab music. They were the cramped, flat-fronted kind of dwelling from which life spilled out into the street, but fortunately it must have been too late for many people to be sitting out of doors; too late, as well, for the usual horde of Arab children to come skipping after me. I was conspicuous enough as it was, a foreigner with damp, salt-wrinkled trousers and no shirt. Outside one door there were two men in turbans sitting on hard chairs. They stopped talking to watch me. A dog with its ribs showing sniffed at me and cringed away. The place smelt of dogs, wood-smoke and urine.

Halfway down the street a woman in a white burnouse flitted off into the shadows and I saw she had been at a water pump. It was a rickety thing with an elaborate cast-iron handle. I had the presence of mind to stop and wash as much of Johnny's dried blood as I could off my neck and chest. A little further down was a yellow-plastered building with barred windows, a limp flag hanging

169

on a pole above the door and a peeling sign painted in Arabic and French. I stopped twenty yards short of it, lingering uncertainly in the dark patch between two street lamps. The next lamp was right in front of the building and I could read the sign clearly, as well as the large print on a wall poster next to the door. The sign said GENDARMERIE. The poster carried a portrait of a man I recognized and the inscription, HOUARI BOUMEDIENNE, PRESIDENT DU CONSEIL DE LA REVOLUTION. I'd learnt something, anyway: I was in Algeria.

It was just as well I had stopped. An amber-skinned man in a khaki uniform with a web belt and pistol holster came to the door of the police station. He stood there looking out for a minute, then yawned and went back inside. Keeping to the other side of the street I hurried past.

The panicky feeling had returned. If I'd been asked to guess what country I was in I would have said Tunisia. Algeria was rather different. They weren't exactly friendly to the cause of the exploiting British imperialists. I couldn't even be sure that we had an Embassy here and I certainly couldn't expect any help, let alone sympathy, from the authorities. From what I'd heard they tended to put people in jail and forget to try them.

But there was still a phone call to be made. Until that was done I had to avoid being accosted by anyone official, and in the meantime I'd have to try not to arouse the suspicions of ordinary people. Difficult, in the circumstances. For all I knew the boat might already have been found.

I passed a row of shuttered shops and reached the end of the street. Just before the jetty it was intersected by a tarred road that curved away from the bay and led inland. So the village wasn't as isolated as I'd thought. And on this corner was the obvious and perhaps only place to find a telephone — a café. It had a wide veranda supported by wooden props above the slope of the street and backing onto a row of cypress trees. From where I was I could hear men's voices but I couldn't see onto the veranda. Six steps led up to it under a crudely-lettered sign, CAFE MOGAMAT KERCHA. I took a deep breath, crossed the street and went up the steps.

The veranda was mostly in darkness, with the only light coming through a door from the interior of the café. An old Arab sat

170

motionless over a cup of coffee at the nearest table; his watery eyes followed me as I reached the top step and started for the doorway. When I saw the other two men, the ones who had been talking, I had to control an impulse to turn and run. They were soldiers in camouflage uniforms. Their rifles was leaning against the wall and they had been fooling around with their bayonets, throwing them into the planking on the veranda floor. They stared at me.

It was too late to turn back. I could only hope that soldiers here didn't make a habit of asking civilians for their papers. I let my glance stray casually past them, and on quaking legs I walked into the Cafe Mogamat Kercha.

Only four men were inside, one of them behind the bar, and they were all civilians. I had that much to be thankful for. The café had dirty yellow walls that reflected the hard neon lighting. A garish jukebox stood in one corner and a dozen strips of flypaper held the day's catch suspended from the ceiling. Some flies that had escaped that fate were trapped behind the glass of a display counter full of sticky cakes.

There were a few tables inside but the three customers all stood at the bar that ran down the left side of the room. They had been eating snails, tearing out the meat with their teeth and letting the shells fall in little heaps on the floor. The man behind the bar had been writing something on a notepad. I say 'had been' because it was one of those scenes where everything stopped. I expected the curiosity. I went to the bar and said, 'Telephone, *patron*?'

He went on looking at me and then glanced at the other men, as if to confirm that I was real. At a guess, he was Mogamat Kercha. He wore a vest and an apron and had a bad-tempered face.

'Have you got a telephone?' I said. I spoke French with enough confidence to sound impatient. He still said nothing but one of the customers detached himself from the group and sidled along the bar towards me. He was a lean Berber with sad brown eyes and a drooping moustache. He wore a shirt with dramatic vertical black and scarlet stripes. He said, 'Do you have any dollars?'

'No.'

'American cigarettes?'

'I'm English, not American.' They might as well know it. Studying my bare torso the man nodded, as if my being English

171

explained something, and sucked another snail thoughtfully from its shell. Behind me someone came through the door and I knew it would be the young soldiers, their surprise having given way to curiosity. I might not have much time left. I said to the man who had spoken, 'Can you make the *patron* understand that I want to use the telephone? I have to make a call to Algiers.'

He nodded again, turned to the man behind the bar and translated my request into Arabic. The *patron* must have understood French but he chose not to. He gave a quick, abrasive answer. The interpreter grinned at me unexpectedly and said, 'He wants to know, have you got money for the call?'

'Of course,' I lied quickly. I'd already decided to bluff my way past this point if it arose, but the lie seemed to need some embellishment. 'Have a drink,' I said recklessly.

'Thank you.' The Berber became confiding. 'I have a great respect for the whisky of Scotland. We will have a double whisky and a *citronnade.*' I was about to say something cutting when he pointed to a notice on the fly-spotted mirror behind the bar, next to another portrait of the President. It was the usual thing in Arab countries: the purchase and consumption of alcohol by Muslims was forbidden. 'We will share the whisky,' he said, 'but if the police come then I am drinking lemon juice.'

I caught sight of myself in the mirror. There were purple bruises and red weals on my throat where Johnny had tried to throttle me. 'Do the police come often?' I asked casually.

'Sometimes two or three times in the evening, but it is all right. As long as I am with you it is all right.'

I almost laughed. If he knew anything about me he'd be running, whisky fumes and all, up the road to the police station.

The *patron* had no trouble finding whisky, Johnny Walker in an American quart bottle. He put a double measure in a greasy glass on the counter between us and poured half a glass of *citronnade* for appearances' sake. The Berber looked round furtively before drinking his half in a swallow, then I emptied the glass. It tasted marvellous. I ordered another: if a bill was going to go unpaid it might as well be a good one.

'My name is Toumi-Taieb Ben-Ahmed,' the Berber announced. 'Few Europeans come here since the French left, so I have rarely the

172

chance to taste Scotch whisky. That is why I am enchanted to make the acquaintance of an English gentleman.'

'Then perhaps you'll give me a cigarette, Toumi-Taieb,' I said, 'even if it isn't American.' He gave me an imitation French one, loosely packed with villainous black tobacco. The atmosphere in the café had relaxed visibly: I'd bought my way in. The landlord had gone back to his notepad; Toumi-Taieb's friends were eating snails and talking again. The two soldiers were still slouching about behind me but one had put some money in the jukebox and Arab singing droned through the room. And I was wasting time. 'I must make that call,' I said.

'But of course.' Toumi-Taieb hesitated. 'You are on holiday here from England?'

'Yes. I had an accident with my car. I tore my shirt and fell in a ditch.'

'Lamentable. You were not injured? And the police ...?'

'The police have been there,' I said hastily. 'No-one was hurt. But now I must telephone to arrange to go to Algiers. Excuse me.' I walked down the bar to where the *patron* squatted on a low stool behind it. 'Your telephone?' I said.

He looked at me and shrugged, presumably deciding that if I could afford to buy whisky for strangers I could afford a phone call as well. He lifted the phone from a shelf beneath the counter. It was the old-fashioned French country type with a winding handle.

'How do I find a number in Algiers?' I asked.

Forced into French, he said grumpily, 'Turn the handle. The exchange at La Calle will tell you.'

I lifted the receiver. Even before I turned the handle I knew the phone wasn't working. There were no atmospherics, nothing.

'It's dead,' I said. The landlord took the receiver from my hand, listened and nodded agreeably. 'Yes, it's dead.'

The old fear was coming back into me, quickening my pulse. 'What's wrong with it?' I said.

'Sometimes it is like this. For an hour it is off, for an hour on. On, off, on.' He extended his fingers and spun his hand back and forth like the balance wheel of a clock then shrugged again, philosophically.

'Where is there another telephone?' I asked, controlling my

173

impatience. I silently cursed the time I had wasted.

'Only at the police station. Maybe they will let you use the phone there. Here is the man to ask.' He jerked his head, looking past me to the door. I turned, and froze. The village policeman had come in.

He'd been yawning again as he came through the door, but the yawn turned into a gape as he saw me. He glanced round uncertainly at the other men, then approached the bar, his gaze drawn back to me. He looked rather slow-witted.

The *patron* stood up. 'I'll ask him for you, *camarade*,' he said with sudden affability.

'It doesn't matter,' I began, but he was already gesturing at the policeman and talking in a stream of guttural Arabic. The gendarme said something briefly and the *patron* turned to me. 'Ah, his phone does not work as well,' he said. 'Half an hour ago it went dead. Now there is no phone in the village. *Tant pis!*'

I acquired that piece of useless information at the price of increasing the policeman's interest. His curiosity was thoughtful rather than idle now, but still he did nothing but stare. He might have been thinking of an excuse to ask me something. But it was not fear of him that urged me to get out of the café and out of the village before it was too late. I knew why the phones were dead. I knew they would not be fixed in time to make any difference. The people I was trying to fight were too thorough.

The *patron* was pouring coffee for the policeman from an enamel pot. I said, 'Where is your toilet?'

I'd already made sure that it wasn't inside the café. 'Out on the veranda, to the right,' said the *patron*. I started to move casually to the door.

Everything might have been all right if it wasn't for Toumi-Taieb. I was his find, his benevolent whisky-buying foreigner, and it must have been hard for him to resist laying some claim to me. Unless it was because he knew instinctively that when I'd gone through that door I wasn't going to come back. And there'd be no more whisky. He said something to the policeman, who was standing next to him.

'Wait!' the policeman called. I turned slowly.

He pushed himself away from the bar and approached me. Now he had the excuse he needed. 'You had a crash with your car?' he asked.

174

'Yes.'

'Where?'

'Near La Calle,' I said, desperately remembering the name the *patron* had mentioned. I had no idea where La Calle was.

'I heard nothing of a crash,' the policeman said. 'Was only your car involved?'

'Yes, it overturned.'

'And you are English?'

'That's right.' Here it came, the crunch.

'May I see your passport?'

I thought of groping for it and pretending to discover I'd lost it, but that would have been stupid. I had an idea that might make sense to him. 'The police took my passport,' I said. 'The police from La Calle, I think.'

'They must have given you a receipt, then. Show me the receipt.'

I tried to look surprised. 'They gave me no receipt,' I said. 'How stupid of me — I should have asked for one.'

He might have been slow-witted but he wasn't buying that one. His eyes narrowed suspiciously and he fingered the flap of his canvas holster. The jukebox had stopped. Everyone in the café was silent; I could even hear the flies buzzing behind the display counter. Outside, a car door slammed.

'That is not easy to believe,' the policeman said. 'You must come to the police post and wait until I can phone La Calle and ask them.'

If I was innocent, I told myself, this would be the time to start getting indignant. I tried to. 'I have urgent business in Algiers,' I said. 'You can't detain me because of the inefficiency of your own police.'

'It will be better not to argue,' he said. His hand moved from the holster to a long truncheon clipped to the other side of his belt. I weighed up the chances of running for the door before he could get his pistol out. They weren't good: and the soldiers had rifles. Then, suddenly, it was too late to matter because two men were coming into the café. The one in front was Wolf-Dieter Kranz.

He paused in the doorway, taking in the situation, then came forward with a self-important waddle, like a head waiter. He stopped in front of the policeman and gave the slightest hint of a formal bow. When he spoke it was with the assurance of a man accustomed to settling problems. 'Is something the matter, officer?' he said.

22

He seemed sleeker and plumper than he had been when we met in Jerusalem, but the face was as I remembered it, olive-complexioned with a blue shadow on the chin, the features packed neatly and tightly together in the centre – a nose with black hairs growing on it, a rather prim mouth and bright eyes of an indeterminate colour. They didn't match the complexion: they might have been blue, grey or green, depending on the light in which they were seen. He was a very well-preserved fifty. His dark hair was trained carefully over a balding patch in the middle of his head.

The other man stood behind and to the left of Kranz. He was one of the hatchet men, the same kind I had seen walking in pairs among the crowds staring at the Russian tanks in Prague. He had hard uncommunicative eyes that wandered from the policeman to me with some distaste. The gendarme had been looking the two men over and noticing, no doubt, their expensive lightweight suits and Kranz's air of authority. He said doubtfully, 'Are you a friend of this man?'

'A business associate, more accurately,' Kranz said. 'I can vouch for him if necessary.' He turned to me with a thin smile and said in English, 'What story have you told him?'

I didn't see why I should say anything. The knot of fear was twisting and tightening in my stomach again and quite irrelevantly I'd become aware that my throat was still hurting. 'You'd better tell me, Mr Mannis,' Kranz prompted. 'I don't know how to start convincing you that it's for your own good. The boat may be discovered quite soon.'

'That means the police will be looking for your bright boy,

176

Goodwin, as well,' I said.

'On the contrary. They don't know that Goodwin exists. They will be looking for the man who killed Johnny Roth. I notice you still have traces of blood on your chest.'

'Is Johnny dead?'

'He is, Mr Mannis.'

I knew Kranz was right, or partly right anyway. Once he'd cut the telephones in the village any chance I had of stopping Goodwin had gone. And that left me, the way Goodwin himself had been left in Jerusalem, facing a possible charge of murder. To the hostile eyes of the Algerian police the facts would look nasty: I'd wounded Johnny with a dangerous weapon and left him to bleed to death. There were no witnesses to say I'd acted in self-defence or escaped from the boat in fear of my life. On the other hand Kranz hadn't made this detour to save *my* neck. He was thorough. He was mopping up behind him: he would rather deal with me himself than leave it to the police, because I knew too much.

The policeman, who had become impatient with the byplay in a foreign language, said to Kranz, 'Show me your papers.'

'Certainly.' The German reached into his pocket and handed over two passports and a folded sheet of paper. The policeman unfolded it and began to read with frowning concentration.

'The letter is from your Ministry of Commerce,' Kranz said. 'It requests the utmost co-operation from officials with whom I may have dealings. As the visas will show, my assistant and I are here to do promotional work for the Leipzig Trade Fair. My English associate here, Mr Mannis ...' He looked at me and raised his eyebrows rhetorically.

'He thinks I'm a tourist,' I said. I was bitterly marvelling at Kranz's smug, type-cast German thoroughness. 'I told him that I crashed my car near La Calle and that the police have taken my passport.'

'Mr Mannis also is engaged in promoting Algerian exports,' Kranz said. 'It seems there has been some regrettable mix-up over his passport.'

The policeman folded the letter and handed it back. He didn't bother to look at the visas and he seemed unsure of himself, as Kranz meant him to be. But he said, 'I must check with the police at

La Calle about the passport.'

'I am rather well acquainted with the Prefect of Police in Annaba,' Kranz said. 'Surely we could save time and trouble by making one phone call to him? He will be able to iron out any misunderstandings.'

'The phones are not working,' the policeman said with some relief.

'Well, what are we to do?' Kranz demanded with an elaborate shrug. He managed to convey an impression that he was a tolerant but busy man, that he understood the policeman's problem but that there were limits to his patience with the foibles of bureaucracy. Already he had dropped the names of the Ministry of Commerce and the local Prefect of Police. Perhaps he would call in the authority of the President next. 'I heard of Mr Mannis's accident when I came through the frontier from Tunisia,' he said. 'As a colleague I thought the least I could do was to help, and perhaps take him back with me to Algiers. I know his time is as valuable as mine. Could I not, perhaps, drive to La Calle with him and settle matters with the police there? This is a very trivial matter, after all.'

So that was the idea. If I'd ever had any doubts that Kranz intended to kill me they were gone. It might have been a curious situation, this, if it hadn't had a ghastly air of unreality about it – two sides arguing over which was to take its revenge on me. Some of the tension must have been communicated to the Algerians in the café. They went on staring at us silently; Toumi-Taieb plucked nervously at his shirt sleeves. The room was a surrealistic set-piece; it seemed as if none of it would ever change. And the idea that Johnny Roth was dead and that I had killed him was just as unreal.

The policeman said stubbornly, 'The Englishman must wait here. Soon the telephones should be fixed.'

'And what if they are not fixed till tomorrow?'

'We will see,' the gendarme said evasively.

'Very well,' Kranz said. He was annoyed but he was clever enough not to be too defiant. 'We will have to think of some other plan. But I warn you, my friend the Prefect will hear of this delay.'

The policeman shrugged, moved back to the bar and sipped his coffee. Kranz looked at me.

'You amaze me, Mr Mannis,' he said in his precise, humourless

English. 'It seems it did not even occur to you that you would be pursued once you had left the boat.'

'No, it didn't,' I said with some attempt at sarcasm. I was suddenly irritable and I wanted it all over and done with. 'I forgot about the radio. Then when Goodwin didn't try to follow me I thought you and he would be too anxious to get moving to worry about a small detail like me. All right, I'm naïve.'

'Details are important, Mr Mannis. Goodwin is safely on his way now but you might have got a message through to his people in London. Which opened the further possibility that they would make some attempt to retrieve the films in the next few hours. An Incident, Mr Mannis. Incidents are best avoided. I think we should have a drink.' He leaned against the bar in a neat sort of way and signalled to the *patron.*

'I'll have a double Scotch,' I said. 'I watched a very interesting Incident in Czechoslovakia the other day. Your people didn't go out of their way to avoid that.'

'Ah, Czechoslovakia is the exception that tests the rule, to give that saying its correct sense. Things are very delicate as a result. It was important that this operation should be performed smoothly, with a minimum of violence. You have not helped. Nor has Goodwin, for that matter.'

'Goodwin?' I said, and I must have looked surprised.

'There are two dead men on board that boat, Mr Mannis. A few more in Albania, including a valuable agent of our colleagues in the KGB. It does not matter that Goodwin did not kill them himself, they died as a result of his actions. Two of them in particular, Wicks and Varthis, died quite unnecessarily. In the eyes of many people Goodwin is a murderer. He comes to us with blood on his hands and we must protect him. In these times, that's not good for us. We take him because we have promised to and because we want the films. We take Goodwin on sufferance.'

'High-sounding sentiments,' I said. 'You forget that you put Goodwin and Johnny up to killing in the first place. He told me about Schloss, in Jerusalem.'

'They needn't have killed Schloss,' Kranz said complacently. 'There were other ways around the problem and Goodwin would have found one if he had used his intelligence. You see, there is a

179

point in every one of us at which we see violence as the only solution to a particular problem. Usually, in fact, there are other solutions, but under stress it requires a great strength of personality to search them out. I knew Goodwin didn't have that strength. It was only a matter of finding his flashpoint, finding the point at which he would do something stupid instead of something reasonable. The flashpoint was fairly low.'

The drinks arrived. Kranz took a sip of Pernod and rolled it round his mouth. The hatchet man, who leaned on the bar behind him, had ordered a glass of water.

'Schloss hadn't long to live anyway,' Kranz continued. 'He'd been playing us off against the Americans, and sooner or later one side or the other would have made him answer for it. Still, I don't deny my responsibility. I turned something to my own advantage, that was all. I trapped Goodwin. I started to use him. I have used him up, Mr Mannis, sucked him dry.' He took another delicate sip of his drink. 'This Pernod tastes rather stale, somehow.'

I felt sick — whether from drinking too much whisky too quickly, from delayed shock or fear or a sudden loathing for Kranz I didn't know. I closed my eyes and leaned back against the wall next to the bar, waiting for the nausea to pass. When I opened my eyes again sweat had broken out all over me. The German watched me dispassionately. 'However,' he said, 'I did not come here to reminisce.'

'No, of course. You came to kill me. But it looks as if the Algerians have got the first option.'

He shook his head. 'What made you think I wanted to kill you, Mr Mannis?'

'I've been a nuisance. I nearly upset your plans. There's no good reason for keeping me alive.'

'You make several false assumptions, Mr Mannis. If I had wanted to kill you I would have left it to Ludi' — he indicated the hatchet man, who was starting to look bored. 'He is very competent. Secondly, you did not upset the plans. Goodwin is on his way to Algiers as arranged: you have merely caused some small inconvenience. But you are right about the Algerians, unfortunately. Johnny Roth was a stupid lout who understood nothing but violence: it's a pity that you should be held responsible for killing

180

him. Like Schloss, he got what he deserved. If I could convince that idiot the policeman to let you go, you would be spared all the consequences. Perhaps I still can.'

Kranz, I realized, was superbly talented at taking advantage of situations. Out of this one he'd extracted a small carrot to dangle in front of me. It could only mean that he wanted something in return. He might have been telling the truth about not intending to kill me but I had lost the will to believe anyone.

When he had paused to let his point get home he said, 'There is something I would like to know from you, Mr Mannis. You are a newspaperman. In Tunis tonight, before I came across the border, I received a report that the London evening papers had news of Goodwin's disappearance. That is not unexpected: he has been missing more than twelve hours now. Naturally, the true details were not given, but the authorities had to explain the magnitude of the air and sea search that is being conducted from Malta. They described Goodwin as an official of the Ministry of Defence who was testing radio equipment on a boat. The reports did not receive much prominence, but one of them let something slip.'

'That sounds unlikely,' I said. 'On delicate stories like that they issue things called D-notices advising the newspapers what to publish and not publish.'

'I am aware of that,' Kranz said. 'There was a statement made by the Ministry, but in one edition of one paper there was an extra paragraph that was very significant. It came from an enterprising correspondent in Istanbul and apparently the editor did not think it necessary to refer it to the censors. But it was omitted from the subsequent editions.'

'They're not censors,' I said.

'This paragraph said only that the Turkish Navy was keeping watch for the boat in the Bosphorus.'

Perhaps for the same reason as the editor, I failed to see the significance of this. 'Well?' I said.

'Don't you see? Number one, if the Turks knew about it there must have been a NATO intelligence alert. Somebody talked to that reporter in the confusion before secrecy was imposed. Number two, the Bosphorus is the entrance to the Black Sea. It is the only access from the Mediterranean to the Soviet Union.'

It dawned on me. 'They know he's defecting, then. They didn't swallow his story about the boat breaking down.'

'They believed the story of the boat at first,' Kranz said. 'But sometime today they learned, or guessed, that he was coming over to our side. It was as good a guess as any that he might take the boat through the Bosphorus. What I want to know is, how did they learn?'

He was watching me intently. 'How should I know?' I asked, but I was disturbed and excited without knowing exactly why.

'It is too late to matter,' Kranz said. 'Goodwin is safe. But I still want to know how they found out so soon.'

'The Americans have suspected Goodwin for some time,' I said. 'You know that better than I do. They were following him around the night he met you, the night before he and I left London.'

'And the Americans may by now have told the British of their suspicions,' Kranz agreed. 'It is still a big jump from a vague suspicion of treachery to a certain knowledge of defection. I will tell you exactly what the Americans know: they know that three months ago Goodwin met a courier of ours in Cairo. That is all, nothing more than that. It was a chance observation by a nosey-parker of the CIA. It proved nothing, it did not even justify their passing the information on to the British 3 Committee. Goodwin knew he had been seen. He was very careful after that and he gave nothing away. The Americans learned nothing more, and above all they learned nothing of me. It was something else, Mr Mannis, that led the British to this conclusion today.'

I wished he would stop calling me Mr Mannis. I said, 'What makes you think I can help you?'

'It's only an idea, Mr Mannis. Goodwin and I had very strict security arrangements in all our dealings. We never came face to face unless there was no other alternative, and then we took the utmost precautions to ensure that our meetings were secret. Only in London, when it was necessary to make our plans for the Albanian operation, and when it became evident that Goodwin would have to come over to our side, were we forced to meet several times within a few days. I have come to the conclusion that it was in London that the security leak happened. The biggest risk we took in London was in employing *you*, Mr Mannis. Unfortunately you were the only choice. Goodwin thought you were indiscreet, an opinion fully confirmed by the episode at the Horse and Hounds public house.'

'Of course ...' I thought I had something. 'The American who was following Goodwin must have seen you at the Horse and Hounds. That's where the leak happened.'

'No. We led him there specifically because it was a large and crowded place. I was only one of two hundred people there. The important thing, when carrying out surveillance, is not so much to see your man meeting people as to be able to identify those he meets. I am unidentifiable. I have a completely clean record in the West, there is no file on me anywhere, no photograph. If they saw me there it made no difference. I have ruled out that and also the photographs you took of the American agent who was following Goodwin.'

'Those photographs were stolen,' I said. 'And they weren't taken by your own people, were they?'

'No. The Americans stole some photographs of their own man, that was all. Goodwin managed to put the idea in your head that the communists must be behind it. What else was there, Mr Mannis? Whom did you tell about that incident, or what other indiscretions did you commit?'

I tried to remember, then wondered what the hell I was helping Kranz for. 'Why don't you figure it out for yourself?' I said.

'Just because you know more about it than I do. I have plans for the future: it will not be good enough to base them on guesswork.'

'And don't tell me there's any place for *me* in your plans,' I said. 'I know about you and that won't do, will it? Come on, Kranz, you don't expect me to give you any help for the price of a bullet in the skull, do you? Not that I can help you anyway. Why don't you run along and look after the Leipzig Trade Fair and leave me to the Algerians? Or if you insist on staying you'd better buy me another drink.'

Maybe I was getting drunk already, and suddenly it seemed like a very good idea. Ludi looked at me unpleasantly over the rim of his glass of water.

And then I had the answer Kranz had been looking for. I knew what had happened and I wondered why it hadn't occurred to me at once. I spluttered into my drink.

'What is it?' Kranz said.

'You've been tumbled to, old boy, that's what it is. I'm bloody sure of it. Your lily-white record has got a blot on it and Mr Mannis is glad to take credit for putting it there. Next time you pop your head up outside the Berlin Wall you'll be seized very smartly by the short and curlies.' I found that idea funny, and laughed.

'What are you talking about?' Kranz demanded.

'Er ist betrunken,' Ludi observed.

'Yes, I'm drunk,' I said. 'And in my drunken half-witted way I've just realized there was a picture of *you* on that spool of film, Herr Kranz. I'm convinced of it. And that picture is now in the hands of the CIA or whoever stole the spool from my office. *And,* I daresay, that's what has set off the recent alarms and excursions in Istanbul and points west. So there.' I downed the fresh drink the *patron* had brought.

Kranz had lost his composure. He stood clenching and unclenching his fists and he seemed to have gone blue around the mouth. 'When did you photograph me? And why did Goodwin not know?'

'I never told him. I've just realized, to be quite honest. You see, I wasn't taking the pictures at the Horse and Hounds, it was a friend of mine — female. I forget the details. She didn't know who to look for so I told her to photograph everyone who came out. And of course you came out first, you'll be fair and square on the first frame. And if the same lads who were following Goodwin had pinched the spool and seen you against that background they'll have put two and *zwei* together, so to speak. Once you've got a picture it's not too difficult to put a name to it, much easier than the other way round if you're well enough organized.'

I was enjoying myself. I thought Kranz was outraged mainly by my alcoholic levity, but slowly I realized that the implications of what I'd said were worrying him. He spoke quickly in German to Ludi, who shoved himself off the bar and went out of the café. From the other end of the room Toumi-Taieb giggled: he'd watched me, with what could only have been envy, getting plastered. The policeman leaned on the counter and kept his bovine gaze on us. Kranz turned to me.

'You have explained something, anyway,' he said coldly. 'An

American came across the border ahead of us. I thought it must be by chance, but now I realize they are closer than we expected. They will not stop Goodwin.'

Something seemed to constrict my throat and my mouth went dry. 'An American?' I croaked.

'They followed me to Tunis. But it's obvious from what you have told me that they know very little. I will make sure they know nothing more until it is too late. So. I must go.' He straightened up and involuntarily his heels came together, 'Goodbye, Mr Mannis.'

'You're leaving me to the tender mercies of the police after all, then?'

'You should consider yourself lucky,' he said. The smugness had gone out of his voice and it had a hard, icy edge. 'They will deal with you by the due process of law, and that's a privilege not often accorded to those who meddle about in this business. You are guilty of one unforgiveable crime — stupidity.'

'Careful,' I said, 'your flashpoint is showing. There's one point you haven't considered. If I tell the police the truth, from the beginning, and convince them that it *is* the truth, they'll be interested in Goodwin as well as me. He's entered the country illegally as well. They'll stop him if they move fast enough.'

'Mr Mannis, you may tell them what you wish, because the fact is that they *won't* move fast enough. The point where he intended to beach the boat is only ten kilometres further along the coast from the place where you wrecked it. Both are in the prefecture of Annaba, where I have friends. Neither your story nor the news of the boat's discovery will be relayed to other prefectures until it is too late to matter.'

'What did you bribe them with?' I said. 'Dollars or American cigarettes?' But the sarcasm was lost on Kranz. He said, 'I must not waste further time here,' and turned to go.

'Don't forget to pay for the drinks,' I said. He stopped irritably and took a purse from his pocket.

'Does he pay for all?' the *patron* asked me shrewdly.

'All, yes.' Kranz gave me a dirty look, slapped a hundred-dinar note on the counter and walked out. In a few seconds a car engine raced and headlights arced away down the road that led inland. The policeman had watched him go with some surprise, but had said

185

nothing. He resumed staring at me. We seemed to be back where we'd started before the Germans came in, except that I now knew something that had set my pulse racing and made me curse the policeman's presence. The Americans were after Goodwin. The Americans, even if they didn't know much about Goodwin's escape plan, were close behind Kranz and his men.

The policeman stirred. 'Where has he gone, your friend?'

'To the police at La Calle,' I said. Why not keep up the pretence that Kranz had started? It would be suspicious if I suddenly dropped it. 'He will bring the passport to show you, or at any rate a receipt.'

'He'll have to come to the police station, then,' the gendarme said. 'I can't wait here all night.'

'No, of course.' If I was going to do anything it would have to be soon, before I was marched off to the police station; and before somebody came in with news of finding Johnny's boat, making me into a criminal suspect instead of just a foreigner who behaved strangely. Kranz had already failed in one bluff to get me away; it was unlikely that I would succeed in another. The only alternative was to escape: to run away, quite simply, at the first opportunity I saw. But with my body battered and my energy sapped by exhaustion, fear, hunger and too much whisky, how far would I get? And where should I go?

The policeman brought out a coin and dropped it on the counter, then turned to me. 'We'd better go,' he said.

I remembered what I'd been going to do before he stopped me leaving the café. 'Let me go to the toilet first,' I said.

'All right.' I went to the door and realized in a panic that he was following me. I walked to the end of the darkened veranda with him close behind. Beyond the rail it was a long drop, perhaps twenty feet, to the ground that sloped down to the tarred road. Even if I'd been able to jump I could hardly have done so without breaking a leg.

The lavatory door was at the end of the veranda. The policeman seemed inclined to follow me in but I slammed the door behind me. It didn't lock, and when I tried the light switch I found that didn't work either. The place was a single cubicle with a squat pan choked with paper and smelling foully; by the soft starlight that came in through the window I could see some artless graffiti on the walls. On

186

one wall the light threw a ragged shadow, and I turned to look out of the window. There was a cypress tree standing next to the wall, not two feet from the window.

It was my one and only God-given chance to get away with a minute's grace, but I had to work quickly and quietly. The window was at shoulder level and rather small, but fortunately it opened sideways instead of upwards, and there would be just enough room to squeeze out. The rusty handle grated slightly. I eased it open, then hoisted myself by the elbows onto the sill and peered along the wall to the left. The policeman wasn't leaning over the veranda rail, thank God, or he would certainly have seen me.

I got my shoulders and chest out of the window and squirmed as far as I could without toppling out, then made a grab for the tree. Being a cypress it had no boughs to speak of and the trunk at this height seemed dangerously slender. It bent like a sapling as I got one hand around it and drew it towards me. I took a firm grip with both hands and heaved myself off the sill, swinging with what sounded like a thunderous crash into the foliage. The tree swayed crazily. I hugged the trunk and got my legs around it, but the swaying loosened my grip and I went slithering down, cracking a million twigs and tearing my skin on the rough bark. Only one thought occurred to me — that I must have been drunk to try it. I fell the last four feet to the ground.

I scrambled to my feet and looked up. The top of the tree was whipping back and forth against the wall. The lavatory door crashed open. I turned and ran diagonally for the road.

The road may not have been the right place to run to. I should have headed for the hills behind the village, but instinctively I chose the quickest way of putting some distance between me and the policeman. I heard him shout but I'd covered fifty yards before he fired. The bullet hit the road behind me and came whining past. He didn't shoot again: he was running back along the veranda and down the steps.

I'd got my one minute's start and I had to make the best use I could of it. I was in no state to be running and already my breath was coming in agonized gasps. Pretty soon I'd have to get off the road and hide, but as it wound away from the village the road cut between the low coastal cliffs: if I didn't get beyond them I might be trapped between them and the sea.

My speed fell rapidly as I ran, from a sprint down to a miler's pace, and a very slow miler at that. I couldn't draw enough breath; my feet seemed to be pounded numb and my legs turned to jelly. Then the road went sharply uphill and I had to double my exertions just to keep moving. I glanced frequently over my shoulder: there'd been a dozen shouts coming from the village at once, but now they had faded away. And no-one was running after me, which might be ominous. The policeman might have a car, or at any rate be able to commandeer one in the village.

There was a hairpin bend ahead where the road turned to cut across the landward side of the cliffs. I didn't see or hear the car until it swept round the corner and transfixed me like a rabbit in a glare of yellow headlights. It bore down on me with the dazzle blossoming into great circles of light that swam and overlapped across my vision. I flung myself off the road to the left, feeling my ankle give under me as I went. The car braked, slewed onto the gravel and stopped as I tumbled down the steep bank of caked earth. I started to roll: my head hit something and my hand grabbed at a tree root and gripped it. I lay there with the world spinning around me. My mouth was full of sand and I could hear my own harsh breathing.

From above me came voices, and the beam of a torch played down the bank. I thought: This is it. But I hadn't the strength to move. I saw the silhouette of a man coming over the edge of the road. In a few seconds the torch beam fell on me.

He slithered down, squatted next to me and muttered, 'Oh Jesus.' Then, 'Are you hurt?'

'No,' I said. It wasn't true: my head was ringing with pain and my ankle seemed to be twisted, but these things had suddenly receded to the back of my numbed mind. I knew the man who was bending over me, who was now getting his arm round my shoulders to draw me into a sitting position. I knew him from an evening in London when he'd been driving a Mini Cooper. I focused with difficulty on the spectacles glinting faintly in the starlight. He said, 'I'm Lewis Noonan. How the hell did you get off that boat?'

'Rip Kirby,' I said.

'Who?'

188

'Never mind. Have you got a cigarette?'

'Yes, sure, sure.' Lewis Noonan spoke with a grating Mid-West accent. He fumbled in his shirt pocket, found a cigarette and lit it for me. This time it was American.

23

We went clumsily to the bank together. I hobbled on my twisted left ankle and Noonan supported me. The car was a big Citroën: it had been turned around and stood with its lights glaring up the hill. A large blonde man in a dungaree jacket and trousers was leaning against the nearside door. He sent a cigarette end spinning off into the darkness as we reached the road, and walked over to us.

'This is Alfred le Seuer,' said Noonan, 'who damn near ran you down. It's Michael. Michael Mannis.'

'Hello!' said Alfred le Seuer. 'I am sorry I made you a fright.'

'Alfred's a pilot,' Noonan said and gave a nervous laugh. 'He thinks this car is a plane. Is that right, Alfred?'

'Yes, Lew-ees,' said Alfred patiently.

'You must catch up with Goodwin,' I said urgently. 'He's got at least an hour's start.'

'That's not necessarily a problem,' Noonan said, sucking on his cigarette.

My head had started to clear but now questions were crowding into it, thick and fast. Noonan held the back door open for me and I eased myself in, propping my left leg on the seat. The damaged ankle had already swollen. Noonan sat in front, Alfred got behind the wheel and started the car and we surged up the hill. There was still no sign of pursuit from the village, but once the local policeman got a message out the search would spread pretty quickly.

'Well, what happened?' Noonan demanded.

'I wrecked the boat. On some rocks about ten kilometres east of where it was due to be met. Do you ...?'

'That explains why Comrade Kranz came down this road,' Noonan said, snapping his fingers rapidly. 'I guess you don't know what his plans are?'

'He told me some of them,' I said. 'Do you know where he's taking Goodwin?'

'He *talked* with you?' Noonan stared at me incredulously for a moment, then said, 'Goodwin is going west. I know that much. Kranz and the other krauts came through the border in two cars, you see, him in one and a heavy mob in the other. Then they split up and it was a toss-up which one to follow. Kranz came down this road. The krauts in the other car had a transceiver, they were using it to communicate with Goodwin, so we stuck with them for a while. Then they turned off the main highway a little west of here: I figured they'd be picking Mr Goodwin up there, but it was no good going after them, there were too many for a showdown. Kind of guys you wouldn't follow down a dark alley, you know? I was curious about Kranz, anyway. I wanted to know why he came down here, and we had enough time spare to come take a look. I figured he was the key man ... '

I began to understand Alfred's patient tone with Noonan. He talked with compulsive, nervous animation. He drew on his cigarette till the ash formed a long glowing needle, illuminating his plump cheeks and the vertical worry-lines between his eyebrows.

'You followed the wrong car,' I said carefully. 'The other one is taking Goodwin to Algiers.'

'Algiers!' The American bounced up and down in his seat, but with pleasure more than surprise, it seemed. He punched Alfred on the shoulder. 'Did you hear that, Alfred? Algiers — what did I tell you? I said they'd have a plane waiting for them there, didn't I? So where is Kranz now?' he asked, turning back to me.

'Following them, I suppose. He drove back along this road.' Deflated by the way Noonan's knowledge seemed to have overtaken mine, I leaned back in the seat. I could feel tiredness creeping up on me.

'We came by a short cut,' Alfred said. 'We missed Kranz.'

'If you use the same route you may still be able to stop him,' I said.

'Who needs to stop *him*?' Noonan said. 'Goodwin still has the films, correct?'

'So you're going to chase Goodwin to Algiers?'

'Chase? Who said anything about chasing him?' Noonan drew on his cigarette as if he were sucking life out of it, and looked at me in a comical parody of tried patience. 'We're going to be waiting for him, my son. Algiers is six hundred kilometres from here by road. On these roads, no matter what kind of car you have, that's seven, maybe eight hours' driving. By air it's a comfortable two and a half. I told you Alfred was a pilot. Alfred le Seuer, Croix de Guerre, ex-Foreign Legion air reconnaissance wing, veteran of Indo-China, the Algerian war and, last but not least, the Organisation Armée Secrète. He never got caught. Since my Government has no representation here, we have to resort to friends like Alfred when we need a little help.'

Alfred drove with a laconic, deadly skill, coaxing the Citroën like a roller coaster through the dips and bends of the hilly country. The yellow headlights glanced off dark bushes, telephone poles and ragged wooden fences at the side of the road. I said, 'I killed Johnny Roth, and pretty soon his body is going to be found on board that boat, if it hasn't been found already. The police are after me.'

'Maybe you'd like me to ditch you, then?' Noonan chuckled. 'The further you get from that boat the safer you'll be, son. There's no reason for anyone to be curious about Alfred's plane or his passengers. He does a lot of charter work between Annaba and Algiers and we're just two more customers. I'll dig out a clean shirt for you and you'll look as innocent as a baby.'

Remembering Kranz's claim to have bribed the police in Annaba I said, 'Algiers may be safe enough for a few hours, but what then? I've still got no passport.'

'That can be taken care of. Listen, you want me to tell you things. Let me start by saying I owe you a favour.' He reached into the glove box and tossed a pile of photographs into my lap. They were eight-by-ten enlargements of the single picture Claire had taken of Kranz, coming out of the Horse and Hounds. 'Remember the occasion?'

'I remembered the existence of this picture exactly half an hour

ago,' I said, 'just in time to give Kranz a fright. He knows you're
after him.'

'He had to find out sometime.'

'You stole the spool of film from my office?'

'Not me, Michael, not me.' He shook his head at me, grinning
mischievously.

'Who, then?'

'Who else but your friend and mine, Tom Blakeney?'

I stared stupidly at Noonan's face for a few seconds. I understood
now the feeling that had been growing ever since I'd got into the car:
it was as if I'd been performing on a stage for the past week with no
idea of what was going on in the wings. Or among the audience,
because there *had* been an audience and I had been unaware of it. I
said, 'Tom? Is he working for you?'

'Tut-tut-tut,' Noonan said mockingly. 'You don't want to go
saying things like that. Tom is a newspaperman. He has good
contacts, that's all. They do him favours and sometimes he feels
obliged to return them.'

That remark was curiously repetitious and I remembered
Goodwin saying something similar the week before. 'Goodwin,' I
said, 'was careful to cultivate an impression that Tom was doing
favours for someone – but not for you. Without actually saying it,
he suggested it was someone like the Russians. It made me nervous.'

'Sure. It would suit Goodwin to emphasize that Tom knew
people from the other side, and forget the fact that he has a few
good friends at Grosvenor Square as well. Including me, whenever
I'm in London. Goodwin had a shrewd idea about Tom's relationship with us, and he couldn't afford to have him shooting his mouth
off about the big job that was coming up. Curiosity didn't matter,
he's used to that. What counted was evidence, and you provided that
with the picture of Kranz.'

'You'd better give me another cigarette and start at the
beginning.' I said.

The car went gliding on as Noonan talked, picking up speed when
we turned onto the main road westward to Annaba. The headlights
swept miles ahead into the darkness.

Processing intelligence is rather like breaking a compound down
to its elements: if there is truth in it, it is best to assume that

192

half-truths, ambiguities, evasions and downright lies will be found as well. It is dangerous to jump to conclusions before they have all been analysed. So when Lewis Noonan, in May of that year, was sent to Cairo with information suggesting that a certain Egyptian hotel clerk was a courier of the KGB, his brief was simply to keep a watch on him. When the Egyptian had a rendezvous with Joe Goodwin, Noonan came to no conclusion except that Goodwin was worth watching as well. He told no-one but his immediate superior, the CIA station chief in Beirut.

Then the hotel clerk, whose name was Fazeed, vanished without trace. Noonan went back to Beirut: there were more important things in the Middle East to worry about. But when the pressure of other work permitted, Noonan began to compile a record of Goodwin's movements. It took time and patience, but he built up a fairly accurate picture of what Goodwin had been doing in the past year. Only one interesting point emerged: the Englishman had been in Jerusalem at the time Schloss was murdered. Schloss was known to the Americans as a sort of intelligence tout of uncertain loyalties. Was it coincidence that Goodwin had been in the vicinity twice when men suspected of working for the Russians had been disposed of? There seemed no earthly reason why 3 Committee should want Fazeed and Schloss out of the way, so there was only one other possibility, that 3 Committee had nothing to do with it. The Jew and the Egyptian had been killed to ensure their silence, but what did they know that was important enough to keep them silent about?

Noonan discovered that Goodwin went abroad only two or three times a year, so that if he was communicating with the other side his contact must be in London. There was still not a shred of evidence, nothing that the CIA could tell 3 Committee, but in July Noonan got himself seconded to Grosvenor Square for a month in an attempt to run Goodwin's contact to earth. Inevitably, Goodwin became aware that he was being watched. He'd been very careful but now he knew he must soon be blown, and he started making plans to leave. About this time, apparently, the Albanian job came up.

Kranz was spending a lot of time in London now, and everything Goodwin learned went more or less directly to him — including, of course, the substance of Terry Wicks' report on System V. Kranz must have insisted on Goodwin seeing the mission through before he would help him defect. Goodwin was sweating on the top line and he put his plans together hastily. Fortunately he was able to recruit his old comrade, Johnny Roth. But the question of a photographer wasn't so easy. At short notice I was the only one available, and that meant dragging Tom Blakeney into it.

Goodwin tried his best to win my confidence and keep Tom in the dark. Up to a point he succeeded, but that night in the Press Club Tom had sensed that something was wrong. The next day he invested in a lunch, three drinking sessions and a series of telephone calls, casually dropping Goodwin's name at appropriate intervals. The hostile curiosity that this aroused in Whitehall was enough to tell him that Goodwin was engaged in extremely delicate work. Then he moved on to some friends in Grosvenor Square.

'It was one of those situations,' said Noonan, 'where each side is damned eager to hear what the other side knows, and pretends like hell not to be. Bit by bit it all came out: Tom's suspicions and our suspicions. Still there was nothing to go on except we now knew Goodwin was working on something big. We still hadn't found his contact. At that moment I wasn't in on the proceedings, I was following Goodwin to the Horse and Hounds.'

'And I was following you,' I said. 'You really should have checked the number plates on that Cooper before you hired it. They were very distinctive.'

'Hell, I was so sick of changing cars and driving around London I didn't even notice.' Noonan offered me another cigarette. 'So then I lost Goodwin and found you – snuck away in a cellar taking pictures of me. What was I to think? Goodwin knew we were tailing him and he must have put you up to it. I got back to Grosvenor Square and found Tom there and we had a real strategy conference. We decided not to bring you in on it. Tom said you were – well ... ' Noonan cleared his throat in embarrassment. 'Tom said you might not be able to bluff Goodwin very well. We still didn't have the evidence we needed; we hadn't found his contact. On the other hand we weren't specially keen for Goodwin to be able to identify me, so Tom ... '

'Tom agreed to lift the spool of film,' I said. 'But you didn't know I'd accepted the Albanian job anyway.'

'We – ah – we took the liberty of searching your apartment while you were out,' Noonan said. 'We found the cheque for five hundred pounds. Anyway, we got hold of the film and developed it, and apart from me there were pictures of six strange men, all outside the Horse and Hounds. We were damned if we could figure it out. Then you and Goodwin left. He was still in the clear as far as 3 Committee were concerned, and here he was setting off on some big job that we knew nothing about. We couldn't call on the resources of the British, not yet: they would have asked a lot of nasty questions that we had no answers for. We tried casing the Horse and Hounds, we found four out of the six men and checked out their backgrounds; nothing. Finally we decided to take your lady friend into our confidence.'

'Claire!' I said incredulously. 'She helped you?'

'She was very helpful. She remembered that one of the six men, Kranz, had driven away from the Horse and Hounds in Goodwin's car. That was all we needed: Kranz was Goodwin's contact. At that stage we brought in 3 Committee.'

'But you still didn't know who Kranz was,' I said. 'He told me he had a clean record in the West.'

'We couldn't identify him, but it was a fair bet that if Goodwin was going to do anything that wasn't in the script, Kranz would be at his shoulder, feeding him lines. The Special Branch were brought in. They kept a watch on all the airports and ports, and as soon as Kranz headed out, I was behind him. That was on Wednesday – two days ago. He came via Brussels, Frankfurt and Marseilles, and arrived in Tunis this afternoon. His movements were watched all the time and I was one flight behind him. He picked up his heavy mob in Tunis and headed west. By now I knew, of course, that the boat had allegedly disappeared on its way to Malta. We had a rough idea where Goodwin was heading for.'

'Why the story in one of the evening papers tonight, then? Kranz told me about it – the Turks seemed to expect the boat to go through the Bosphorus.'

Noonan's eyes twinkled behind his glasses. 'Your newspaper editors in England are very co-operative. That story was meant for Kranz's eyes only, to hurry him but not worry him, get it?'

I opened the window of the Citroën and took several deep

breaths of the cool air that rushed in; to understand the connection between the episode of the photographs and Lewis Noonan's and my presence in this car required a leap that my imagination wasn't quite up to. But Kranz had realized the danger. 'What now, then?' I asked.

'Now comes the tricky part, the part that makes all that paperwork useless if we don't do it right. Goodwin and the films are still on the loose. Alfred and I will get on the blower to some friends in Algiers. London is waiting to hear of Goodwin's whereabouts — your side as well as mine, that is — and I guess they'll be flying some people out as soon as they can.'

'They won't be here in time,' I said.

'Exactly. Goodwin is still my responsibility. So we fly to Algiers and get a little welcoming party ready. Right, Alfred?'

'Yes, Lew-ees.'

In the short silence that followed I dozed off in a corner of the back seat. When I awoke we were pulling up in the forecourt of a small airport. It was late now; no-one seemed to be about but the building was lighted and the entrance open. I was nervous of a policeman appearing.

'Annaba airport,' Noonan said. 'You wait here, Michael. Alfred and I will go get cleared for take-off.'

They got out of the car. Noonan fiddled in the boot for a moment, then tossed a clean silk shirt through the window to me. 'Get that on, it'll make all the difference,' he said.

They were gone ten minutes before Alfred came back and signalled for me to get out. He collected Noonan's suitcase from the boot and we walked into the airport. There was no-one in the building but an Algerian leaning tiredly on a broom and a French flight controller who exchanged some words with Alfred.

'Call to Algiers made. All systems are go,' Noonan chuckled, rubbing his hands together. 'Let's get airborne.'

The plane was a Piper Twin Comanche parked at the edge of the apron alongside an old Dakota with no visible markings. It made me think of something as Alfred held the single door open for us.

'What if Kranz has the same idea?' I said. 'To fly to Algiers instead of driving?'

Alfred seemed to find that funny. 'Who will they use for a pilot?' he said. 'We are all French, the pilots, and all friends. We are *pieds-noires,* you know that word? French Algerian: this country is still our home and we must work together – like that.' He rubbed his two forefingers together. I took his point. We buckled ourselves in, Alfred pressed the self-starter and the radio squawked at him as he tested the rudder and flaps. We trundled out onto the lighted runway, stood there building the revs up to a crescendo of engine noise, then raced forward and took off. I was asleep in the back seat before the plane levelled out.

Noonan shook me awake as we made a landing approach at Dar-el-Beida airport. Ahead of us to the west, the lights of Algiers rose in shimmering terraces from the bay. It was two o'clock and I'd been sleeping just long enough to want to carry on. We landed and parked; in a daze I let myself be led across the tarmac and into the terminal. Four men were waiting to meet us. They were different in size, complexion and colouring but in some indefinable way they were physically similar, like members of a separate sub-species. They were fit and strong, and fitness and strength were important to them, even if the collective cynical expression they turned on us pretended otherwise. The hotel touts and carpet pedlars who were pestering other travellers left them alone.

Alfred introduced them: 'Gaston, Louis, Gunther, Raymond. Ancient Legionnaires, like me.' Their handshakes were identical, offered like a challenge. 'Glad to know you, fellows,' Noonan said. He'd been studying them and nodding approvingly. 'I think with your help we can pull this off. You're happy with my terms?'

'One thousand United States dollars apiece?' Gaston said. 'Yes, that will be satisfactory.'

'Payable on completion. And it's understood that violence is to be avoided if possible. That's in your interest even more than mine: you want to go on living in the goddam country.'

'No violence,' Gaston said, but he smiled slowly and pointed past us to the sheet-glass window. 'I think that is here for the man you want, yes? It arrived one hour ago, carrying a crew only.'

On the tarmac a compact little jet was parked. It bore the Aeroflot insignia on its tail. 'Yak-40 executive plane,' Noonan said. 'The red-carpet treatment for Goodwin. When he gets here without the films he'll probably have to hitch rides to Berlin.'

Something seemed odd about that statement. 'You're going to let

Goodwin go?' I asked.

'I can't stop him. My job is to get the films, that's all. Like I said, no violence. If the British want to settle a score with Goodwin they'll have to find their own way of doing it. Once I've relieved him of the films, he's a free agent.' With a sudden convulsion of laughter Noonan dug me in the ribs. 'Free agent — not bad for this time of night, huh?'

Gaston, whose English fortunately wasn't up to appreciating the joke, said, 'Shall we go now?'

24

The inland road to Algiers from the east winds through the Grande Kabylie range, descending slowly and magnificently to the fertile Tell and the coast. From where we waited, we saw the peak of Lalla Kredidja drenched with yellow light from the rising sun. Around us the daylight gave some perspective to the scenery, the flanks of brown old mountains falling away in interfolding curves to the right, where the Tell began. But our attention was focused, rather monotonously, on a strip of road at the foot of the forty-yard slope on which we squatted.

Noonan restlessly flicked pebbles down the slope. I lit yet another of the cigarettes he'd given me; the squashed ends of a dozen lay in a little nest between my feet. Gaston, unscrewing the top of the coffee flask, came back from the car and sat on the ground between us. He said, 'A long wait, eh?' He had a habit of licking his lips when he smiled. 'I am used to waiting. A soldier's life is three-quarters waiting, believe me.'

'I can believe you,' Noonan said drily. 'I was a company commander in Korea, myself.'

'Ah, Korea — I sympathize. I was in Indo-China.' Gaston poured black coffee into plastic cups and passed them to us.

'Sympathize?' Noonan said.

'The profession of a soldier has been destroyed,' said Gaston with sudden bitterness. 'Destroyed by communists and liberals with weak stomachs. What is it worth any more? Korea and Indo-China: in those two campaigns, the fate of the West was sealed. If the fighting had been left to the soldiers – *pouf*! We could have put the communists in their place forever. Instead the politicians interfered, the liberals and fifth-columnists got what they wanted. The same here, in Algeria. The Legion is broken up and the Arabs spit on me. At one time they would not have dared cross the path of a Legionnaire.'

I hadn't actually seen any Arabs spitting on Gaston, but I was prepared to believe they might if they heard him talking. 'Spoken like a true soldier,' said Noonan ambiguously.

'These people we make the ambush for,' Gaston said. 'They are communists, yes?'

'Yes,' Noonan said cautiously, and Gaston gave one of his lip-licking smiles. Noonan watched him. 'Don't forget I'm paying you, and I'm telling you what to do, Gaston. Unless they shoot back, nobody does any shooting except Gunther.'

'Okay, Lew-ees,' Gaston said and fell silent, sipping his coffee. I turned to look at the metalled road again. Kranz may have been right, I reflected, in saying he could detect people's potential for violence. Gaston's flashpoint would be low, perhaps as low as Johnny Roth's. In some ways they were similar. Gaston and his pals spent their time loitering around the remaining French bars, hoping another war would break out.

We were eighty kilometres from Algiers. We had come in two cars, an old Pontiac that seemed to belong to Gunther, and a Renault 4 van that carried the supplies we needed. Gaston knew the road well. He'd had no difficulty finding the spot he wanted in the dark and setting up the ambush.

The critical strip of road ran almost straight for three hundred yards between two sharp bends. After crawling down a cliff face to our left it crossed what amounted to a small plateau set on the shoulder of the mountain, before the next bend took it winding down again. Down a bank on one side it was flanked by a field of ripe wheat, on the other by the slope on which we had based ourselves. The cars had been reversed into a gulley behind us and were hidden from the road. We hoped we were too, though the mountain scrub provided precious little cover. On the other side the wheatfield gave no cover at all, so the ambush had to be set up on one side of the road only. This, as Gaston had explained at unnecessary length, was quite contrary to the cross-fire principle, but since the wheatfield would give no cover to the ambushees once they were forced off the road, it should not be a major disadvantage. The purpose was to secure the films intact, not destroy the car.

Unlike most mountainous areas the Grande Kabylie is highly populated. There were villages within three or four kilometres to either side of us, and even this early in the day the road was moderately busy. Gaston had taken account of the fact that civilians in peacetime couldn't ambush a car in broad daylight without a certain amount of curiosity from passers-by. Our equipment, therefore, included some items intended to distract the curiosity. The full list had been read out impressively, checked and distributed as follows:

Raymond and Louis: One Algerian police officer's uniform each, complete with truncheon, web belt and 9 mm automatic pistol.

Raymond: One pair of binoculars.

Gunther: One 7.62 mm FN automatic rifle, with 50 rounds of ammunition.

Gaston: One 9 mm Uzi machine carbine, four canisters of tear gas, one gas mask.

Alfred, Noonan, and myself: Side-arms of various makes and calibres. Mine was a .38 Smith and Wesson revolver.

In addition there were five field telephones and a thousand metres of cable linking them. Noonan, sucking a cigarette and shaking his head in wonder, had muttered, 'Where the *hell* ...?'

'Our souvenirs,' Gaston had said triumphantly. 'Inherited from the O.A.S. They had either to hide it or leave it for Ben Bella's monkeys to find.'

The dew evaporated from the grass and the day grew warmer. Idly I watched the passing traffic: an ancient red bus rattling towards Constantine, a workhorse deux-chevaux, a couple of cyclists in turbans whose loud laughter rang across the plateau. There were

200

occasional pedestrians too: they would be the biggest threat to our secrecy if any were in the ambush zone when the car entered it.

Noonan knew the cars that Goodwin and Kranz were travelling in, a Hudson Hornet and a Peugeot 404. From the point where Goodwin had been picked up, the Hornet had had about an hour's start, but it was quite possible that they had rendezvoused since and re-allocated drivers and passengers. If they had teamed up to form a convoy, we were ready to stop both of them.

Gaston, Noonan and I were positioned about halfway down the three-hundred-yard strip of road. On the slope just around the bend to the east, Raymond in his policeman's uniform was stationed. With the binoculars he could see about two kilometres up the road, and when he saw what we wanted he was to alert us all on the field telephone — one long buzz for one car, two to indicate both together. There would be no time for conversations. As soon as the car or cars had passed him, he would run down onto the road and stop all following traffic with the excuse that blasting was underway ahead. That would explain the noise. Louis, also in uniform, waited around the bend at the western extremity, and on the same signal he would halt the eastbound traffic. So with a little luck we would have the whole stretch of road to ourselves, out of sight from either end, for about five minutes.

Gunther, the marksman of the party, waited with his rifle and a telephone by his side fifty yards to our left. The car would have picked up speed for a hundred yards on the straight before he fired, aiming for the two nearside tyres. If the driver knew what he was doing he'd be able to keep the car upright and bring it to a stop, with his passengers badly shaken, just about where we waited for them. Gaston would fling tear gas into the car and we would cover and disarm the Germans and Goodwin as they were forced out. In case Gunther missed his target, or for some other reason the car managed to keep going, Alfred would drive the Renault van out of the gulley to block the road just before the bend. If there were two cars instead of one, exactly the same tactics would be employed in duplicate.

So much for the theory. Now, all we could do was wait and see how it worked out. Kranz's men would be armed, and they'd be expecting an attack: those two points were worth bearing constantly in mind. As Gaston said, rather wistfully, an orthodox ambush in which we shot to kill would be a good deal easier. In one thing we were on common ground with the Germans: they didn't want the Algerian authorities interfering any more than we did, so as far as possible whatever happened on this road would remain the business of the participants.

We waited. I was exhausted, there seemed to be grit behind my eyeballs and no strength in my limbs, but sleep was out of the question. My twisted ankle hurt like hell. Gaston poured more coffee and offered round bread and some sweaty sausage that Noonan and I refused. The Frenchman ate heartily, licking crumbs off his lips. The clopping of horses' hooves came from the road and I watched for a minute as a peasant rode by on his cart.

Then the field telephone behind us gave three short buzzes. My blood ran cold before I remembered that was not the alert signal. Somebody wanted to talk. Gaston answered, listened for a few moments and said something briefly. He replaced the receiver, frowning. 'It was Louis,' he said. 'There are soldiers coming up the road.'

'Soldiers ...?' I began, but Gaston said, 'On a training run. Nothing to worry about if we keep out of sight. As long as the car does not come.'

We flattened ourselves down on the ridge, looking out through the scrub. I felt my heart pounding against the stony ground and the sun was warm enough now to send trickles of sweat down my face. We heard the rhythmic pounding of boots and in a minute the platoon of troops came round the bend on the right. They wore Castro caps and fatigue uniforms; their dark faces shone with sweat but they laughed and chattered as they ran by. When the stragglers were passing out of sight I turned and saw Gaston's lips curled in a sneer.

'The National Popular Army,' he said. 'Monkeys in uniform!'

'We'd have been the monkeys if the car had come by then,' Noonan said. 'How do we know there won't be more of them? And d'you think they'll be persuaded to stop by a phoney policeman? *Jesus*!' He drew frantically on his cigarette and nervously tapped at it a dozen times. The waiting was getting on his nerves; I was too tired for anything much to upset me.

202

'Patience, Lew-ees,' Gaston advised. 'It will be all right.'

'It's nearly eight,' Noonan said, looking at his watch. 'They should have been here by now. And when they get here all we need is a squad of troops joining in the action.'

But it wasn't troops that upset the ambush. Lying on the ground with my hands behind my head I'd somehow gone uncomfortably to sleep for a few minutes in spite of the tension. When the telephone gave one long buzz it startled me awake and for a second I had forgotten where I was. Gaston was scrambling on hands and knees to get his Uzi gun. I groped for my revolver. Then I heard Noonan, who was peering through the bushes towards the bend in the road, mutter with absolute despair, 'Oh, *Christ!*'

I looked. Coming round the bend with a cacophony of bleats and bell-ringing was a huge flock of sheep. Raymond must have seen the car too late to stop them, but perhaps they were unstoppable anyway. They blocked the road completely, some of them scampering up the slope and others spilling over the bank into the wheatfield, with the figures of two shepherds darting about at the edges of the flock. Then the Hudson Hornet lurched round the bend behind them.

It was a big black monstrosity of a car. It squatted behind the sheep like an evil flat bullfrog and the driver gave a long blast on his horn. The sheep trotted a bit faster but there was no way past them; there must have been four or five hundred across the road. The car crawled at five miles an hour and the shepherds waved their sticks and shouted at it. Already Gunther would have it in his sights.

For about twenty seconds we did nothing. We all seemed to come to our senses at once, as if someone had snapped his fingers. I discovered I'd been holding my breath, Noonan uttered a long stream of curses, but it was Gaston who acted first. He said, 'Gunther must not shoot!' and dived for the telephone. I realized what he meant: shooting the tyres when they were moving at that speed would do nothing but warn them prematurely of the ambush. We'd have to wait till they were level with us and deal with them as best we could. Gaston seized the telephone but Noonan shouted, 'No – wait!' He was pointing to the right. Alfred, unaware of the new development, had driven the red Renault van across the road as instructed. To the man in the Hornet, nothing could be a clearer warning.

The sheep had kicked up a pall of yellow dust from the sides of the road and we could hardly see the car behind them. But it had stopped, that was certain. We stared at each other wildly, realizing whatever move we made would be wrong.

Between them, Gunther and the driver of the Hornet settled the course of events. The driver, seeing the Renault drawn across the road ahead, stopped and reversed rapidly to make a three-point turn. Then Gunther, having held his fire for as long as he could and in the absence of new instructions, acted as originally planned.

We were about fifty yards from the car. We heard the four sounds merge into one — two sharp cracks from the rifle, two thumps as the tyres burst — and saw the Hornet slump heavily to the right. The driver must then have reacted instinctively, but his instincts were wrong. He gave up his three-point turn, slammed into first gear, and with the car tilting and the flat tyres flopping, drove straight through the flock of sheep.

The next few minutes had the hideous quality of a nightmare that refused to end at its climax. The shots had startled the sheep into a run. When the car scythed into them they scattered as well as they could, up the slope towards us and down into the wheat, but a solid wedge of them were still trapped in the middle of the road. The car gathered speed as it caught up with them. The first one it hit was flung twenty feet in the air; more went under the wheels and the crippled Hornet bumped over them. The urgent, hysterical bleating, the insane ringing of bells, the screams of the shepherds came from everywhere at once. Dust billowed up from the road. As the car drew level with us Noonan grabbed my arm and shouted, 'Come on!'

We broke cover and slithered down the slope. Gaston was alongside us, snapping open the retractable butt of his Uzi. Then we were waist-high in milling sheep that bleated and skittered away from our feet as we went after the car. The smell was sickening and I could hardly see for dust. One of the shepherds, a boy in a turban, ran towards us but stopped when he saw the guns. He'd been eating watermelon and he stood there with juice glistening on his chin, staring at us. Favouring my sore ankle, I hopped after Noonan.

The car drew away from us, leaving gouges from the wheel rims and a trail of dead and broken sheep. It had got up to thirty miles an hour and was rocking and swaying across the road. Most of the sheep had scattered; the road was clear for eighty yards to where the Renault blocked it. But one old ram was hobbled and too slow to get out of the way. The front bumper lifted him and flung him backwards across the bonnet. His horns cracked against the windscreen, frosting it over.

The Hornet, tilted at a ridiculous angle to the right, went on in an almost straight line for forty yards. Then all control seemed to go. The back slewed round to the right and the car turned a complete circle before stopping at the edge of the road, teetering and rolling slowly down the bank into the wheatfield. The dead ram slid off the bonnet and rolled after it.

For a few seconds as we raced down the road the car was out of sight behind the embankment. We heard glass breaking and metal tearing. Then it appeared, still rolling, with its doors burst open and leaving a path of crushed yellow wheat behind it. It turned over four times before it stopped, upside down, showing a great rectangle of rusted underside to the sky. One of the Germans had fallen out and lay next to it. The roof seemed to have been flattened to the level of the bonnet. We scrambled down the bank and trotted towards the wreck.

A man wriggled out through the twisted back door before we got there. It was Goodwin. On his hands and knees he moved a little way through the stalks of wheat, picked up something that had fallen out of the car, then stood upright and turned to face us. Involuntarily we all stopped. We were about twenty yards from the car. Gaston levelled the Uzi gun on Goodwin and cocked it.

I had somehow not expected to see him again – not close up, at any rate – and it startled me slightly but didn't scare me. There was nothing left in Goodwin to be scared of, even though he held the packet of films in one hand and his revolver in the other. It wasn't pointing at us, it hung by his side as if he'd been holding it and forgotten it was there. Under the sickly veneer of brown his face was as grey as his hair. The tic still flickered across his eyebrow. Puffy red lids half-hid his eyes, which blinked at us two or three times. He wore his orange shirt with the buttons ripped off the front, and standing in the waist-high wheat he looked strangely small and vulnerable. The gun seemed too big for his hand. Nobody did anything for a few seconds, then Noonan walked a couple of paces forward and said, 'Give us the films, Goodwin.'

Now the Germans were crawling out of the car on the other side. There were three of them. They stood up with their hands in the air and I realized Gunther had come up on our right and was covering them with the FN. He signalled for them to move away from the car, stood them in a line and ordered them to throw their guns to the ground. Sullenly they complied. They were all Ludi's type and they wore thick dark suits that looked utterly incongruous. But their attention too was fixed on Goodwin.

He did nothing but stare at us. Noonan said, 'Come on, Goodwin, let's do it the easy way. Hand over your gun and the films. That's all we want.'

'We are wasting time,' said Gaston flatly.

On the road behind us a fierce altercation began. I glanced round and saw that the shepherds — the boy and a woman in a burnouse — had collared Louis in the police uniform and were demanding retribution for the slaughter. They shouted and pointed at the car and the dead sheep, and he was trying to restrain them from coming down the bank.

Goodwin suddenly laughed. It was a harsh cackle that died out almost as soon as it began. 'That's *all* you want,' he called — *all* you want, these? He shook the packet of films. 'Tell me another.'

'That's all,' Noonan said calmly. 'I'm not interested in what you did to get them, or what you do after this. You're beaten, and you may as well admit it. Give me the films and we'll go. Kranz will be along soon to pick you up.'

'You don't know anything about it.' Goodwin tried to laugh again and shook his head, as if he were trying to explain something to backward children. Suddenly it occurred to me that he'd been concussed in the crash: he seemed quite remote from the reality of his situation. 'Kranz doesn't want me,' he said. 'He wants these. These are my ticket. If you take them I'm worth nothing to him, don't you see?'

Noonan changed his approach. He pushed his revolver into the waistband of his trousers and said clearly, 'You don't have to go with Kranz. You can go wherever you like. We don't want to harm you or take you with us, Goodwin, understand? But I'm afraid we

206

must have the films.'

The German who was lying on the ground stirred and moaned. Gunther knelt quickly beside him, extracted a pistol from inside his jacket and jerked the man to his feet. He had a cut across his forehead.

'*Do* something,' Gaston whispered fiercely.

The twenty-yard gap between us and Goodwin had become a psychological no-man's-land. Someone was going to have to cross it. Noonan stepped forward, talking as he went: 'Quite a number of people have died already, and we don't want that to happen again. Those films aren't worth all that. It's better that they should go somewhere safe.'

Suspicion flashed into Goodwin's eyes as Noonan approached. The American stopped about ten yards in front of him. Goodwin's stare settled on me. 'There's Michael,' he said. 'I didn't kill Michael, did I? I had the chance but I didn't, and then I tried to and still I couldn't.'

'That's right,' Noonan said and stepped forward again.

'But Michael knows a hell of a lot about me.' His voice rose to the edge of hysteria. 'Michael knows about Schloss and Nikos and Wicks. What use is it for me to be free of Kranz when Michael knows all that?'

Goodwin looked down at his hands and became aware that he was holding a gun. Standing there in the baking heat I knew that something awful was going to happen. The air hummed with it. Goodwin stared at the revolver briefly, weighing it in his hand, and looked at the film again. He spoke quite calmly. 'I can't give you these. They cost me too much, do you understand? They cost me all the fight I had left after Kranz had taken his share. You've only got so much of it, and after a time even your instinct for survival runs out, do you follow?'

'I think so,' Noonan said.

Then Goodwin turned and ran. Noonan started after him. I sprang forward.

Gaston didn't move. He fired from the hip, a burst of four shots that rattled across the plateau. Goodwin had taken three strides, and on the fourth his arms and legs became strangely disjointed and flailed at the air. Then he went like a big broken woolly-haired scarecrow in a nose-dive through the wheat to the soft earth.

Frozen with horror, I stared at the spot. There were bright flecks of scarlet on the yellow ears of wheat. Noonan rounded savagely on Gaston. 'You murderous bastard, you didn't have to do *that!*'

Gaston licked his lips furiously. He snapped the safety catch on his Uzi and lowered it. 'It was a trick,' he said.

'No, God damn you! Couldn't you see he was out of his mind?' Swearing softly, Noonan turned away from the Frenchman and strode through the wheat to where Goodwin lay. I didn't follow him: seeing the effects of Gaston's work could only add to my part in it. The Germans stared at us.

'He had his gun,' Gaston said defensively. 'I thought he was going to use it.'

Noonan was crouching by the body and extracting the packet of films with some difficulty from Goodwin's tightly-clenched fingers. Then he picked up the revolver, opened the breech and examined it.

'Empty,' he said. He flung the gun towards Gaston. 'I guessed it was empty. He couldn't have used it if he'd wanted to.'

Everything around us was still and hot and silent, like a dead moment in time. The German prisoners stood in a neat, dark row; the two shepherds lingered by the roadside. But there was a car standing next to them now, and Louis had come down to join us.

'Kranz is here,' he said. 'He must have driven right past Raymond.'

Kranz was there, standing at the door of the Peugeot and staring at us. 'Screw Kranz,' Noonan said, and stood up. His voice was tired. 'Will the shepherds take money to shut up about this?'

'They think we are all special police anyway,' Louis said.

'Pay them whatever they want for the sheep. Now let's get moving.'

Gunther covered the Germans from the rear as we went in single file across the field and up the embankment to the road. Kranz stood implacably by his car, watching us. He turned his dark expressionless face away from me to look at the spot where Goodwin lay.

'He's yours,' I said. 'You'd better take him.'

In a minute our party was assembled and ready to go. In an hour we were in Algiers, driving through the gates of the British Embassy in the Chemin des Glycines. Tom Blakeney was waiting to meet us, together with a group of men from the CIA and a man who was introduced as the Secretary of 3 Committee.

25

That evening Tom and I sat in a café overlooking the Old Port in Marseilles, waiting for Noonan to join us. I carried a new passport in the pocket of a borrowed suit. It had been thought advisable for us all to leave Algiers on the first available flight.

Tom was saying something but I'd been looking at a red-haired girl standing at the other end of the bar. She returned my stare boldly over the top of an anisette glass.

'What was that?' I said.

'I was *saying*,' Tom said primly, 'that Claire was very worried about you.'

'Oh.'

'She wanted to know if you had life insurance.'

'Matrimony sneaks up on one in the most unexpected disguises, doesn't it?'

'You've got a phobia about it,' Tom said. 'It's not all that bad, really. Look at me ... '

'There's something I still want to know from you, Blakeney,' I said.

'What?'

'How did you know about Czechoslovakia?'

He gave a patient sigh. 'It was a guess. A big, fat, blind guess, that's all, whatever Goodwin may have implied to the contrary. You're malleable material, Michael. When are you going to learn to leave the thinking to me?'

Noonan came shouldering his way through the café and flopped into a seat at our table. He sucked at his cigarette and made a face, realizing it had gone out. 'The films got to London okay,' he said. 'I just heard.'

'What are they doing with them?'

'They want you back tomorrow to help sort them out. They have some kind of working party drawn from our side and yours making an assessment, then it'll go up to NATO level for a decision. That's promising: it may mean there'll be positive action.'

I'd already been through a three-hour grilling from the CIA men and the Secretary of 3 Committee. Obviously the point Tom made hadn't yet gone home – that my talents in life were better directed to taking pictures than talking about them. 'I'd much sooner stay in Marseilles and recuperate,' I said. The redhead was still at the end of the bar. 'What sort of action will there be against Albania?'

'Who the hell knows? An invasion, an ultimatum? We've got a chance to show we can be tough, and I hope we're going to take it. Thanks to people who prefer to remain anonymous, the initiative is ours and not the Russians'. I trust we'll make use of it.' He grinned, then punched me on the shoulder. 'Hey, I almost forgot! Do you know some guy called Lagoudis of the *Asphalea?*'

'Slightly,' I said, remembering the impersonal stare of the dark glasses.

'I had a message from Athens. He hauled a man out of the water on the east coast of Corfu on Thursday morning. Your friend, Nikos Varthis.'

'Alive?' I hardly dared to ask it.

Noonan nodded. 'Only just. In hospital now with pneumonia, and he had to have two fingers amputated. But recovering.'

Relief and joy welled up in me. 'Thank God,' I said, feeling myself lift to the ceiling. 'Thank God. The tough old bastard made it. He must have swum all the bloody way.'

'Have you two given up drinking?' Noonan asked.

I signalled to the waiter and ordered three double Scotches. 'Let's drink to the health of Nikos,' I said. 'Look, Marseilles is great at this time of year, and maybe you've got business back in London but I haven't. I feel like staying here for a week. The CIA and 3 Committee don't really need me anyway, they can take a jump at themselves.'

210

'Did you look at that new passport of yours?' Noonan asked, in what I should have realized was a dangerously casual tone.

'Not very closely,' I said.

He stared sadly at his glass. 'It's valid for exactly two days. If you don't leave tomorrow the Sureté will come and fetch you. That was 3 Committee's idea,' he added, 'not mine.'

I should have guessed. I sat there for a few seconds and finished my whisky. 'In that case there's no time to waste,' I said. 'Excuse me.' I stood up and approached the girl with red hair.